Advance Acclaim for *The Wishing Tree*

As I started reading *The Wishing Tree*, I was instantly drawn into a story filled with complex family relationships and characters I cared about. I felt Ivy Marshall's pain as she faced past issues and cheered her on during her happier moments. Marybeth Whalen has earned a place on my must-read list.

—DEBBY MAYNE, AUTHOR OF *PRETTY IS AS PRETTY DOES*, *BLESS HER HEART*, AND *TICKLED PINK*

A betrayal, a bakery, and a beach: all three combine to woo you through Ivy Marshall's conundrum. Will she forgive? Is that enough? Or is it time to move on with her love life? Strong characters, a terrific setting, and stunning baked goods make this a terrific beach read.

—MARY DEMUTH, AUTHOR OF *THE MUIR HOUSE*

Sink your toes in the sand, let the salty breeze tease your hair, and be swept away to Sunset Beach. Marybeth Whalen writes with an authentic voice, full of deep introspection and insight into relationships and the questions we all have about whether or not we've made the right choices. And there are cupcakes! *The Wishing Tree* delighted me from start to finish. Highly recommended!

—CARLA STEWART, AWARD-WINNING AUTHOR OF *CHASING LILACS* AND *STARDUST*

Marybeth Whalen writes with a light hand, skillfully blending issues of faith and the realities of modern life into a compelling and believable read.

—MARIE BOSTWICK, NEW YORK TIMES BEST-SELLING AUTHOR OF *BETWEEN HEAVEN AND TEXAS*

An engaging story of true love and the power of forgiveness. Thoroughly enjoyable!

—ANN TATLOCK, CHRISTY AWARD-WINNING
AUTHOR OF *PROMISES TO KEEP* AND *SWEET MERCY*

Like a beach at ebb tide, Marybeth Whalen's latest novel reveals itself in layers. From challenge comes strength, from struggle, self-discovery, from the sweeping away of old things, new beginnings. Readers will cheer Ivy's season of growth in all the things that matter most.

—LISA WINGATE, NATIONAL BEST-SELLING
AND AWARD-WINNING AUTHOR OF *BLUE
MOON BAY* AND *FIREFLY ISLAND*

A tradition of wedding wishes takes on new meaning for Ivy Marshall as she searches for truth and faith. Marybeth Whalen delivers a classic story of healing, redemption, and forgiveness, reminding us the best days are ahead. Not in the past.

—RACHEL HAUCK, AWARD-WINNING,
BEST-SELLING AUTHOR OF *THE WEDDING
DRESS* AND *ONCE UPON A PRINCE*

A lovely journey of discovery and forgiveness. Here's to wishes!

—SHEILA ROBERTS, BEST-SELLING
AUTHOR OF *WHAT SHE WANTS*

Marybeth Whalen explores a question in the hearts of many married women at one time or another, but one rarely on their lips: "What if I had chosen differently?" Ivy Marshall, in her journey toward that answer, comes to redefine herself and learns what it really means to wish, to forgive, and to love. *The Wishing Tree* is a novel not to be missed.

—CHRISTA ALLAN, AUTHOR OF *WALKING ON
BROKEN GLASS* AND *THE EDGE OF GRACE*

THE WISHING TREE

Also by Marybeth Whalen

She Makes It Look Easy
The Mailbox
The Guest Book

THE
WISHING
TREE

by MARYBETH WHALEN

ZONDERVAN.com/
AUTHORTRACKER
follow your favorite authors

ZONDERVAN

The Wishing Tree

Copyright © 2013 by Marybeth Whalen

This title is also available as a Zondervan ebook. Visit
www.zondervan.com/ebooks.

Requests for information should be addressed to:

Zondervan, *Grand Rapids, Michigan 49530*

Library of Congress Cataloging-in-Publication Data

Whalen, Marybeth.
  The wishing tree / by Marybeth Whalen.
    pages cm.
  ISBN 978-0-310-33488-0 (trade paper)
  I. Title.
  PS3623.H355W57 2013
  813'.6--dc23
                                    2013002819

Scripture quotations are taken from the Holy Bible, *New International Version®, NIV®.* Copyright © 1973, 1978, 1984, 2011 by Biblica, Inc.™ Used by permission. All rights reserved worldwide.

NEW REVISED STANDARD VERSION of the Bible. © 1989 by the Division of Christian Education of the National Council of the Churches of Christ in the U.S.A. All rights reserved.

Any Internet addresses (websites, blogs, etc.) and telephone numbers in this book are offered as a resource. They are not intended in any way to be or imply an endorsement by Zondervan, nor does Zondervan vouch for the content of these sites and numbers for the life of this book.

Published in association with the literary agency of Fedd&Company, Inc., Post Office Box 341973, Austin, Texas 78734.

Printed in the United States of America

13 14 15 16 /RRD/ 20 19 18 17 16 15 14 13 12 11 10 9 8 7 6 5 4 3 2 1

*To Curt, who reminds me
where to hang my wishes*

I need your grace
To remind me
To find my own.

—Snow Patrol,
"Chasing Cars"

One

Ivy Marshall didn't have to pick up the phone to know who was waiting to speak to her. Her father, Simon Copeland, had called to deliver bad news. She looked toward the ceiling at the buzzing fluorescent light hanging above her head, allowing a few empty seconds to tick by before glancing over at the phone. The light that indicated the waiting call was still blinking. She groaned aloud in her empty office and reached for the receiver. Not answering was only putting off the inevitable.

"Ivy?" Simon Copeland's deep timbre was unmistakable. He had the voice of a radio announcer or politician. Instead he was a commercial real estate magnate, but in the recent economic downturn, not a very good one. His failure had surprised everyone, most of all him.

"I'm here, Dad," she responded, not bothering to hide

the strain in her voice. They both knew what he was calling about; it had been coming for months.

"You kept me waiting long enough," he harrumphed. There was a time when no one kept Simon Copeland waiting.

She was grateful they were not in front of each other so she was free to roll her eyes. *Just get on with it*, she wanted to say. Instead she chewed her lip, pulling away a stray piece of skin until she tasted blood, sharp and metallic. "Didn't mean to," she mumbled her lie.

Ignoring her, he launched into his (rehearsed, she suspected) speech. "As you know, we had our board meeting this morning." His tone was official instead of parental. "And some unfortunate decisions were made that affect all of us."

But me most of all, she thought, but again, refrained from saying. "Okay." Her voice was barely loud enough to hear.

"We're closing the Asheville office," he said, making it official.

"Yeah, I figured." She closed her eyes, felt the tears stinging behind the lids.

There was a long silence. She could hear her father breathing, and her mind wandered back to her childhood when she used to hear him snoring behind her parents' closed bedroom door before their marriage ended. She opened her eyes. That was a long time ago and certainly not relevant anymore.

"So what do we do next?" She blinked, clearing away the tears with a few rapid movements. That was all it took to clear her vision so she could see the new future that waited for her. She took a deep breath as she listened to her father outline his plan for closing the Asheville branch of his company, for ending the job she'd held for nearly four years. It would take at least two months to wrap up their current projects and close down the office, giving the employees time to look for other jobs. That was some consolation.

Last night at dinner she'd told her husband, Elliott, she had a feeling that this would happen. He'd smiled as though it meant nothing, told her she worried too much and left the table abruptly. Maybe now he'd face reality. Without her income they wouldn't be able to keep the house or be members at the club or participate in the church building campaign they'd recently committed to.

"I won't make you tell the employees," she heard her father saying. Their faces flashed in her mind as he spoke: Delores, who had worked there since the first day and kept them all straight. Pete, who was a nice guy more interested in skiing than working; he'd be fine. Beck, whose real name was Walter, but went by his last name because it just fit him better. Beck was no Walter. She'd miss the way his harmless flirtations always made her feel pretty even when her husband hardly noticed her.

She thought of Elliott's late nights on the computer, and that nagging suspicion tried to work its way up her spine. No time for that now. She had to gather everyone in the conference room for her father to deliver the bad news via conference call, all standing together staring at the phone on the large table as Simon Copeland's disconnected voice came out of it.

Tears filled her eyes—just yesterday Delores had been tittering about plans for a trip to Italy with her husband,

Bob. Ivy hoped she could still go. She should probably be the one to tell them. But she was a coward and her father was giving her the easy out. She took it gratefully.

They ended the call with the promise that she would call him back once everyone was gathered. "Ivy," he said before they hung up. "This wasn't anything you did. You were good at your job. This should be a beginning for you, not an ending."

She rose from her desk, her eyes falling on a framed photo of her and Elliott taken at the party her best friend, April, had given them after they married. April was Elliott's cousin but she made her allegiance to Ivy clear almost immediately, becoming the sister Ivy didn't have, even though Ivy had a sister. When this was all over she'd call April, fill her in on everything. Then, maybe, if she felt up to it, she'd call Elliott.

Lately her conversations with her husband had boiled down to the business of life—what groceries they were out of, what bills needed to be paid, when they were expected to be somewhere. She supposed that losing her job would qualify as part of the business of life. She studied the photo for a second, noting how happy they looked that summer, how love seemed to shimmer in the very air around them. When had the air stopped shimmering? When had they stopped smiling like that?

She turned away from the photo and left the room. As she closed her office door she could feel the picture shift on the wall like it always did, hanging crooked until she straightened it. Maybe this time, she thought as she walked away, she wouldn't bother to fix it.

⌒

Ivy was nearly out the door, purse over her shoulder and car keys in hand. In light of the bad news her employees had just absorbed, she was attempting to leave work early, already anticipating a long soak in a warm bath as soon as she got home. She hadn't been able to reach Elliott since her father's call and had almost decided to freeze him out for the rest of the evening as punishment. Let him wonder.

"Ivy Marshall," she heard Delores yell as she started to step out the door, "don't you dare sneak off without a piece of your very own cake!"

Ivy froze in her tracks and grimaced before turning around with a fake smile to replace the grimace. She took a few steps back into the office, knowing her escape was hopeless under Delores's eagle-eyed gaze.

"Oh . . . you're having . . . cake? Now?" She'd hardly expected her employees to go on with the celebration of Delores's birthday.

She entered the conference room where, just an hour ago, they'd all stood around with sober expressions and stared blankly at the phone as their jobs were ended without their consent. Now, instead of the phone sitting center stage on the conference table, the cake she'd baked for Delores was there. The cake, she noticed, had still managed to bring a bit of brightness to the room, magically dispelling the somber air. The sad faces were now smiling as they took bites of cake, the smell of flour and sugar and butter filling the room, making them all forget for a moment what had just taken place.

Beck smiled at her, his eyes crinkling as he did, the way she liked. He pointed at the cake with his plastic fork. "This is good stuff, Ivy." He took another bite and continued talking to her with the cake filling his mouth. "You could go into cake baking as an alternate career." If Elliott did that she would scold him for talking with his mouth full. But on Beck it was somehow . . . cute.

"I'll keep that in mind," she said. Her mind flitted back to Sunset Beach, North Carolina, and her aunt's Seaside Bakery, where as a teen Ivy had learned to bake and decorate cakes. She could remember coming out of the bakery at the end of the day, the sunshine warm on her skin, the smell of ocean breeze mixing with the sweetness of confection. "You smell good enough to eat," Michael used to say, lifting her off her feet and spinning her around.

She ignored Michael's appearance in her mind, focusing instead on Beck and Delores and Pete and the temp they'd hired, who really didn't have a job to lose since she could just get assigned somewhere new. Ivy smiled at her, the one person in the room she didn't feel guilty about. Ivy couldn't even remember the girl's name.

She accepted a piece of cake from Delores, thinking that this was far from the scene she'd imagined when she'd baked the cake. Last night she'd listened to Bruce Springsteen in the kitchen while she worked and even danced a little bit as she slathered the yellow cake with white icing, creating little peaks and swirls with her spatula. She'd looked up to find Elliott watching her dance. "I like seeing you like this," he'd said. Instead of responding, she had immediately stopped dancing, looking intently at the cake until he walked away without another word between them. She'd noticed the disappointed look on his face but pretended she didn't. Once upon a time, she would've reached for him, they would've danced together, and the cake would've been forgotten. For a moment, it seemed as if he also wished things could be that way again.

Now she forced herself to take a bite, chew, and swallow, the icing like glue in her mouth as everyone looked on. They were, she knew, waiting for her to say something that would make it all better, add some bit of humor or wisdom or perspective to this unfortunate situation that she didn't possess as their fearless former leader. She even tried to think of a Bible verse she could quote, but it all just felt like platitudes. Instead she sucked the icing from her teeth and proclaimed the first word that came to mind, "Delicious!" But she didn't taste a thing.

∽

Her cell phone rang just as she was finally making her escape from the office. She pulled out of the parking lot, past the large blue-and-white For Sale sign in front of the building. It had been the first indication of what was coming, though she hadn't realized it at the time. At first her dad had told her he was merely looking for another place to house the office, but she'd noticed him pulling at his ear as he spoke, a clear sign he was lying. She hadn't lived with the man since she was sixteen years old, but that didn't mean she couldn't read him. Still, she'd gone along with the lie, not wanting . . . what? To rock the boat? To catch him in a lie? To deal with the real issue?

Her mother's number popped up on her smartphone screen, along with a photo she'd chosen to represent her mom—Vivien Leigh as Scarlett O'Hara, her own little joke that had gone right over her mother's head. "I don't even like *Gone with the Wind*!" she'd said. Ivy had bit back a smile as she'd pictured her mother saying "Fiddle-dee-dee, I'll think about that another day!" Even if she didn't see it, her mother was the quintessential Southern belle. Margot Copeland clung tenaciously to the Southern way, which included daughters answering the family matriarch's phone call in a timely mannuh.

Talking to both her parents on the same day was a rare event. She guessed her mother had heard about her dad's decision and was calling to check on her. In spite of their rather bitter divorce years ago, somehow her mom still kept track of her father's every move. Ivy suspected she had a mole planted inside his company and had said as much to her father. He'd laughed and agreed but seemed mostly unfazed by Margot's continued interest. The sad part was, her mother could spy on her father all she wanted—all she was going to watch was a man moving on with his life as fast as he could. But perhaps the business falling apart would slow him down.

"Hey, Mom, I guess you heard?" she answered the line.

Her mom drew in a loud breath. "Well, now, how did you hear?"

Ivy held the phone out and looked at it quizzically, then put it back to her ear. This wasn't going to be a quick conversation. She would drive in a big circle while she chatted with her mom. She turned away from home, her warm bath and good book getting farther and farther away. "Umm, Dad called and told me? Just a few hours ago?"

"Well, now, how would he know?"

Ivy frowned. Clearly they were talking about two different things. "Mom, how would Dad know what? I'm talking about him closing down the company."

"He's closing down the company?" Margot shouted in her ear. "Why am I just now hearing about this?" This time when Ivy pulled the phone away, it wasn't out of confusion but an intense desire to protect her eardrums.

"Mom, *Mom.* He's closing down my company, my office, not the entire operation." *Though that might not be far behind*, she thought but didn't say.

A beat of silence followed as Ivy took another wrong turn, meandering down a street that hosted a line of retail shops and funky apartment buildings, one of those parts of Asheville she always told herself she'd visit "when she had time." In five years of living there, she'd never once had the time. Her father's news hit her all over again. Perhaps now she would. Though, ironically, now she wouldn't have the money to spend in those shops.

"I'm sorry to hear that," her mom said. But Margot Copeland was not one to extend sympathy for long, much as Ivy needed it. Instead she plunged headlong into a familiar theme, taking the opportunity as Ivy expected she would. "So, does that mean you'll have to come home now? Forget your little mountain adventure?" Her mother had a way of saying the word *mountain* with such disdain; she made her feelings clear, even as she sounded harmless.

She was glad that Elliott was nowhere near, that he

couldn't hear this. She'd told him her parents had stopped asking her to come home, that they'd forgiven him and all was well. He'd probably known she was lying but he'd gone along with it.

"Not sure what I'm gonna do, Mom," she said, trying to sound as bright and chipper as possible. She worked hard to sound happy whenever she talked to her mom. No sense giving off even the slightest hint of weakness. Her mom was like a wolf—she knew when to move in for the kill. That was the thing about Southern belles; they seemed sweet and innocent, but that was part of the ploy to disarm you entirely. She changed the subject. "So if you didn't call about the Asheville office, why did you call?"

The excitement returned to her mother's voice, any remnants of sympathy for Ivy's plight completely erased as she gushed, her entire speech marked by exclamation points. "It's the most wonderful thing! Your sister is being proposed to on national TV! Tomorrow morning! You simply have to watch!"

Ivy gripped the phone tighter as she gripped the steering wheel just as tight with her other hand. She swallowed, wishing she could just hang up the phone on her mom and not bother making nice polite conversation. For a moment she tried to pinpoint exactly what she felt: anger at her mom for not being more caring, jealousy for Shea's good news in light of her own, loss over her job, or all of the above? It was a cocktail of emotions, poured into a tumbler and then given a good shake. Her cup overflowed . . . and not in a good way.

"Aren't you happy for your sister?" she heard her mom's voice saying. Ivy had pulled the car over into a parking lot on a side street. She'd ventured deeper and deeper into an unfamiliar part of the city and would have to use GPS to navigate her way back home. Stupid. She should've just driven home, filled the tub with water so that she'd have an excuse to get off the phone. She closed her eyes, rested her head on the steering wheel. It was an unseasonably warm day for February. She opened her eyes. February the 13th. Valentine's Day was the next day. Great. Salt on the wound. She couldn't imagine celebrating love with Elliott right now. Not when he hardly ever came to bed with her, spent way too much time on the computer, and no longer even acted like the man she'd fallen in love with that winter six years ago.

"Ivella Margaret Copeland, are you there?"

The stubborn part of her rose up. She hated when her mother called her by her full name, the name they shared. *There has been an Ivella Margaret in my family for every generation as long as we can remember*, she could still hear her mother say with pride.

"Mom, it's Ivy Marshall now. And yes, I'm still here." She had officially changed her name to Ivy Copeland Marshall after she married Elliott, but she'd never told her family that—they hadn't been speaking at the time and it had just never come up once they did start talking again.

"I'd expect you'd be happy to hear about your sister. Excited for her."

"Sure, Mom, of course. That's great news." Go along to get along: it was their family motto.

Her mother huffed. "You don't *sound* all that excited."

Ivy could tell she wasn't giving her mother what she was looking for. Her mother wanted someone to celebrate with. Ivy wasn't going to be that someone.

"Mom, it's just been a hard day." *What with me losing my job and all.*

"I'm sure it has, honey. But maybe this will be a good *distraction.*" There was a long pause, which meant Margot was scheming. "Maybe you could come home to congratulate your sister in person? Maybe even this weekend? I was thinking about having a little engagement party. A surprise."

The last time Ivy had talked to Shea had been three months ago. She'd dutifully called her on her birthday because Margot had asked in that way that only Margot could, where asking equated with commanding. Shea had sounded less than excited to hear from her, and when Ivy had pulled the phone away from her mouth to press End, she'd been surprised to notice that the call had lasted a mere fifty-nine seconds. Fifty-nine seconds in three months does not a sister make. The truth was Shea would never really forgive her for marrying Elliott, no matter how much water flowed under the bridge.

"I'll have to see, Mom. I can't really commit to anything with everything that's happened." Plus, what would it look like to leave her husband on Valentine's weekend?

She could actually hear her mother pouting through the phone, but Margot quickly recovered as she remembered what she had to be excited about—her other daughter. "At least call her tomorrow. But afterward! She has no idea!" Margot giggled. "Owen has set this whole thing up without her knowing! And I even get to be there as a witness! It's going to air on *Have a Nice Day USA* at 8:00 a.m., so have your TV on!" They were back to exclamation points.

She promised her mom she would watch the show and

that, yes, she would call Shea after it was over, much as the mere thought pained her. Shea was smug on days she wasn't being proposed to on national television in front of a live audience by the perfect guy. Ivy ended the call with her mother and focused on the GPS as she pulled out of the parking lot, trying to figure out where she'd wandered to.

But it wasn't being lost that was bothering her. It wasn't feeling like a stranger in this place she wanted so badly to feel like home. It wasn't even her job loss or talking to her parents or the thought of Shea's good news. It was what Shea would surely say yes to in front of the nation. It was the thought of what was coming. Shea would have her wedding at Sunset Beach. She'd have the right location, the right flowers, the right dress. The right groom. What was nagging at Ivy wasn't that her sister was getting married; it was that Shea was having the wedding Ivy had never had.

༚

Ivy drove her car with caution, trying to pay attention to the street signs and traffic signals, instead of getting distracted by the cute little apartments mixed with kitschy little stores. She could imagine herself living here, waking up early to walk to that funky little coffee shop, buying those perfect little knick-knacks in the window of that store for her single-girl apartment on her way home. She could buy a dog. Elliott was allergic. She was thinking about what to name the dog as she passed by Elliott's car, her eye reflexively picking out the familiar make, model, and color, as recognizable as a face. The car was pulling out of one of the apartment complex parking lots, the kind of place where a single girl would live the kind of life she was just envisioning.

Her heart beat rapidly as she drove past. She looked over to see if it was him, taking in his distinct profile as he scanned the street for oncoming traffic, his face turned away from her as it seemed it always was these days. She knew his profile too well. But she didn't really know him.

Although everything in her wanted to double back and tail him all the way home, she kept driving, thinking as she did about what a record-breaking bad day it had turned out to be. Bad things happen in threes; isn't that how the saying went? If that was true, then all the bad stuff that was going to happen that day had happened. She'd lost her job, had her nose rubbed in her sister's success, and confirmed something she'd suspected but been able to ignore about her husband up until now: there was someone else. She'd just witnessed him leaving her apartment when he was supposed to be at work.

She could imagine what he would say if she confronted him. "That's absurd! You're overreacting! Just what exactly do you think you saw?"

But still she could remember her mother talking to her own sister, Aunt Leah, the year Ivy's parents split up. Her mother had packed her and Shea up suddenly and taken them down to Sunset Beach in the fall, long after the tourists were gone and there was nothing to do but go for bike rides with Shea. Aunt Leah had met them there, her brows knit together even though she wore a smile on her face around the girls. Though Margot hadn't divulged much to her daughters, there'd been many whispered conversations between Margot and Leah. Ivy had overheard them. "A woman just knows, Leah," her mother had said, her hand gripping her sister's sleeve, the fabric of her blouse crumpling under her fingers.

All these years later, Ivy was finding out exactly what her mother meant. A woman did know. Ivy didn't need proof. She didn't need a confession. She didn't need a private detective or any of the other things she'd seen on TV. Instead the truth about Elliott settled inside of her, like a rock tossed into the ocean, falling and falling and falling until it landed with a soft but certain thud, lodging in her stomach and staying there as she drove home, parked in the garage, and let herself into the house, all the while wondering where this steely resolve was coming from, and where the tears she would've expected were.

She climbed the stairs, ran her long-awaited bath, and waited for the tears to come as she sat on the side of the tub and watched it fill, steam coming off the water. She slipped out of her clothes, leaving them in a messy pile where water was sure to splash them. Her mother would disapprove. A wry smile filled her face as she slipped into the water, welcoming the burning sensation hitting her skin. At least she could feel something. She tilted her head back in the water, wetting her hair and then, sliding under the water, holding her breath.

She thought of being a little girl and bathing with Shea. They would play mermaids, braiding each other's hair and pretending to have fins instead of legs. They would dream of all the adventures they'd have once they became real mermaids and could live under the sea all the time. They'd even made up mermaid names. Shea's mermaid name was Coral and Ivy's was Oceana. That tub had been their own little world, a world they'd once believed in as surely as they'd both believed in happily ever after.

Ivy sat up in the water as she heard the beeping noise that meant the door downstairs was opening. As she listened to Elliot's feet walking around below, she tried not to think about who he'd been with, or what he'd been doing. She felt her eyes sting with those unshed tears she'd been staving off all day. Ivy's life was a far cry from happily ever after. But it looked like tomorrow on national television, Shea would be getting hers.

"Congratulations, Coral," Ivy whispered into the empty room, her voice bouncing off the water, her tears slipping into it and disappearing.

Two

April called that evening while she was standing in the kitchen, debating dinner. The girl had a sixth sense, could always tell when something was wrong with Ivy. "Your timing is impeccable," Ivy said as she answered the phone.

"What's wrong?" In the background she could hear one of April's new puppies whining.

"Is that Barnes or Noble?" she asked.

"Don't try to change the subject," April teased. She knew Ivy was trying to divert the conversation. And besides, April knew Ivy took little interest in the puppies she'd impulsively brought home from a recent Adopt-a-Pet event. Ivy had warned her she'd bitten off more than she could chew—and, slowly, April was admitting it.

Ivy heard April's squeaky back-porch door open and shut. "There," April said, "I've escaped to the outdoors."

Ivy could imagine relief spreading across April's elfin face, her blond pixie cut framing it. Ivy was betting she had on jeans and a loose flannel workshirt at that very moment, her bangs clipped back with pink barrettes to expose her wide, innocent eyes.

"I thought you were supposed to put the dogs outside."

"They're not exactly outdoorsy-type dogs."

"April, only you would pick out dogs that don't enjoy being outside."

"Why I'm still single is making more sense to you now, isn't it? My picker is broken, clearly."

April was just coming off a yearlong relationship with a youth pastor who ultimately decided to move back to Michigan to be near his family. While he'd offered to see where it went from long distance, he'd made it clear that living in Michigan was part of any future with him. April had turned him down, but not without more than a few tears. The dogs, Ivy was certain, were a reaction to the loss. A noisy, messy reaction that she was sure April regretted.

"So, shoot. Tell me everything," April said.

Ivy sighed. Where did she start? "Okay, suffice it to say that this day is going down as one of the worst days of my life."

"Really? Worse than the day you told your family you were breaking up with Michael in order to marry Elliot?"

Ivy nodded as she answered. "Yes. Worse than that. I think this day just took that one's place."

April was silent for a moment. "Wow. Must be pretty bad."

"You have no idea."

"Okay, before you start, I'm going back inside because

the dogs can see me, and they're going crazy barking at me through the window. I'm just going to throw some food down for them and hope it diverts them. Hang on." Ivy listened while the door squeaked and the barking reached a crescendo, then suddenly quieted at the sound of kibble filling a metal bowl.

April sighed loudly into the phone, and Ivy could hear the squeak of the couch springs as she sat down. "Okay, they're quiet. Do tell. But talk fast because I know the quiet won't last."

As succinctly as she could, Ivy ticked off the three things that happened—the call from her dad, the call from her mom, and seeing Elliott's car.

"I'll kill him," April breathed into the phone. "Seriously. I'll sic these dogs on him."

Ivy couldn't help but smile at the thought of the little mutts going after Elliott, attacking his ankles with gusto while he hollered. "I'll keep in mind that I can call on their services if needed."

"You really think Elliott would . . ." April breathed.

"I don't know, April." Ivy found herself backpedaling. "Maybe he was running some papers over to a colleague who's sick at home." She could come up with a dozen excuses for what she'd seen, so she was sure Elliott would too. "I'm sure it's nothing, and I won't ask. Don't want to be the crazy accusing wife, you know."

A heavy silence fell. Apparently single friends didn't do too well with news that all was not bliss on the marriage front.

"Anyway"—Ivy decided to change the subject—"talking

to both my parents in one day has wiped me out. I'm going to eat something and go to bed early so this day can be over."

"Ivy?" April said. "Take my advice and don't answer any more calls from your parents."

She sighed. "I wish it were that easy."

"Yeah," April said. "Your life was much easier back when you weren't talking to them."

"Back when you and I were first figuring out each other's brand of crazy."

April laughed. "Did you figure mine out yet? 'Cause I'd love to know."

"Not even close." They both laughed. Ivy loved how April could always make her laugh, no matter what. It was April, after all, who'd gotten her through that rough patch with her family, helped her see that she could make it even if it meant making it alone. April had taken her back to church, got her praying again, made her see that, really, she wasn't alone at all. Back then, Elliott and April had seemed more like family than her own blood.

She leaned her head against the phone, feeling the connection to April that was always there. At least she could count on that.

"So, what are you going to do?" April asked.

"Well, I'm going to get out of bed every morning, and I'm going to put one foot in front of the other . . ."

"Breathe in and out all day long," April finished with a giggle. *Sleepless in Seattle* was their favorite movie, and they often found reasons to quote lines to each other. April was convinced that she'd find her Tom Hanks character in some magical way, just like Meg Ryan had. It was Ivy's job to affirm that she would. But sometimes Ivy wondered if April wasn't better off single. The trouble with finding Mr. Perfect was that he wouldn't stay perfect.

"So are you going to watch your sister on TV tomorrow morning?"

Ivy laughed. "What do you think?"

"Guess you have to."

"Pretty much. You know I'll be quizzed on it later."

"How bad can it be, right?"

"Right. I mean, it's just my sister getting her dream proposal so she can start planning her dream wedding—"

"The one you were supposed to have," April interrupted.

"Thank you for pointing that out," she replied.

"Meanwhile your dream has kind of . . ."

"Fizzled," Ivy finished her sentence.

"Well, just because something fizzles doesn't mean it can never spark again."

Upstairs, in the bonus room they used as a gym, she could hear Elliott running on the treadmill, his feet pounding out a rhythm. Lately he'd become obsessed with working out. She could pick up almost any women's magazine and learn what *that* indicated. She wondered what kind of spark could possibly ignite the passion between them again. She could hardly admit to her best friend that she was starting to believe there was no hope for her marriage, that the spark she was referring to was impossible.

"Well, I better go," she said. "I just heard Elliott's treadmill switch off."

"Look, whatever happens, you know I'm on your side, right?" April's dogs were getting louder in the background. She had to yell over the barking.

"'Course I do," Ivy responded. April was someone who would never lie to her, never throw her over for someone else, never hurt her. She had proven that over and over. But Elliott was her family, and Ivy knew April loved him. That was the thing about family—you never really stopped loving them no matter how mad at them you got.

"Okay, good. Now if you were a true friend, you'd come over here and rescue me from these dang dogs!"

They said good-bye and she hung up the phone with a smile on her face that lasted until she saw Elliott come down the stairs, his phone in his hand as he texted, his thumbs flying over the miniature keyboard. He passed by her without even looking up.

∽

Dinner was a quiet affair, as always. Elliott seemed to write off tonight's silence to the news of her job loss, squeezing her shoulder as a form of solidarity as they were dishing up their plates. But "It'll work out" was all he said before he took his plate and went to eat in front of the computer.

Ivy sat alone at the kitchen table, picking at the leftover lasagna she'd pulled out of the fridge, her mind flitting to their first Valentine's Day together—and how different tomorrow night's would surely be. Back then they'd been newly in love, both startled by their attraction to each other, by the similarities, by the need they had to be together all the time. "I've never felt like this about anyone," were words they both threw out, equally as often. It had been real then. Of that she was sure.

She looked in the direction that Elliott had disappeared mumbling something about finishing some work as he slunk away with plate in hand. "I'll just bet," she said to herself, studying the candleholders they'd received as wedding gifts, wondering when was the last time they'd eaten by candlelight or skipped dinner altogether in a rush to fall into bed, eating sandwiches in the kitchen much later, famished and grinning at each other.

She yawned loudly, covering her mouth out of habit even though she was alone, her eyes taking in the view they'd loved off the back of the house—the trickling stream, the expanse of mountains beyond. His arms had gone around her as they stared at it together the first time they'd looked at the house. "This is the house we'll grow old in," he'd said and kissed her as the Realtor looked away, shuffling his feet awkwardly.

Elliott walked back into the room, carrying his empty plate, streaks of red and pieces of noodles and cheese clinging to the china. He laid it in the sink and started to walk away.

"You could at least run some water over that," she remarked, looking down at her mostly full plate.

He stopped walking, strode back over to the sink, and pulled dramatically on the spigot so that the water shot out at full blast, filling the plate. "There," he pronounced, sarcasm lacing his voice as he shut the spigot off just as abruptly as he had pulled it on. She watched his back as he walked away and tried to come up with the words to confront him about what she'd seen that afternoon. Words that wouldn't make her sound crazy. Words that he couldn't twist. Words that would get to the truth.

But no words came. She carried her plate to the sink and rinsed it, watching the uneaten lasagna slip down the drain. Then she sank into the couch, laptop open. She needed to get on some job search sites, start typing her résumé, or do something productive. Instead she got on Twitter, escaping into whatever other people were talking about. She clicked on some links, read up on some celeb news, and added a book someone was tweeting about to an online bookstore cart. The novel was about a woman making a fresh start and finding triumph in the midst of heartache. She stopped and listened to the sound of Elliott in the next room, typing. That sounded like a story she needed to read.

She was about to log out of Twitter when she saw a tweet from their pastor. He had quoted Psalm 84:5, "Blessed are those whose strength is in you, whose hearts are set on pilgrimage." She wanted to find her strength in God, as if it were that easy. And the idea of a pilgrimage sounded good at that moment—but a pilgrimage to where? She usually found such comfort in the Psalms but tonight she just felt hollow, wrung out.

She heard Elliott's footsteps behind her and opened her eyes.

He stooped down and peered at her laptop. "Twitter, eh?" He wore that amused grin on his face she was growing to hate. He stood back up and scratched his head, leaving the top of it sticking up like a rooster's comb. There was lasagna sauce dried on his cheek. She realized looking at him that she didn't find him attractive like she used to, didn't want to reach for him just because he was close enough to touch.

She closed the laptop and stood up. "Yeah, was just goofing off." She tucked the computer under her arm and took it over to the kitchen counter to charge for the night.

Elliott continued. "I just don't get the whole Twitter thing. I mean, who wants to listen to a bunch of people yammering on about nothing?"

She shrugged, refusing to engage in whatever he was trying to stir up—a debate? A spat? An odd attempt to start a conversation? When had they stopped knowing how to talk to each other? They hadn't said more than ten words about her dad closing the office. And she hadn't even told him about her sister's televised proposal the next morning. Instead all she could think of was driving past his car that afternoon, seeing his profile, his hands on the wheel—hands that had just touched someone else. She was sure of it.

"I mean, why do you like that Twitter so much?" he pressed. He always called it "that Twitter," like he was so above it, when who knew what all he did, what sites he was visiting during all that time he spent online. He crossed his arms in front of himself, and she avoided looking at those hands she always used to want touching her. She chose not to answer his question and knew that he wasn't really interested in the answer anyway. Somehow he'd stopped being concerned with what she liked, or why she liked it.

"I'm going to bed," she said. "Lots to settle tomorrow."

"Think I'll stay up for a while," he called after her. "Got some stuff I need to finish before I call it a night."

She didn't even respond, just trudged up the stairs to their bed and climbed in alone.

∽

The next morning she rolled over and peered at Elliott's side of the bed. It hadn't been slept in. Lately he'd been falling asleep on the couch, making excuses about not wanting to wake her when he came to bed late. She didn't press but she knew that wasn't the real reason. He didn't come to bed because he didn't want to, plain and simple. His absence was just another indicator of the bigger problem in their marriage, the widening gap that, more and more, they couldn't cross.

She rolled onto her back again and stared up at the ceiling, thinking about tackling the task of telling their remaining clients that they were closing up shop, selling off properties, and leaving town. She wasn't looking forward to the day at work any more than she was looking forward to going downstairs, turning on the TV, and watching her sister get proposed to on national television.

But duty called, so she slipped out of bed, wrapped the fluffy robe that Elliott hated around herself, and padded down the stairs to the kitchen, her feet encased in bunny slippers that April had bought her for Christmas as a joke. "In case the rabbit dies," she had said as Ivy opened them, her face barely containing her mischievous smile. April had seen the look that passed between Ivy and Elliott, apologizing later for joking about something so private.

She made coffee. After stirring in a generous amount of

hazelnut-flavored creamer, she settled onto the couch and turned on the massive television that Elliott had bought himself for Christmas. She propped her feet up on the coffee table, wiggling the rabbits back and forth. "Don't feel bad, guys," she said to her feet. "It's not your fault."

The host of *Have a Nice Day USA*'s face filled the screen, holding a mic and bantering with the weather person. Ivy took a sip of coffee, then blew on it and sipped again. The screen flashed to Owen holding a ring box and grinning for the camera, then flashed to Shea inside her school surrounded by smiling children, also grinning. How strange to see her sister on national TV. She was probably scared out of her gourd.

Ivy turned off the mute feature just in time to hear "When we get back!" Then Owen and Shea's faces disappeared, and the screen went to a commercial about antacids. She scurried into the kitchen to refill her coffee, which Elliott had made and left for her that morning, just as he always did. There were still parts of her marriage—little glimmers—that reminded her that it wasn't all bad. In her heart she could make excuses for why he was over on that side of town yesterday afternoon. She could tell herself that she was jumping to conclusions without even asking.

She looked around, wishing that she'd told him to stay home this morning and watch this ridiculous display of Copeland family drama with her. Once upon a time he would've. They'd have laughed together over it, sipped coffee side by side, then kissed lovingly before they headed off to work, teasing each other over who had the worst coffee breath. They might even have planned to meet for lunch.

Valentine's hearts rained down from the sky in the *Have a Nice Day USA* studios as they returned from commercial break, reminding her. It was Valentine's Day, after all. Lunch together should be on their agenda. But there had been no card, no plans, no single rose waiting by her coffee mug . . . nothing to signal that a day devoted to celebrating love was a priority for him. Ivy blinked away the tears and focused on the television, her sister's face swimming in front of her. The announcer was talking.

"We've got something so exciting for you today, folks! A live proposal to get your Valentine's Day started off with a big dose of romance."

Pictures began scrolling by as the announcer kept talking, describing how Owen and Shea had known each other all their lives, their families spending summers together at Sunset Beach, North Carolina. There was Shea on the beach as a little girl, posing proudly by a sandcastle. Owen and Shea as teens, posing on the roof deck of the beach house wearing matching braces; Owen's dad and mom with Shea and Owen at their college graduation; Owen and Shea posing outside some European landmark. And then, the picture she'd sensed was coming, she and Michael with Owen and Shea on the night Michael proposed, Ivy proudly displaying the diamond ring he'd given her, the facets catching the light from the flash and throwing it back. She studied the photo for a second before it faded into a shot of the studio and the smiling host, Dick Byrnes. She could remember that night with such clarity, the scene playing out in her mind as crisp and large as the televised image in front of her.

Dick Byrnes turned to Owen with an artificial laugh. "Seems like you've known Shea forever!" His smile was plastic and insincere. But Owen's smile *was* sincere as he agreed that, yes, he had known Shea for most of his life. He looked . . . excited. There was no denying it. And Ivy knew it wasn't just because he was on TV. He was finally going to ask Shea—the great love of his life—to marry him. After the ups and downs of a teenage romance, they were going to head to the altar as adults, ready to face the future together. They were going to do what she and Michael had not.

Dick Byrnes turned to his virtual audience. "Folks, this is the moment we've all been waiting for. Shea Copeland is a teacher in North Carolina who thinks she's being interviewed about the importance of parental support in schools. She has no idea that waiting just outside her classroom is her childhood sweetheart, Owen Bradshaw, with a ring in his hand!" The camera flashed to Owen, who gave the thumbs-up sign with a big, goofy grin. Oh, Owen.

"Here we go!" There was a moment of silence as another camera focused on Shea, blinking and smiling, an earpiece in her ear. "Shea? Dick Byrnes here. Can you hear me?"

Shea glanced over at what Ivy guessed was a monitor, nodding. "Yes, Dick, yes, I can."

"Good. So are you ready to talk about the importance of parental involvement in the schools?"

Shea started to say yes, but Dick cut her off. "Or, would you rather talk about love on this special Valentine's Day?"

Ivy saw her sister's cheeks color slightly and could feel her own heart begin to pound in time with Shea's.

"Umm?" Shea looked around, probably searching for

some indication of what she was supposed to do next. "Sure?" she finally answered.

Ivy hoped for her sister's sake that this didn't turn into a nationally televised train wreck. She felt herself feeling less and less jealous and more and more sympathetic.

"Well, that's good news!" Dick Byrnes said. "Because we've got the ultimate romantic surprise planned for you!"

Right on cue, the children around Shea started singing "I Can't Help Falling in Love with You." The children's voices added a sweetness and innocence to the song that brought tears to Ivy's eyes and, she could bet, everyone else watching. The camera kept panning from the faces of the children to Shea's face as she covered her mouth, her eyes widening and filling with tears as the children made room for Owen to enter the room, carrying red roses and a black velvet box. He wasted no time getting down on one knee as the camera angle widened to show the children's smiling faces and Owen's parents and Margot fanning out behind them, the picture of solidarity and support. Perhaps, Ivy thought, if things had been different, she'd have been there too.

Owen opened the ring box, the diamond glinting in the light, like it was winking at the viewing audience. "I can't help falling in love with you, Shea," he said. "I never could." Ivy leaned forward to watch as Owen told her sister how much he loved her, how he wanted to make her happy, and how he'd spend the rest of his life doing so. The sincerity in his eyes as he spoke was real and so intense that Ivy found herself wanting to look away. It hurt to see that much love in someone, especially when she didn't have it. Not anymore.

As Shea nodded vigorously in answer to his proposal,

Owen slipped the ring onto her finger. The camera panned the tear-streaked faces of her mom, Owen's parents, then Owen and Shea as they kissed and embraced. Ivy raised her now-cold coffee in a toast to her sister and Owen, the ones who had made it this far. "You did it," she said aloud in her empty house. "Good for you."

Three

On the way to the office, Ivy turned off her cell, knowing her mother, and probably April, would call. She also turned off the radio after she heard a few too many references to Valentine's Day by overly enthusiastic announcers. As she drove she wondered about Michael, if he'd watched Owen propose and if he felt saddened by what he saw. Or if his life was happy, wherever he was, whatever he was doing, whoever he was with. Her heart clinched at the thought of him with someone else, and she had to laugh at herself. This whole proposal nonsense had clearly messed with her head.

She pulled into the parking lot and steered her car into the parking space with the sign marked "Ivy Copeland." The day the sign had gone up, Delores had come into her office with a confused look on her face. "Ivy? I think the sign people made a mistake." Her voice had sounded almost apologetic.

"Yeah?" She got to her feet and followed in the direction that Delores waved her. She stood beside Delores and peered out the window at the sign bearing her former name.

"If you'll excuse me." She turned on her heel and marched back to her office. Picking up the phone, she punched the phone buttons with unnecessary force as she dialed her father's number. When his secretary answered for him, she had said, "It's Ivy. Put me through, please" with none of her usual pleasantries.

"Ivy?" Her father sounded concerned, tipped off by his secretary, no doubt.

"Would you please explain why you had the sign people put Ivy *Copeland* on my parking-space sign?"

Her father sounded genuinely puzzled. "Because that's your name?"

She growled, "Dad, my name is not Ivy *Copeland*. My name is Ivy *Marshall*. It's time you respected my marriage. I won't have my family continue to treat me with this kind of disrespect." Her face was flushed, her heart beating. This confrontation had been long in coming and she was ready for it. This was the sand she'd plant her flag in.

Now her father was getting a little angrier. "Ivy, I simply forgot. You've been a Copeland to me all your life. You need to give me a chance to get used to this . . . this change. I wasn't trying to make some sort of statement. If you'd like, I'll call and have a different sign made. But let me remind you that I started this branch of the company for you, so that you could stay involved in the family business even though you insisted on joining *him* in Asheville."

She interrupted him. "*He* has a name, Dad. It's Elliott.

I know you'd rather it be Michael but it's not. I suggest you learn his name because he's going to be around for a long, long time."

Her father was silent on the other end. "Well," he finally said, "if his name was *Michael*, you'd still be with us."

She'd hung up on him, but for some reason, she'd never followed up on changing the sign. Maybe because some part of her—however small—wanted to hang on to Ivy Copeland as much as her father did.

Now as she got out of the car and walked into the building, she felt a little surge of pride in the sign, a little "take that" to Elliott. *I'm Ivy* Copeland, *after all. How ya like me now?* She dropped her keys in her purse and entered the office, her face immediately assuming the penitent expression that she had been wearing around her colleagues since her father's call.

Delores was not at her desk, but her desk calendar was turned to the new day and new Bible verse. Today's, Ivy noticed, was Psalm 84:5, same as the verse she'd seen on Twitter, the one about finding strength in God and going on a pilgrimage. It seemed God didn't want her to miss the message. God often spoke in stereo so she wouldn't miss what He had to say.

She was pondering what the verse meant as she passed by the conference room to find Delores waiting with Pete and Beck and the temp, all smiling. They moved out of the way to reveal a table full of breakfast goodies—fresh-squeezed orange juice, a dish of cheese grits, a plateful of bacon, and an egg casserole. "Surprise!" they all sang out in unison. Delores reached for her, and Ivy let her wrap her in a hug. "We knew you wouldn't have eaten this morning, so we fixed up this nice little Valentine's Day celebration to share."

Tears filled her eyes, threatening to engulf her as the emotions of the morning rose to the surface, ushered there by this unexpected small kindness. "Thanks, everyone," she managed to say. She caught Beck's eye and he winked. "Let me just put my things down." She hurried out of the room and into her office, where she put her purse on her desk, sat down, hung her head, and let the tears flow, knowing it was useless to try to blink back the torrent waiting to be released.

∽

After a good cry and a good breakfast, Ivy was ready to face the day—even the unpleasant parts. She talked to clients and contractors, explaining the demise of the business, spouting like a seasoned pro the platitudes that had escaped her the day before. It was amazing what you could accomplish when you put your heart aside and ran on autopilot.

She mostly forgot it was Valentine's Day, mostly forgot that she hadn't heard from her husband, mostly tried to forget the proposal altogether. She also ignored the second call from her mother, a desperate message from April, who was worried about her, and she tried to ignore her aunt Leah's call too. But her aunt was smarter than everyone else and bypassed her altogether, choosing to sic Delores on her.

"Your aunt called again," Delores said. She stepped into Ivy's office waving a piece of paper in the air before plunking it down on Ivy's desk. On it was written Aunt Leah's name and number, as if Ivy didn't know it by heart.

"Okay, thanks, Delores," she said, not looking up, a non-verbal cue that she didn't feel like talking at that moment. A cue that Delores chose to ignore.

"I saw your sister on TV this morning," she said. "That was exciting."

Ivy refrained from groaning out loud. "Yeah, it was great." She hoped she somehow sounded convincing.

"So you know that young man she got engaged to?"

"Yeah," Ivy replied. She looked up from her computer screen to find Delores's filmy hazel eyes fixed on her intently. "We all grew up together. His family had the beach house next to ours for as long as I can remember." In her mind's eye she could see Owen in blue swim trunks running along the sand to catch a Frisbee, his blond hair flopping over one eye.

"That sounds nice," Delores replied. "I love the beach. What beach did you all go to?"

Ivy sighed. "Sunset Beach. On the coast, kind of near Myrtle. If you've ever been to Calabash—"

Delores interjected, "Yes, I've been there. We ate seafood there once, I believe."

Calabash, North Carolina, was the self-proclaimed Seafood Capital of the World. She forced herself to make a joke. "I'm sure the seafood was fried." Her laugh was fake but Delores seemed not to notice.

"No, no, I can't have fried. Not good for my cholesterol. I got broiled. It's just as good."

"Uh-huh. Well, I'm going to call my aunt now." Ivy didn't want to get into a discussion on the benefits of broiled fish—not when she had so much else on her mind—so she picked up the phone message and waved it like a ticket out of the conversation.

Delores smiled. "She seems to really want to talk to you. So much excitement over that proposal this morning. I guess there's lots to do now that you all have a wedding to plan."

"I'm sure there is." Planning a wedding was the last thing Ivy wanted to think about, but Delores didn't need to know that. In another few weeks they wouldn't even be seeing each other anymore. The thought made her sad.

Delores paused before she left the room. "I wanted you to know I'm not going to look for another job." She clasped her hands together. "I'm going to retire."

"That sounds nice," Ivy said. Part of her wanted to retire too. Forget her MBA, her years of experience. Just retreat from the world of commercial real estate and corporate success and do something mindless. She thought of dancing in the kitchen as she frosted Delores's cake the other night.

"Well, it's time. Now I'll let you get to your phone call." Delores gave her a little wave and ducked back out of the room, leaving Ivy alone to stare at the phone message bearing her aunt's name and number.

Ivy loved her aunt Leah, who had managed to stay neutral in spite of everything that had happened. Leah had encouraged Ivy to mend fences, to forgive, to remember why she loved her family even though she was angry. But she'd also understood the hurt she felt and let her process all of it without pushing. She'd been the mediator who ultimately led Ivy to talk to her mother after several months of silence, the one who'd urged her to enter into business with her father as a way of mending the rift.

Ivy sighed heavily as she looked around the office at the things she would have to box up. Did that mean she should blame Leah for where she was now? She smiled at the irony and dialed the phone to the bakery, figuring that was where she would find her.

The Seaside Bakery was started by her aunt and mom after her parents' divorce. Her mom had gotten a lot in the settlement and didn't really know what to do with it, so she invested it in her sister's crazy dream of starting a bakery in the place they all loved most—Sunset Beach. It gave Leah and Margot a chance to live there year-round and helped them become more a part of the community instead of mere summer guests. They were full-blown citizens now, even though her mom had become less and less involved in the bakery in recent years. The shop was her sister's dream, and she'd been happy to fund it.

"Seaside Bakery," an unfamiliar male voice answered.

"Umm, I'm looking for Leah?"

"Yeah, she's around here somewhere. Hang on." She heard his muffled voice calling out for Leah.

Leah picked up the other extension, the one in the kitchen where she was probably rolling out a batch of cinnamon rolls or icing some eclairs. Ivy's mouth watered at the thought. "Hi, Aunt Leah, it's Ivy," she greeted her aunt.

"Ivy, I'm so glad you called! It's been crazy around here and none of us could get you!" By "none of us," Leah meant her and Margot.

"Well, I don't know if you've heard but Dad had to close the Asheville office. So I'm pretty busy here with that." *The world doesn't stop just because Shea gets engaged*, she thought but held her tongue.

Leah was unfazed. "Yeah, I was sorry to hear about that, but actually the timing is kind of good, don't you think? It'll free you up to be involved in planning Shea's wedding." Leah was trying to sound confident, but Ivy detected the doubt in her voice even as she said it. Leah was engaging not in just wishful thinking, but wishful talking.

"Oh, Leah, I doubt I'll be able to be involved from long distance. I mean, I'll have to find another job."

"Well, if it's a job you need, I could use you here at the bakery. You always were my best employee."

This was more wishing on Leah's part, yet her words brought back the smell of sugar clinging to her as she left work each day, dashing out of the bakery and into Michael's arms. She closed her eyes until the image faded away.

"Well, that would be kind of hard considering I live across the state." She worked at keeping her voice light and carefree. She was just fine, all was well. The last thing she wanted was for her family to figure out how bad things were with Elliott.

"Ah, yes, but I can dream, can't I? You know we'd love nothing better than for you to decide to come home."

Home. The word struck her with its power. How long had it been since she felt at home somewhere? From Charlotte to Sunset to Asheville, she'd traipsed around the state of North Carolina, chasing love and happiness . . . and come up empty. She felt a pull toward the coast she hadn't felt in a long while, just as sure as if Aunt Leah had tugged at a string tied to her heart that she hadn't known was there. And yet, Elliott was in Asheville. Her home should be wherever her husband was.

"Well, I can't very well do that, Aunt Leah. I have a life here."

Her aunt laughed, but Ivy knew better than to think the matter was settled. Aunt Leah had an intuition where Ivy was concerned, and she knew that her offer to return home wasn't offhand. "So you do, so you do." Aunt Leah's voice was nearly melodic. "Well, I called to tell you some news. I'm sure you saw the big proposal this morning."

"Of course. Very exciting." Ivy played along.

"The part you don't know is that the producer of the show had some sort of flash of brilliance and decided that it would be wonderful if they followed up on the happy couple." She was silent for a moment. "By broadcasting their wedding."

"What?"

"Yeah. Apparently he was taken by the Southern charm of the location and the story of these two kids growing up together. He said it sounded like a storybook. So he asked Shea and Owen if they would consider, and apparently Owen agreed right then and there." She snorted. "Men. He has no idea what it takes to pull a wedding together. There's just not going to be time to do it when that show wants them to do it."

Ivy could feel her heart begin to speed up on her sister's behalf. "When are they talking about doing it?"

"Apparently they're wanting to broadcast the wedding in June."

"That's less than four months away! And it's a morning show. Do they expect them to get married that early in the morning? On a weekday?"

"No, it would be taped, then played back. If you ask me, it's the last thing your sister needs to deal with. Planning a wedding is hard enough without the added craziness of putting the thing on TV." Her aunt knew about planning weddings. She worked with brides on their wedding cakes all the time.

"How is she going to plan a whole wedding that fast? Don't they know weddings take a long time to plan?" She felt a twinge as she thought of her own speedy wedding, but mercifully her aunt did not point that out.

"That's what I told Shea. But she doesn't want to make Owen look bad by declining the offer."

"What about her students? Is she going to finish out the school year?"

"Thankfully, her principal is giving her a leave of absence the last week of school, so she'll have two weeks to focus exclusively on the wedding. And she'll need it. With her teaching schedule, she's not going to have time to do much before the wedding. Personally, I think she's going to live to regret it."

Ivy was learning there were lots of things in life you could live to regret.

Leah continued. "So will you just call her? Offer your support, even if you can't come home to help."

Though she knew Leah didn't intend to heap on the guilt, Ivy felt it anyway. "Yeah, sure. I'll give her a call later."

"Thanks. And I'll tell your mom I finally got ahold of you."

"Yeah, please do." With any luck that would save her from yet another family conversation.

"And, Ivy? I really am sorry about your job. I hope everything else is going well for you. That you're happy."

"Oh yes," she lied. "Going great!"

As she said her good-byes and hung up with her aunt, she felt bad for lying to her. But telling the truth would be admitting far more than she was ready for. She and her family might be back on speaking terms, but they were nowhere near the kind of openness they once had.

Four

Over the next months, the quick succession of business-filled days was a welcome relief to Ivy, who needed the distraction that closing up the office—and the details that seemed to multiply when she wasn't looking—allowed her. It was much easier to fall into bed at night and let exhaustion overtake her than to face the fact that Elliott might be cheating on her. Somewhere in all the chaos, she fielded calls from her mother and aunt, had coffee with April weekly, and even managed a few brief but civil calls to Shea.

Her sister had asked her to be the matron of honor, and Ivy knew that obligation, not emotion, was behind her sister's request. Once upon a time, she and her sister had been as close as sisters could be, regardless of the three years separating them. Perhaps that was what had made Shea ask—a tribute to their shared past. Because they certainly didn't share the present. And with Shea married to Owen and Ivy married to Elliott, there wouldn't be much chance at the future either. Not with Owen still taking up for Michael the way he did, giving her that look that was a mixture of pity and disdain the last time they saw each other. She had to admit that avoiding Owen had also meant avoiding Shea.

Now Ivy looked out the window of her office at the empty parking lot. Her colleagues had been gone a few weeks now, and she had only a few more details to mop up before she shut down this office for good. She stirred her first cup of morning coffee absently, listening to the clink of the spoon echo in the empty office.

The phone rang and she picked it up, expecting her mother checking to make sure she'd given Shea the appropriate answer. With her mother, appearances were everything. Even if her girls were no longer close and the family barely resembled the family they once were, for one day she wanted to stand up in front of their friends and extended family and pretend. And now that television was involved? That only upped the ante.

Instead she saw April's number, which was odd, considering they'd just seen each other the night before, when April had stopped by her house with her wild dogs. April hadn't stayed long, rushing off to meet some girlfriends for dinner. After she'd gone, Ivy and Elliott had shared a laugh about the hyper puppies and how April had gotten herself into a mess but was unwilling to concede defeat. For a fraction of a second it had felt like old times between them, and she'd clutched at the hope the moment had given her. They'd even sat and watched a movie together. He'd held her hand, and she'd rested her head on his shoulder, crossing more emotional distance in those simple movements than it would appear.

April's voice was odd when she said hello. "Do you have some time to talk?" she asked, her voice strained.

"Have you been crying?" Ivy responded. She wondered if something had happened last night while she was out. Maybe she'd run into an old boyfriend who was now engaged. That always got her down.

"Could you just meet me at my house?" April avoided the answer, a tip-off to Ivy that more was going on than she was saying.

Ivy looked at the time and calculated how much of her day an impromptu visit to April's house would take. It wasn't like she lived just down the street. April lived a bit outside of Asheville, working as the caretaker of a collection of cabins for tourists while living in one of them. The property was gorgeous, with a stream running through the landscaped gardens and wildlife frolicking all over the place. It was a place where Ivy could lose herself, and had many times, swinging on a porch swing while overlooking the water. April had given her a place to stay when she first moved to Asheville, and the locale had been a perfect place to start her new life. Other than Sunset Beach, she'd never felt more at peace anywhere.

"Sure," she said. She hung up and surveyed the work on her desk. Some phone calls still to be made, a smattering of emails to be returned, and several contracts she needed to read through and sign. Only a few days' worth of work, really. And just yesterday her father had called. "You know," he'd said, "if you'd rather go help with the wedding, I can finish all of this. I never intended for you to take it all on."

She couldn't tell him what a relief the work was, what a welcome distraction it had been. She was nervous about the final paperwork being done, the remaining deals being closed, the door being locked behind her when the last day came in a few days. She worried about what she would do with herself then. And going to Sunset to help Shea did not sound like an appealing option. Maybe April would need some help out at the cabins. Maybe she'd let her stay in an empty one in exchange for taking one of the wild puppies off her hands or something.

A lump formed in her throat. Was she thinking about leaving Elliott? After last night that didn't seem as likely. She pushed the question aside and grabbed her keys. First, she would take a break from work and go comfort April. It would be nice to worry about someone else's problems for a change, answer her best friend's questions instead of her own.

∞

Her car tires crunched along the gravel as she ventured off the paved road and up the long winding drive that led to the cabins. A rustic handcrafted wooden sign pointed the way to the Mountain Stream Cabins, as if Ivy didn't know the way. April had worked there as long as Ivy had known her. A few times she'd tried to hire her friend away, tempted her with a big salary and a position helping with scouting commercial property back when the economy was booming and the real estate market in the southeastern US looked unsinkable. *Not unlike the* Titanic, Ivy had often thought to herself in recent months. But April loved where she lived and said that even if the pay wasn't great, the atmosphere was priceless.

Ivy parked her car, got out, and looked around at the sweeping mountain vista, forgetting for a moment all the stresses she had left back at the office. April was smart to stand her ground.

She pulled open the squeaky screen door of April's cabin to a muffled cacophony of barking. But no dogs pounced on her at the door. April sat at the kitchen table, looking mournful, her hands resting on the tabletop. Maybe she'd decided to give the dogs away and needed to be told that she was doing the right thing.

Ivy edged into the room, keeping her eyes on April as she gauged the situation. "Hey, where are the dogs?" she asked, trying to keep her voice bright as she sat down opposite her friend.

April hitched her thumb in the direction of the closed bedroom door. "I locked them in the bedroom so we could talk." As if on cue, Ivy heard one of them fling his body into the door with all his might.

"Not sure your bedroom's still going to be standing," she joked, searching April's red-rimmed eyes for some indication of what was going on. Maybe the pastor had called and said he'd made a mistake, begged her to come to Michigan. Maybe she'd decided to go.

April looked at her and swallowed. "Elliott showed up here this morning," she said.

As Ivy looked back at her friend, she understood. April

wasn't upset for herself. April was upset for her. She nodded. "Okay" was all she said.

"It's what you thought a few months ago." April's voice broke and she pressed her fingertips to her temples, looking down. "He had an affair." She said the news to the floor.

Ivy sat up taller, refusing to enter into exactly what April was saying, to watch from afar, as if this was happening to someone else. "So why'd he come to you?"

"He said you all had a nice night last night. That it made him feel so guilty he couldn't go one more day without telling someone." April looked back at her. "He knew if he told me, I'd either make him tell you or tell you myself."

Ivy took a deep breath, held it, then exhaled loudly. "I guess I know which one you all decided on."

"He's waiting at your house. To talk. He wants to fix this."

Ivy laughed. "Fix this? How exactly? How do you fix months of sneaking around, lying, betraying me—breaking our vows?"

"It wasn't months. It happened only once, but he felt so guilty about it, he's been avoiding you. A month ago he went to see a counselor at church, and the counselor told him he would have to tell you. Ivy, Elliott knows what he did was wrong, and he wants to work on the marriage with you."

"Well, give the man a medal." Ivy hated the sound of her voice, the bitterness that was there, waiting to escape at the first provocation. From behind the closed bedroom door, they heard the sound of scratching, dog toenails clawing into the wood.

"Did you tell him I suspected as much?" she asked,

looking in the direction of the bedroom so she didn't have to make eye contact. Though she knew that April would love her through this, she also felt a deep sense of shame. She couldn't keep a husband.

April nodded. "I told him you thought something was wrong."

A woman just knows. She remembered her mother's words. She'd vowed she'd never end up in her mother's position. And yet, here she was. She'd run from Sunset, from her past. But it had found her anyway.

Without warning she stood up and walked out through the screen door to stand on the porch, gulping in the fresh mountain air as if it would heal her. She scanned the mountain range, and a verse came to mind: "I lift up my eyes to the mountains—where does my help come from?" She thought of a hand mighty enough to carve those majestic peaks, a power big enough to tell the tides at Sunset Beach when they could come and go. And yet that power felt powerless to her just then, as far away as the coast of North Carolina—her real home—felt. She had once believed that God had led her here to Asheville, had brought her Elliott. But what if he'd never been involved, and all of this—the whole of the life she'd built—was a mistake?

April had come to stand behind her. "I need to go," Ivy said without turning around.

"I figured."

"What's that supposed to mean?"

April's eyes darted away. "You just always seem to run when things get uncomfortable."

Ivy ignored the remark because she couldn't disagree

with her friend. She turned around, her gaze falling on the cabin's door, avoiding April's eyes, which had come to rest upon her again. "What was her name?"

April shrugged. "I didn't ask. I got the feeling it was someone from work."

She wanted to scream, to run and run and run and never stop, just like April said, to climb that mountain in front of her and, at the apex, shake her fist at the heavens.

"But," April continued, "he knows he has a problem. Isn't that what they say? That admitting that is the first step?" Ivy could hear the defensiveness in April's voice, the piece of their friendship she'd always feared coming into play. Elliott was her family. Was it right to ask her to choose between them? Yet how could she not?

Ivy laughed a bitter laugh. "Don't hand me that Twelve Step stuff. That's for alcoholics. For people who have actual addictions. You can't have an addiction to screwing around on your wife. I'm sorry. That just doesn't cut it." From inside she could still hear the dogs, their barks reaching a frantic pitch as they heard the angry voices on the porch. She heard another thump as one flung himself at the door. "I'm a little disappointed in you, frankly," she said to April. "It sounds to me like you're taking his side."

"I'm taking both your sides. I care about you both," April said, a little too quickly for Ivy's taste.

"Look, I get that he's your cousin, but right now I just need someone who's for me. Just me. Not him. I'm the one who got wronged here. I'm the one who was betrayed." She jabbed her index finger at her own chest.

"I just know how much you both loved each other. I

know—" April broke off and looked away for a moment, inhaling deeply before she spoke again. "I know how your parents' divorce hurt you, how your dad's leaving affected you. And I just thought that if Elliott's willing to do whatever it takes to put things back together, it would make a difference. He's truly sorry and he really wants to make things right. He's trying!"

Ivy snorted, her anger keeping any real feelings about what April had said at bay. "Maybe I don't trust men because of my dad. Maybe I've had trouble believing in marriage because of what happened to my parents. But Elliott certainly hasn't helped that now, has he? And you—" She jabbed her finger in April's direction, taking note for the first time of the way April had stepped back and was looking at her with wide, fearful eyes. She ignored April's shocked expression and finished speaking. "You should understand that I need someone who's not going to point out how sorry he is. The poor little thing." She spat the words and spun on her heel. "I can't be near either of you right now."

She stomped off the porch and ran to her car, diving into it and slamming the door shut. She jabbed the key into the ignition and turned the engine, throwing the car into reverse and accelerating out of the drive, her back tires spitting gravel as she raced away from April and all she represented.

The truth was, she couldn't think about her past hurts or her present ones. She couldn't look at the shock and sadness on her best friend's face. She couldn't look, or she'd have to face her own. Better to hang on to the anger. The anger would protect her. The anger would fuel her. The anger would get her home.

She drove and drove, not wanting to go home and not wanting to go back to the office. As she drove she thought about all that had happened in the past months—Elliott's increasing distance, Shea's televised proposal, her dad's decision to close the business. None of it was her call, but everything involved her, changed her life. Her hands longed to grab hold of even one of the elements and take control, but they remained empty, powerless. She squeezed the steering wheel, debating what her next move should be.

For lack of a better place to go, she drove to the church she and Elliott had attended since they married, her belief in God and knowledge of the Bible more a birthright than a decision. It was as much a part of the culture she'd grown up in as sweet tea and magnolia trees. And yet, the older she got, the more she considered her faith—whether it was something she accepted or questioned, something she embraced or rejected. And if the answer was acceptance and embrace, what did that mean? *God is great, God is good*, she used to pray before meals. But as she parked the car and focused on the cross at the top of the steeple, appearing to touch the blue skies and white clouds, she wondered if He really was. In light of all that had happened, did she trust God's goodness? Or did He seem as far away as that blue sky?

"I can't do this alone," she whispered in the silence of her car. "Please show me what to do." She tried to focus on good times and happy memories, but they pounced away like the deer in her backyard.

She thought suddenly of the verse from months ago—the

one she'd seen the same night she'd spotted Elliott's car, and again the next day. The verse had been coming to her mind off and on ever since as she puzzled over what it could mean: "Blessed are those whose strength is in you, whose hearts are set on pilgrimage." The only place she could think of taking a pilgrimage to was the home that still called out to her no matter how many years went by. But that was a dumb idea.

You can't go home again. Fitting that Thomas Wolfe was from Asheville. When she'd first moved there, she'd done all the touristy things—the Biltmore House, the Mast General Store, the Thomas Wolfe home. Elliott had taken her to all of it, helping her dig into her new home-that-didn't-feel-like-home. She'd been determined to make Asheville feel like home, but so far it hadn't. There was something still inside of her that hearkened back to that place she could never quite work out of her system.

Her heart stirred at the prospect of returning to Sunset. Just yesterday her dad had told her she could stop working so hard, go to Sunset and help with Shea's wedding preparations. From the sound of things, her mom and Aunt Leah could use the help. The speedy timetable demanded by the TV people had put everyone on high alert. They would welcome her. They would be happy to see her.

And they would know nothing about what was going on with her and Elliott. Nor did they have to. She drummed her fingers on the steering wheel as she thought it over. It could work. With her job done and the wedding only a few weeks away, she certainly had a good excuse to go— nothing to raise her family's suspicions that anything was amiss between her and Elliott. She'd have to guard that secret for sure. But if she played her cards right, she could take the time she needed apart from Elliott, feel useful as she helped out her family, and maybe even reconnect with her sister.

A smile filled her face. Maybe going home again—to her summer home—was just the answer she needed. An answer she'd asked for, and gotten, just when she needed it most.

$\backsim$

She walked into her house with a sense of purpose, her mind focused on the packing list she'd started composing in her head as she drove from the church parking lot to her neighborhood. She was starting to warm to the idea of Sunset. It was May, and spring would be in full swing there, the first tourists starting to show their faces, the promise of summer in the air. The wedding was coming up soon, a mid-June affair that would air smack-dab in the middle of prime wedding season. Ivy could imagine all the wedding advertising the network was hoping to attract—their primary motivation no matter how much they gushed about being so taken with Owen and Shea's love story and the quaintness of Sunset Beach. It didn't hurt that Owen and Shea were such a striking couple either. The two of them could grace the cover of one of those wedding magazines her aunt had told her were lying all over the beach house as Margot and Shea schemed and planned at breakneck speed.

She was wrestling with the suitcase that was wedged under the bed when she heard Elliott clear his throat behind her. She continued with the wrestling match as if he wasn't there, tugging one last good time to free the luggage and nearly falling over as she did. Hardly the composed, self-possessed façade she was hoping to project.

Ducking her head to avoid his penetrating gaze, she hefted the suitcase onto the bed and busied herself with packing. Her careful packing list went the way of her confident demeanor as she opted for just getting out of there as fast as possible, getting away from the heat of Elliott's gaze burning her back as she worked. She knew he expected her to come back and talk over what April had told her. But she had no intention of doing any such thing.

"Are you going to talk to me at all?" he asked.

She ignored him. Tossed in all the underwear in her drawer. Then added her stack of folded summer T-shirts.

"I take it you're leaving," he tried again. "You're not even going to give me a chance to explain."

She had to respond to that one. She turned and gave him the evil eye. "I don't think you deserve that chance." She turned back to the suitcase sitting there on the bed, so receptive, so open to whatever she threw at it. She could count on that suitcase. She walked over to the dresser and yanked open the drawer containing her shorts a little rougher than necessary. She reached in and grabbed the whole stack, marched over to the suitcase, and added those next to the stack of T-shirts. Then she stood back and pondered the items she'd included so far, thinking over how long she'd be gone and what she could possibly need. There would be the wedding and the bridesmaids' luncheon and—

"Will you at least tell me where you're going?"

She remained silent, walked over to the closet, and pulled out a couple of sundresses without thinking too hard, except to note that Elliott was watching, and it would bug him to see her packing his favorite dresses to wear somewhere else. She pulled the sundresses off their hangers, folded them in half, and lay them across the top of the other clothes. Behind her, she could hear Elliott shifting his weight, crossing and uncrossing his arms as he watched her. She wanted to tell him to leave her alone, but she didn't want to engage any more than necessary.

"If it's any consolation, I'm sorry for what I did," he tried again. "It was just hard between us. You were working and gone so much. Ever since your dad put you in charge of that business—"

Another statement she couldn't not touch. She spun around and glared again. It hurt to look at him. "Don't you dare blame my dad. Or my working."

He took a step back, his back wedging up against the doorjamb. "I wasn't. I was just—"

"Pushing the blame off on someone else." She turned back to her packing. She needed pajamas, toiletries, shoes and walked around retrieving the items from their various places in the room.

"I'd like to talk to you at some point," he said. "When you get wherever you're going."

She thought of the one thing that would worry him, would hurt him. Not as much as he had hurt her, but enough to make her feel just the tiniest bit better. She zipped the suitcase up and turned to face him. "Sunset," she said. "That's where I'm going."

His face registered his surprise. He pressed his lips into a grim line, processing what she'd said. "I guess I've got that coming."

She laughed even though none of this was funny. "That. And more."

He crossed to the bed and she backed away. He held up his hands, a parody of an innocent man. "Was just going to help you carry your suitcase. It looks heavy." Stubbornly, she hefted the huge suitcase with two hands and started to stagger forward. She dropped it after only a few steps, and just as she was getting ready to grab it again, she felt his hands take it from her without another word.

There was a time when just that one little gesture would've been enough to soften her. But not anymore. She followed as he picked up the suitcase, crossed the room, walked out the door, and headed down the stairs to her waiting car, where he stowed it in the trunk. He closed the hatch and walked around the perimeter of the car, inspecting the tires just as he always did when she was getting ready to take a trip of any length. Satisfied with what he saw, he came to stand in front of her, looking sheepish and uncertain.

She kept her distance, her arms crossed protectively in front of herself as he gave her his charming grin, though she didn't miss the sadness behind it. She wouldn't let him disarm her or dissuade her from leaving. Her attraction to him was what had started all of this, what had landed her here, in this driveway with this man she felt like she didn't know at all, running back to the very people she'd once run from.

His smile faded away. "I hope you'll decide to give me

a chance, to give us a chance." His eyes filled with tears he blinked away. "I hope it's not too late."

She watched his arms raise slightly, as if he meant to hug her, then drop just as quickly as he thought better of it. It would be so easy to walk into his arms, to believe all that stuff that April had said about him wanting to work things out. But then she thought of all that waited for her at Sunset, of the people there. People who knew her, loved her, and had never betrayed her. If anything, she had betrayed them. A certain face popped into her mind, a face that had looked so wounded the last time she saw it.

She stiffened, setting her jaw as she looked Elliott in the eye and rose to her full stature of five foot four. "If it is too late, that's not my fault."

As she walked around to the driver's side of the car and got in, she heard, but didn't acknowledge, his response. "Of course it's not." She drove away trying to decide if he was being facetious or serious. But as she exited their neighborhood and headed back to the office to settle the details of her trip, she decided it didn't matter. The only thing that mattered was getting to Sunset Beach, and all that waited for her there.

Five

Ivy spent the rest of the morning back at her office. She made the necessary phone calls, telling her dad she was taking him up on his offer to finish closing the office so she could help with the wedding, then calling her mom and sister to let them know she'd be coming after all. Her mother was ecstatic, her sister polite but distant. Her stomach clenched at the thought of spending so much time with Shea. But when she focused on the alternative of staying and dealing with Elliott, her "pilgrimage" sounded better and better.

After lunch she joined the stream of cars on the highway. Six hours later, just after dinnertime, she pulled into the driveway of her mother's house on 40th Street—the last street on Sunset Beach before Bird Island, a stretch of state-protected coastline, began. Behind the houses on 40th Street lay marsh and, beyond that, the windswept, undisturbed coastline.

She stepped out and closed the car door, stretching her cramped legs and inhaling the beach air, the smell of the sea filling her nose. She couldn't believe she'd denied herself the pleasure of returning for so long. She twisted her wedding ring around on her left ring finger, thinking of why she'd stopped coming, and decided then and there that that had been a mistake.

Her eyes flickered over to the house next door. She half-expected to see two blond boys peering back at her from the front porch, eyes dancing as they concocted their next scheme that would land them all in trouble. She smiled. Whether it was putting crabs in unsuspecting relatives' beach chairs or peeing off the deck, Michael and Owen had always seemed to know how to stir up some trouble. She looked away. With the wedding coming up, she could bet that Owen was staying there, and his parents too.

That had been the draw, once upon a time. Owen and his cousin Michael, the next-door neighbors every summer who became playmates for Ivy and Shea. And then they became much much more. Her heart beat a little faster as she dared to wonder if she would see Michael, when she would see Michael. At the wedding, surely. And probably at the rehearsal dinner beforehand.

She surveyed the front of the house, taking in the changes that had happened while she was away. Wind and salt air had weathered the house, which needed a new paint job. And her mother must've given up gardening because there were no flowers lining the walkway to the house anymore. She walked around to the other side of the car and retrieved her purse, checked her cell phone, switched to silence after

Elliott had called more than once. There was a voicemail from him. She deleted it without listening. Whatever he had to say, she wasn't ready to hear it.

"Ivy!" She looked up to see her mom waving from the front porch. She slipped the phone into her purse and stood up, waved back, pasted on a grin that she hoped passed for authentic. Her job for the next few weeks was to focus on the wedding and keep everyone else focused on it as well, avoiding questions about Elliott until she was ready to talk about it, which might be never. She pulled her purse strap over her shoulder and headed to the house where her mom waited.

"So glad you made it!" her mom hollered.

She put her foot on the stairs and gripped the railing, focusing on her mother's face and how nice it was to see her looking happy to see her. "Me too, Mom. Me too," she said, meaning it with all her heart.

Ivy sat across from her mother, drawing lines in the condensation on the glass of Diet Coke her mother had poured her when they went inside. The two women regarded each other silently, each one struggling for topics of conversation that didn't veer into unsafe territory. Ivy was starting to realize that being at Sunset wasn't going to be quite the escape she'd imagined when the idea first occurred to her. So far she and her mother had talked about Shea (out having dinner with Owen's family), the weather (mild but warming up a bit more each day), the wedding (they were so busy every day and welcomed her help), her aunt Leah (staying busy at the bakery, planning to do Shea and Owen's cake, as expected), and the closing of the business (expected but still unfortunate). They didn't mention the past or her father.

Finally, with nothing left to ask, her mother brought up the one name Ivy didn't want to hear. "How's Elliott doing?"

"He's fine," Ivy said, unable to keep her voice from sounding clipped. "Really busy with work," she reiterated, hoping that explained why she felt free to show up at Sunset for an extended visit, the question her mother didn't ask, yet hung between them.

"Too bad," Margot said, running her hands through her short frosted bob. "I'm sure he'll miss you, though. What with the wedding still a few weeks away. I mean, you are staying till then, right?"

Ivy nodded, trying not to think about Elliott. She wondered if he would really miss her as he'd claimed or if he'd just console himself in the arms of whoever she was. She thought of April's words that morning: *It happened only once.* Well, once was enough to turn her whole world upside down.

Darkness had fallen as she and her mother sat across from each other, but neither of them had moved to turn on any lamps. Margot had tried to feed her when she arrived but Ivy had no appetite. "I ate on the way down," she lied so that Margot would stop trying to push food at her. Sipping on the Diet Coke was all she could manage. She looked at the clock on the kitchen wall, the same one they'd had all her life, little lighthouses dotting each place where a number should be. She wondered if it was too early to turn in for the night.

"Guess I'll bring in my suitcase and get settled," she said.

Her mom stood up. "I'll help."

She waved at her mom to sit down. "It's fine, Mom, I've got it." She headed for the front door. This time there was no Elliott to help with the heavy suitcase.

"Ivy," her mom called just as she was about to go outside.

"Yeah, Mom?" She turned to look at her mother, who had moved into the kitchen and was wiping down the counter.

Margot Copeland smiled at her, a real smile that said more than they'd managed to say up to that moment. "Glad you're here. It's nice to have both my girls home."

She returned the smile. "Me too, Mom. And thanks for letting me come."

Maybe someday she would confide in her mother. But they were a ways away from that.

∾

When sleep eluded her, she threw back the covers and retrieved her cell phone from her purse, checking her messages out of habit, wondering when she'd be able to stop the reflex. She no longer had a job, and after her spur-of-the-moment decision to leave Elliott, she might not have a marriage either. Other than the occasional missive from April, that didn't leave a lot of messages to check. Her caller ID showed several missed calls from Elliott. From the call record she saw that he'd called every two hours since the moment she left.

A flash of guilt traveled through the length of her body. Perhaps it'd been wrong to leave so impetuously. A good wife stayed and fought for her marriage. She tried to remember the moment in the church parking lot, when coming to Sunset Beach had seemed like her best alternative. She didn't need to start questioning the resolve she'd felt then. That could only lead to doubt and waffling. Right now resolution was her best friend.

She systematically deleted Elliott's voicemails without listening to a single one, anger welling in her the more she thought of it. After months of silence and avoidance he suddenly decided—after she left—to pay attention to her. What about all the nights she went to bed alone? What about all the times she begged him to talk, to get off the blasted computer, to face her instead of the television? Where was he before?

Then she thought about his cowardly approach in telling April and letting her do the dirty work for him of telling Ivy. Her anger mounted as she thought about how, in effect, he still wasn't really owning up to what he'd done. He hadn't had the courage to tell her the truth, face-to-face. *He's trying*, April had said. As if trying was enough when really it was too little, too late. He didn't deserve a chance to talk to her, to explain whatever it was he'd done. There were no excuses he could offer her, no rationale for his abhorrent behavior. He'd committed the unpardonable sin. He'd broken their vows.

She hated him for what he'd done. That was all there was to it. Their love had been dying a slow, painful death for a long time. All she had done was deliver the final blow. In truth, it was a mercy killing, like putting a sick animal to sleep. She'd ended both their suffering.

And now they could both move on.

She held the phone in her hand and stared at it, the message blinking that told her she had no more voicemails waiting to be heard. She clicked on the icon that would take her to her waiting emails, and found, other than some work emails, several more messages from Elliott. One had "Since You Won't Take My Calls" in the subject line. She checked the boxes to delete each one of them, not bothering to open them.

He had some nerve. Couldn't he take the hint? She thought about it for a moment. If she didn't want to hear from him, she'd have to do something drastic to get her point across. Something that would show him she was serious about taking the time she needed, serious about how angry she was. She scanned the remaining emails; all were business-related, except for a few from a church committee she'd volunteered for but never made time to follow through on. What was stopping her from just deleting her email account? Cancelling her cell service and buying a prepaid phone at the Walmart in Shallotte?

That would make a statement.

A smile crept over her face as she made a plan to let her business contacts know of her new email, one that only a select few would even know about. And it made sense in light of the business closing anyway. No one would bat an eye over the change, or suspect a thing. No one would guess that she was deleting her email account to dodge her husband. She powered off the phone and tossed it back into her purse, her mind running through a mental list of what she would have to do tomorrow to make it all happen.

She fell asleep debating whether this break with Elliott was temporary or permanent, reminding herself she didn't have to decide right away. This trip was buying her time to decide, letting the answers reveal themselves in time. Beach time.

Six

When her parents split up in her late teens, she and Shea went with Margot to Sunset Beach "to sort everything out." They ended up staying, the two girls splitting their time between home and the beach, their mother and their father. Margot got the Sunset Beach house in the settlement, and the family home in Charlotte was sold, with the proceeds going into an account to support Margot in the manner to which she had become accustomed. Not one to hoard her good fortune (if a divorce could ever be called that), Margot offered a portion of the money to her sister, Leah, to finally start that bakery the family had been saying she should start for as long as any of them could remember.

A year after they arrived at Sunset, shell-shocked and uncertain about the future, Margot and Leah had stood, side by side, and smiled for the grand opening of Seaside

Bakery. The local paper had covered the story and snapped the picture, which now hung, ornately framed, on the wall of the bakery, a place that stood for broken dreams making room for unexpected happiness. When Ivy woke the next morning, that was the first place she wanted to go. Both because she wanted one of her aunt's cheese biscuits and because the bakery was a place that always made her happy.

And she could use a good dose of happiness.

She slipped out from the covers of the bed she'd always considered "hers." In the early morning light she reached into her suitcase and pulled out a pair of yoga pants and a T-shirt from her university days. It took one look in the mirror to determine that her hair was a disaster and she needed a baseball hat. But she hadn't packed one. She thought for a moment and opened the closet, hoping her mom hadn't cleared out everything that was left from the time when this room was solely hers. She smiled when she saw many of her old things still in the closet, including her favorite pair of flip-flops, still sandy. And the baseball hat she stole from Michael. With a sentimental grin, she pulled it on and looked in the mirror, wondering if she could still pass for the girl who used to wear that hat—a girl who was five years younger. A girl who would've never allowed herself to end up in the situation she now found herself in.

She blamed her dad. He'd been the one to talk her into going on that stupid ski trip, after all. *Take a chance, Ivy,* he'd said. *Life is about venturing into unknown territory.* She guessed he'd take all that back now, if he could. She studied the older version of herself in the mirror and wondered if she would still take her dad's advice. She turned away and tugged the hat down lower, to hide her face better. No sense wondering about that now. She was here and Elliott was there, and since there was no going back, she would concentrate on going forward.

She left the house on tiptoe, grateful her mother—or worse, Shea—was nowhere around. She could sneak over to the bakery and say hello to her aunt. Leah would brief her on the real state of things—not the sanitized version her mother presented. Then, fortified with coffee, a delicious biscuit, and the latest family gossip, she'd return home and figure out the rest of her life. That was the plan, at least.

She drove the back way down 40th Street, taking North Shore Drive out to Sunset Boulevard, the only way off the island, crossing over the new bridge that was all the talk among the islanders. There'd been much debate about the need to replace the old bridge, quaint as it was, with one that would allow for better traffic flow and better access for emergency vehicles. Much as she'd hated to hear about the demise of that part of her childhood history, she had to admit it was nice to get in and out of Sunset without worrying about timing her trip according to the top of the hour when the bridge opened and closed. How many times had she sat in the backseat of the car while her father fumed over sitting in traffic because the bridge was up? Ah, family memories.

She passed the familiar landmarks, glad to see that not much had changed since she'd last been there, marveling that it had been as long as it had since she'd come to Sunset. She'd missed five summers, missed the bakery really taking off after years of working to make a name for it, missed

MARYBETH WHALEN

driving over the old bridge just one last time. It was hard to think about all she'd missed.

In mere minutes she pulled up outside Seaside Bakery, putting the car in park and taking in the window display her aunt had created. It featured a large wedding cake painted on the window with the words "Congratulations, Shea and Owen!" written in hot pink across the top. *Et tu, Brute?* She sighed and got out of the car.

She entered the bakery to find an older man behind the counter. "Help you?" he asked gruffly. Ivy recognized the voice as the one that had answered the phone when she called. The man behind the voice was thin and nearly completely bald, a patch of reddish-gray hair ringing his narrow head. He wore khaki pants that were cinched around his waist in such a way that Ivy got the impression they'd slide right off if not for the belt keeping them there. But the most shocking thing about him was that he was wearing a hot-pink T-shirt bearing the Seaside Bakery name and a cartoon cake on the front. The über-feminine shirt was hardly what she expected this man to be wearing. But then again, a man working at the woman-dominated bakery was hardly what she expected either.

She glanced around. "Actually, I'm looking for my aunt? Leah? The owner?" There was a time she would've just walked straight back to the kitchen like she owned the place, but somehow it didn't seem appropriate to do any-more. She eyed the man, wondering when they'd be out of his earshot so she could ask her aunt about him. Perhaps he was some sort of prisoner on work release and Leah had hired him out of the goodness of her heart. She was always doing things like that—sometimes to her own detriment.

"Le Le!" the man yelled. "Someone here to see you!"

Le Le? In all her days she'd never heard Leah called anything but Leah.

Leah bustled out from the kitchen, wiping her hands on a towel, powdered sugar or flour—they looked so similar—dotting the front of a T-shirt that was identical to the man's, except it was about three sizes larger and looked much more appropriate on her. "Ivy!" she called out as their eyes met. "Your mama said you showed up last night!" Leah wrapped her into a suffocating hug, her fleshy arms holding her tight, the human contact so warm and welcoming Ivy was surprised at what it stirred up inside of her. She found that she didn't want Leah to let go, and she wondered how long it'd been since someone had really hugged her. She'd been on autopilot for so long, she'd forgotten what touch could do, how it could melt away all her defenses.

She stiffened and backed away from Leah. "Yes," she said, holding out her arms like ta-da! "It's me!"

"I'm so glad you decided to come!" Leah continued. "But I never thought you would."

"Well, it was a . . . good time to do it. And I knew you all could use the help getting ready for the big day." She pointed to the sign in the window as a reference, as if there could be any question what she was referring to.

"I guess you met Lester?" Leah asked, using the towel in her hand to wipe down the display counter even though it was already in pristine condition. Her aunt was always busy.

Ivy nodded at Lester. "I did," she said, even though she hadn't really.

"Lester's been working here for—what is it?—six months

already?" She turned to Lester for approval and gave him what Ivy could only call a flirtatious smile. He blushed and nodded, standing a little taller under Leah's gaze. Was something going on between Leah and Lester? Her long-widowed aunt and this little wisp of a man? The first thing that popped in her mind was what a field day she and Shea would have with this. Then her heart sank as she remembered. This wasn't old times. This was five years later and things weren't the same between her and Shea. Not by a long shot. She looked from Leah to Lester. More than just the bridge had changed at Sunset Beach.

"So you gonna help me out around here? You know I could use it," Leah said, turning from making googly eyes at Lester. "You always were one of my best employees." She turned back to Lester and hooked her arm around Ivy's shoulder. "Ivy was actually my first employee."

Ivy smiled, remembering the day of the grand opening. She and Michael had made themselves sick sampling all the goodies. Later they'd tried to walk off their full stomachs down by the ocean. That had been the night he'd told her all about their shared future, the way he saw it. He'd been so full of plans. And she'd been so full of fear. She'd told herself then it was because of her parents' recent divorce, that the fear would subside. But it never really had, and ultimately she'd elected to run from it instead of face it.

"Yeah, those were the days," she agreed with Leah. Lester studied her with a confused look on his face.

"Where you been keeping yourself since then?" he asked. His deep voice belied his small frame.

"Oh, I live in Asheville now," she said, wondering if that

was actually true. "With my husband" she was quick to add. She glanced over at Leah to be sure she heard that part.

She did. "How is Elliott?" Leah asked. She looked around dramatically, as if she'd missed him. "Where is Elliott?"

"Well, he had work." She waved her hand in the air with a smile. "And he knew he'd just be underfoot down here with all this wedding business. He'll be here for the wedding, though." She suppressed a grimace after the words were out of her mouth. Why had she said that?

"That's good to hear," Leah said, a strange look on her face that Ivy ignored. "Seen your sister yet?"

"No. She and Owen were out last night when I arrived, and I pretty much passed out after my long drive down." *I went to bed and watched the ceiling for hours as I tried to figure out what to do about my cheating husband and adjusted to the reality that I was actually back in Sunset.* "But I'm sure I'll see her when I get back home in a bit." *I can't avoid her forever.*

"I really just popped by for one of your cheese biscuits. It's been too long since I've had one." Her stomach rumbled as she said it. She couldn't remember the last time she'd eaten. Up to that moment, the thought of putting a bite of food in her mouth, chewing, and swallowing had seemed like too large of an undertaking. Suddenly, though, she could think of nothing else she wanted more than one of her aunt's signature items, the perfect blend of cheese and dough, comfort food at its best. "Think I could get one of those and a coffee?"

Leah was already in motion, ordering Lester to fetch a biscuit from the display case and heading over to the coffeepot to pour a cup of steaming black liquid. Ivy knew there were just Folgers grounds in the filter, but something about her aunt's coffee tasted unlike any other cup of coffee she'd ever had. The closest she'd ever come was that little B&B in Highlands she and Elliott had stayed in that time . . . She blinked until the image of the two of them sipping coffee in bed disappeared. No sense crying over past coffee.

She accepted the cup with a smile and held it up in a toast. Inside she was thinking, *To pilgrimages.* But she didn't dare say it out loud.

∾

After promising her aunt she'd come back to the bakery and help out with some shifts, she drove over to Shallotte to pick up a prepaid cell phone at the Walmart there, then went reluctantly back to the beach house, arriving a little after nine. Her stomach was full even if her heart remained empty, though the hug from Leah had done her good. She wondered when the last time was that someone had wrapped her in a hug that lasted longer than a second, the beat of a hummingbird's wing. Somewhere along the line, she must've started giving off the vibe that she didn't need human contact. Somewhere along the line, she might've even started believing that herself.

Seeing her aunt and Lester flirting had brought a smile to her face, a real smile that wasn't for show. Maybe she would ask Shea about Lester and Leah. Maybe talking about someone else would help the two of them stay in safe territory. That had worked with them when they were kids, when they'd mutually realized that Owen and Michael weren't just neighbors, they were *boys*. The two sisters had become united in their mission to make the boys next door notice they weren't just the girls next door. The joint effort had all but stopped their rivalry. They'd even agreed on who should be with whom. Serious, studious Michael with his brooding intensity and introspective philosophies was perfect for her. Jokester Owen with his charm and ease and sunny perspective was all Shea's. And it had been wonderful, for a while.

She pulled the car into the driveway, lifting her coffee cup from the cup holder and taking the final, lukewarm sip, frowning at the temperature as she got out of the car. She walked into the house, expecting to see Margot and Shea sitting together at the table, talking wedding. She'd seen the expected bride magazines lying around the house, had turned away from the image of the models dressed in white lace on the cover, the headlines boasting about a day where dreams came true. *Whose dreams?* she wanted to know.

But the house looked empty. She stood silently for a moment, scanning the living/dining area, the bank of windows across the back displaying the view she'd been unable to see in the dark last night, the marsh and undeveloped beach land that served as the house's backyard. Soon she would go for a walk down Bird Island, watch the seagulls play, try to find a whole sand dollar, breathe in and breathe out . . . She smiled at the *Sleepless in Seattle* reference.

April would love Sunset Beach. Too bad she had to stay at the cabins and couldn't join Ivy. Though April's job was like being on vacation constantly, it also meant she couldn't leave and go on a vacation of her own. Ivy used to tease her about her rough life. But standing there, looking out at the beach view, she thought about what April was missing.

"Hey, Ivy," she heard her sister's voice behind her, thick with sleep. Shea yawned loudly and Ivy turned to face her, wrapping her arms around herself as if she were cold when the morning was actually quite warm.

"Hi," she said, taking in her sister's appearance up close and personal, without the television between them. Her college pixie haircut was gone. She'd grown her hair out—probably in preparation for the wedding she'd known was coming sooner or later. Still a dirty blonde, her hair had a natural wave, cascading down her back. And her face had lost the baby fat, her cheekbones sharper, her lips more pronounced. She was . . . striking, even first thing in the morning. Once people had made a fuss over Ivy's looks to the point that Margot had fretted over Shea getting a complex, but it was clear now that Shea had come into her own.

Ivy had to laugh at the switch the two had performed without even consulting each other. Shea had slimmed down, grown her hair out, and looked a lot like Ivy had when she left. While Ivy had gained a few pounds—not a lot but enough to look healthier, as Elliott often said, had cut her hair into a short bob, and looked more like Shea had that last time the two of them had been in this room. The thought brought a smile to her face, which Shea returned, inadvertently breaking the ice.

Ivy dropped her arms to her side and took a seat at the kitchen island. "Just waking up?" she asked. Shea nodded and crossed over to the kitchen, busying herself with heating up water in the same ancient kettle Ivy remembered from before, a burnt-orange color that no doubt came from the seventies.

She watched as Shea pulled tea bags from the cupboard, and sugar, and milk. *We drink it like the British do, with milk*, she remembered her mother teaching them when they were little girls. She used to have tea parties with them, training them in the finer things of life because she expected her daughters to have just that. Ivy couldn't remember the last time she'd had a cup of tea, always opting for coffee. But she did always dump a generous amount of cream in her coffee. She guessed that counted.

"So when did you get in?" Shea asked. It was, they both knew, a lame attempt at conversation, dancing around the tension that hung in the air around them. No matter how much they convinced themselves they were fine, that this moment was no big deal, Ivy knew that they were both feeling anxious about seeing each other again. Both nervous about when they would finally say what had gone unsaid all this time. Because it would happen. In some ways, it had to. Because only after it had could they truly move on with their lives.

But now wasn't the time. "Last night. You were out with Owen," she answered.

"Yeah, we were out for dinner, listening to a potential band for the reception." The whistle blew and Shea yanked the kettle from the burner.

"Did you like them?"

Shea shrugged as she hefted spoonfuls of sugar into her

cup. Ivy smiled as she watched. Shea's love of sugar hadn't changed. It was comforting to know that in some ways they were still exactly the same. "They were okay. Not ruling them out but not crazy about them either. Ya know?"

Ivy nodded even though she didn't know. Inside she was coaching herself: *Not everything she says is intended to dredge up unhappy memories. This is what it's going to be like, but it will get better. This is the gauntlet you must run through.* "So are you going to go see other bands?"

"I don't know. We should but I'm not all that excited about any of our options. I said we should just have a DJ, but of course Margot wouldn't hear of it." In her teens Shea had started calling their mother by her first name just to drive her crazy. That had apparently stuck. "She said, 'That is so uncouth, Shealee.'" Shea finished her imitation of their mother and turned to look pointedly at Ivy. "This from a woman who named her daughters Ivella and Shealee."

Ivy grinned back at Shea. This was one thing the two had always agreed on: *what* had their mother been thinking when choosing their names?

"Whatever. I will not be using a single family name for my child. You can count on that." Shea blew loudly on her tea before taking a big sip.

Child. The word stuck in her heart as surely as if Shea had thrown it there like a javelin. Ivy feared at this rate she'd never have a child. She was so far from where she thought she'd be in life by now. She stood up. "I'm just going to go check my phone for messages. I left Dad with some loose ends, so he might've tried to call." She was lying, of course. By the way Shea glanced at her, it seemed like she could tell.

Even after an extended absence, her sister could read her in a way that other people could not. This thought both comforted and disturbed her.

Shea set down her cup and put two slices of bread in the toaster oven. "How is the old man?" She asked.

"Fine, I guess. You know, worried about the economy and his business."

"Yeah, I'm really sorry that the economy affected your job too." Shea caught her eye and held her gaze steady so Ivy would know that she meant it. Just that one small act was enough to bring tears to her eyes, but she blinked them away and sat back down on the barstool instead of making her planned escape.

"Yeah." She shrugged, refusing to dig into how nervous she was about being jobless. "It'll be fine. I'll just figure something else out. It was a good time to come here."

"What does Elliott think about that?" There was that tone to Shea's voice again, almost an invitation to confide in her. But it was too soon for that.

Ivy rested her chin in her hand as she watched Shea butter her toast. "He's good with it. I mean, he understood that it was the right thing for me to come here and help out." She hoped her voice sounded as light and carefree as she was trying to make it sound. "And he's really busy too." She wasn't lying. He was busy, just not with what Shea would think. She dangled her legs, swinging her feet back and forth, feeling childlike on the high barstool.

"That's good. I'm sure you're going to miss him, though." Shea studied her engagement ring and smiled. "I couldn't imagine being away from Owen."

"Well, things change after you're married."

Shea rolled her eyes. "Everyone keeps telling me that."

Ivy stood up again and was about to escape to the safety of her room when Margot came in, wearing a robe and looking surprisingly old. Ivy glanced at Shea to see if she noticed it, but Shea barely even looked at their mother. To Shea she just looked like Mom, Ivy guessed. The beach house, the family members, the view from the back window—it was all familiar to her, as usual as her own reflection. Part of Ivy wanted that again, wanted the sense of home and entitlement that used to come with crossing the bridge into Sunset Beach.

"My girls in the same kitchen," Margot said, squeezing Ivy's shoulder as she passed by her. "Never thought I'd see this again." Ivy focused on the joy in her mother's voice instead of the breach she was referring to, coaching herself again about running through the gauntlet. She was a ways away from making it to the other side.

"And we have my wedding to thank for it," Shea said, grinning as she bit into her toast, piled high with blackberry jelly. A dab of jelly dotted her nose when she looked back up at them.

Margot laughed and wiped it away with a dish cloth. Ivy looked down, avoiding the tenderness—the comfort level—that existed between her sister and her mother. Something she used to have but didn't anymore. Something her heart longed for. *Put it on the list*, she thought.

Margot looked at both girls. "And speaking of weddings . . ."

Ivy and Shea both chuckled in unison at their mother's segue. It was so typical of her to see an opening to talk about what she wanted to talk about and go for it. "I guess some things never change," Margot said, voicing Ivy's thoughts. "I still seem to amuse you girls without even trying."

"You just know how to steer a conversation, Mom, that's all." Shea winked at Ivy. "Even if the conversation steers about as easy as a cement truck."

"I don't care what you two say. We've got a lot of work to do, and now that Ivy's here to help, I think we should divvy up the jobs." She looked from one girl to the other with one eyebrow arched as they both tried to compose themselves and act serious. Even though she looked angry, Ivy guessed that she was secretly thrilled to have them teasing her together. Just like old times.

Her mother grabbed a bulging three-ring notebook from the kitchen counter and opened it, pulling the reading glasses that hung from a beaded chain around her neck onto the bridge of her nose in one fluid motion. She peered through the lenses at whatever was in the notebook.

"What's that?" Ivy asked Shea.

"The Nuptial Notebook."

"The Nuptial Notebook?"

Shea grinned at Ivy's confusion. "Aka the Bridal Binder, the Matrimonial Memo, the Wedlock Workbook, the Girl Scout's Guide to Getting Hitched. Owen and I have several names for it, none of which she likes."

Margot lowered the book and narrowed her eyes at Shea before turning her attention back to it.

Shea yanked her thumb in Margot's direction, smiling at her ability to aggravate their mother. "She made it. It's got all our contracts, brochures, business cards, magazine clippings, stuff like that in it. All filed away within easy reach." Shea grinned. "Even I have to admit it's pretty clever. You know Margot, always properly prepared like a good Southern girl." She laughed at her own joke.

With a pang, Ivy thought about how long her mother had probably been waiting to make that notebook, how grateful she was to Shea for giving her the opportunity. "That's . . . cool," she managed.

Margot looked up suddenly, the glasses slipping a bit on her nose with the sudden movement. "Leah said you're going to be helping some down at the bakery?"

As usual, news traveled fast. "Well, she asked."

Her mother waved her hand through the air. "That's fine, I just need to know how much time you have to commit. There's quite a bit still left to be done, and ever since Owen committed us to this TV thing, everything has to be done at warp speed."

Shea started to speak, probably to defend Owen, but her mother waved her hand again, turning her attention back to the notebook, her face serious as she flipped through pages sheathed in clear plastic protectors. The room was silent except for the sound of the wind blowing against the windowpanes. Ivy longed to get outside and go for that walk. She looked at her mother and sister. Maybe she'd even ask them to go with her.

Her mother closed the notebook with a thump. "Okay." She looked at Ivy. "Today Shea and I have to go see the florist and the photographer—though why we're even paying a photographer, I have no idea. Surely the TV people are going to take enough photos without us adding to it."

Shea looked at Ivy. "Just to catch you up, you'll be hearing a lot about 'the TV people' in the days to come."

"I just don't know why you all felt that we needed to televise your wedding. I mean, the engagement being broadcast was sweet, but I think you should've left well enough alone."

Shea rolled her eyes. "Like we haven't discussed this to death already." She turned to address Ivy as if Margot wasn't even in the room. "As you may already know, Owen agreed to it before I knew anything about it. And once the wheels were in motion, well . . ." Ivy saw a familiar look cross Shea's face, one that she didn't expect to see. But just as quickly as it came, it was gone, a smile taking its place. "But it'll be great! We'll never forget it!"

"It's your wedding day. You won't forget it even if it's not televised for the rest of the world to see," Margot argued, no doubt resurrecting an ongoing argument. She sounded so different from the woman who had called her that day to tell her that Shea was being proposed to on TV. She'd been excited then. But now she definitely wasn't.

Ivy couldn't help but feel slightly relieved that Shea's perfect wedding wasn't so perfect. She didn't wish an imperfect wedding on her sister. But then again, she did.

"So what I was thinking," Margot continued, laying the issue to rest by changing the subject back to the plans, "is that you would take over the wishing tree."

Ivy looked at her mother, blinking as she processed what she had said. A tradition in their family for generations back, the wishing tree was really nothing more than some branches shoved artfully into a pot to look like a small tree. Guests were mailed tags that could be hung on the tree, ideally tucked into the invitations. The ones who attended could bring their tags with a wish for the happy couple written on it to hang on the tree. The ones who couldn't make it were invited to mail their tags in advance. Later the bride and groom could read all the wishes for the future they would, undoubtedly, have. *Yeah, right.* Ivy was more than a little cynical about wedding wishes coming true.

Someone of course had to be in charge of assembling the tree and collecting the tags, making sure they made it onto the branches in time for the big event. The finished product was always a big draw at the reception, with guests taking turns reading the wishes. Some were funny, some poignant, all filled with goodwill toward the couple. If she was correct in her assumption, her wishing tree was still somewhere in this house. Unless her mother had thrown it out in a fit of anger, which was entirely possible.

At least they'd never sent the tags out for her and Michael's wedding.

She swallowed, realizing that Shea and her mom were looking at her. "It won't take that much time," Margot said.

"She doesn't want to do it, Mom," Shea said. "Look at her face. She looks like you just asked her to destroy a sea turtle's nest." Ivy smiled at Shea's mention of sea turtles. Once upon a time the two sisters used to dream of seeing turtles hatch. No matter how many evenings they combed the beach, they never got to see one, though. Once they got there just as the last one slipped into the ocean, making his long swim back to where he came from. Ivy stopped remembering in time to hear Shea prattling on about how she didn't even care about the wishing tree, but Margot was the one insisting. Shea hadn't sent out the tags with the invitations, preferring to keep everything as simple as possible and not fool with one more thing. Margot argued back that the tree was a *tradition* and was about to launch into a historical lesson of marriages from higher up the branches of the family tree until Ivy spoke up and interrupted her.

"No, it's fine," she said. "I can do it." *This is why you came*, she coached herself. *Don't make this a bigger deal than it is.* She gave them a brave smile. "It would be my pleasure."

"You're going to have to send out the tags separately. You know that, right?" Shea asked, her tone expressing her disdain.

"It'll be fine," Ivy responded.

"Oh, good!" Margot beamed. "That was one thing I just couldn't see us getting to unless we burned the midnight oil." She wiped her hands on the front of her nightgown, a flannel one that definitely qualified as a granny gown. "And I'm not much good at that anymore."

A beat of silence passed before Margot announced that she was going to shower and get ready for their appointments. She looked at Shea, ever the mother. "You should get a move on, young lady, if you're going to be ready." She turned to Ivy. "You're welcome to come with us."

I'd rather listen to nails on a chalkboard than hear you two go on and on with photographers and florists. "Oh no, I was thinking of going for a walk, getting reacquainted with the place," she said. But Margot was already walking away, assuming the answer was no.

She shrugged at Shea, who was looking at her with a strange expression. "What?" she asked, wondering if she had coffee spilled down her shirt or something.

"Speaking of getting reacquainted, you know Michael's here, right?"

She knew her panicked expression would give her away if she tried to lie. She had a terrible poker face. "No, I didn't know that." She'd assumed that he'd settled in his hometown of Raleigh, like he'd always planned. Maybe even gotten married. She never dared ask and she'd avoided looking him up on Facebook or googling his name, though lately it had been tempting, proof that two could play at Elliott's game. But it wasn't a game. And even if it was, how did you determine a winner? And what was the prize?

"Yeah . . . Owen suckered him into coming here for moral support, and he got into this house renovation project. You'll see. "

Ivy pretended to be engrossed in the view of the marsh even though she could feel Shea's eyes on her. When she didn't respond, Shea continued. "I think it's pretty amazing of him to come here, considering. . . ." She let her voice trail off. Ivy didn't need her to finish the sentence, didn't need her to point out whose side she was, ultimately, still on.

Ivy dropped her eyes to the floor. "Yeah."

The silence between them stretched out for a few uncomfortable seconds until, mercifully, Shea announced that she needed to get ready and left the room. Ivy watched her go, thinking about what her sister didn't say long after she was gone and Ivy was left alone in the very place she once vowed she'd never return to.

Seven

Ivy walked along the water's edge, hugging herself, shivering a bit as the wind picked up. It was May and warm, but with the breeze coming off the ocean, it could still be chilly at times. And the water was nowhere near ready to swim in. When they were kids they used to dare each other to dash into it over spring break, their lips blue when they emerged. But they always swore they weren't cold at all. She could still see Owen and Michael, teeth chattering as they crossed their hearts, the sun glinting off their blond heads. She smiled.

She wanted to see Michael again.

The knowledge that he was nearby made her shiver all over, and this time not because she was cold. She carried the mental picture of him the last time they were together, a dismal final image to hang on to, but the only one she had. Thanks to choices she had made—choices she wasn't so sure were right in hindsight—she had broken his heart. "Shattered it, then stepped on it" as Owen so eloquently put it. She wondered if he'd managed to put it back together again.

The jetty that marked the end of Bird Island came into view. She made a visor with her hand and took in the vista ahead of her. She was the only person out on the beach for as far as she could see, a feeling that was at once thrilling and terrifying. She loved the solitude but was scared of it too.

"I don't want to be alone," she said aloud, a prayer that didn't begin with "Dear Lord" or end with "In Jesus' name." It wasn't a very official prayer, yet it felt more authentic than any other prayer she'd prayed.

She pressed on toward the end of the island, determined to touch the rocks of the jetty, to navigate her way out to the end and sit for a moment. Like she used to do when she would come out there to daydream about a future she'd thought would look much different than this. As she walked, she felt the answer to her prayer that wasn't a prayer: "You aren't alone."

Then why do I feel like it? she thought.

"You're here to answer that question." The answer surprised her. She wondered if she was really hearing the voice of God or merely answering her own questions on some subconscious level. She watched her footprints in the sand disappear in the path of the waves and figured that one way or the other, she would find out.

∽

When Margot and Shea returned from their appointments late that afternoon, Margot jumped right on to the next item on her list. "I just remembered where I put that wishing tree." She hustled Ivy downstairs to the storage room in the basement. Flipping on the light, they surveyed a jumble of artifacts from her childhood—a red kite with a rip down the center, its string tangled in the handle of a sand pail faded by the sun and missing its shovel, a box of sunscreen bottles long past their expiration dates, a bike with a flat tire, Shea's rusted pogo stick. If she closed her eyes, she could still see her younger sister bouncing around in the carport area, her blond hair bouncing in time with her jumps.

Her mother moved things out of the way to reveal part of a tree branch. Digging farther, she excavated the rest of the wishing tree. Her wishing tree. The one she and Margot had made shortly after she'd accepted Michael's ring, giggling together as they arranged the beach rocks and shells to anchor the branches, turning them just so. As they'd worked, Margot had shared the memory of the wishing tree at her own wedding. She'd smiled as she'd shared some of the funnier wishes, her eyes growing misty as she relayed the memory of Simon reading her the wishes before they stowed them away. Ivy had been surprised by her mother's willingness to talk about her father and wondered where those wishes were now that the marriage was over.

Margot hefted the tree onto a bench so they could both examine it. The branches were askew and most of the beach rocks and shells they'd used to anchor the branches had fallen out. She waited for her mother to pronounce the verdict: DOA. But instead her mother cracked a smile and clapped her hands together. "We've got something we can work with here!"

Ivy's eyes widened. Why not just start over completely and throw the stupid thing away?

"You really want to try to save this?" she asked.

Her mother gave her a knowing look. "No, I want *you* to try to save it." She clapped Ivy on the back. "And you better get to work. Time's a wastin'!" Margot started to dig in a nearby box. "Now, I know we've got those tags we bought in here somewhere . . ."

Her tags. Tags people were supposed to write wishes for her and Michael on. It all just seemed . . . wrong. Perhaps she was being superstitious, but she didn't think Shea and Owen's wishes should be written on tags originally meant for a marriage that never happened. She was all for saving money, but . . . it was bad enough they were using her tree at Margot's insistence. Still, maybe once she restored it, it would be a different tree entirely.

She put her hand on her mom's shoulder. "Mom, I'll just buy more tags."

Her mom shrugged. "Okay, honey. You go ahead and take that upstairs. There's something else I want to look for down here." She turned her back and started digging through more boxes.

Ivy wrapped her arms around the pot and lifted the heavy wishing tree from the bench. She picked her way up the stairs carefully, the tree branches blocking her view as she entered the kitchen.

"I heard it but I didn't believe it," a voice said.

She started, then peered over the branches. "Hello to

you too, Owen." She went past him and set the tree down on the counter before turning to face him. "Good to see you," she offered, even if it wasn't totally true. After everything happened he'd at first been icy cold, then politely distant. Now he seemed to be back to his old cocky self.

He reached out to give her a hug and she went, a bit woodenly, into his arms, forcing herself to hug back, to try to remember what it felt like for this to be natural, easy.

"I'm finally going to be your brother-in-law, like, officially."

She stepped back, creating a comfortable space between them. "Yeah. That's . . . exciting."

He smirked at her. "You're a bad actress."

"What's that supposed to mean?" She crossed her arms in front of her.

"I'd just love to know why you're really here." He crossed his arms too, mocking her. He always did know just how to get under her skin, the brother she never had.

"I'm here to help with the wedding. See?" She pointed at the dilapidated pot of branches on the counter. "I'm in charge of the wishing tree."

His eyes followed the direction of her finger. "If that's where people are putting their wishes for us, we're in big trouble."

"I'm going to fix it," she retorted with an eye roll. Owen always could bring out her inner teenager.

"Where's your hubby?"

"Home." She added, "In Asheville," as if he didn't know where she lived. Of course he hadn't ever visited. None of them had.

Owen just nodded, sizing her up with those knowing eyes of his. Five years ago he was the first one to guess that there was something she wasn't telling them. He'd given her a look a lot like the one he was giving her now.

"Well, tell him I said hi, by all means. I mean, when you talk to him." His eyes darted to the front window, studying the house across the street.

"I will," she said, glancing around the room as she tried to think of an excuse to get away from Owen.

"By the way," he added, turning back to her and fixing her with his gaze. "Shea was trying to call you earlier. Said your service has been disconnected. Isn't it kind of hard to talk to your husband if you don't have a phone?"

"I had to cancel my service. It was a business account and we're closing the business, as you might've heard." The lie tumbled right out of her mouth. Is this what Elliott felt like all those times he lied to her? Was he taken aback by the shock that registered seconds after the exhilaration of coming up with just the right excuse? She didn't want to think about Elliott, and she certainly didn't want to discuss him with Owen.

"Yeah, I heard about that. Tough break," Owen replied without an ounce of sympathy. Looking at him, she knew he was a little glad she had failed. *If he only knew.*

"Which is also why I'm here. Elliott understood my need to get away." *For more reasons than you need to know about,* she didn't add.

"Well, it sounds like you're going to land on your feet, regardless." He clasped his hands together in front of him. "You always do."

She was about to argue with him when Shea came bouncing into the room. She didn't need the pogo stick anymore.

"Hey, you," Shea said, reaching for Owen and planting a kiss on his lips with a loud smack. Ivy looked away. She was never very comfortable around public displays of affection, but especially not now when her own love life was in shambles. When was the last time she'd felt free to walk into a room and simply plant a kiss on Elliott's lips? "Just talked to Dad," Shea said to Ivy. "He said to call him about some business question." She turned back to Owen. "And he said yes to the extra moola we need!" Owen and Shea bumped fists over the news while Ivy secretly wondered why her father would say yes to more funding when he was already facing so much financially.

She slipped away while their attention was diverted, climbing the stairs to her room, fighting to retain control in spite of what seeing Owen, and Owen and Shea together, stirred up. She should have known better than to run back to her family. Because dealing with her family was turning out to be no easier than dealing with Elliott.

The feeling of being alone closed in on her once more.

She flopped down on her bed, looked at her pillow, and felt suddenly bone tired. She curled up and attempted to shut out the world, closing her eyes to block the images of the day: her mother in a granny gown, the deserted stretch of beach, Shea kissing Owen, and a bedraggled collection of bare branches that were supposed to somehow pass for a wishing tree. Just before she fell asleep, she thought of her answer on the beach: she was there to find out how to stop feeling so alone. Somewhere at Sunset was the answer to that question.

~

When she awoke it was dark outside. She looked around for the time, confused about whether it was evening or early, early morning. Maybe she'd slept for hours and hours. She sat up, groggy and disoriented. Maybe she'd slept for days.

Her prepaid phone told her it was after 8:00 p.m. Her stomach rumbled. She'd never eaten lunch and had slept through her normal dinnertime. Never one to miss a meal, she got out of bed and headed for the kitchen, wondering if her mother had cooked. On the way down she grabbed her laptop and decided to see if anyone had emailed her new email address while she ate. She found a handwritten note from her mom that said she and Shea had gone shopping and that there was some soup warmed up on the stove.

She helped herself to a bowl and crumbled saltines over the top. Balancing her bowl and spoon along with her laptop, she set up her meal at the island, taking a seat at the same barstool she'd sat on that morning. She opened her laptop and logged in to her new email account but found not one email.

She slurped her soup and closed the email account page, feeling a little bereft at the thought of all the emails she was missing. And yet, this was what she'd wanted: a nice clean break. She stared at her screen saver, a photo she'd taken of the stream that ran by the cabin she'd lived in when she first moved to Asheville. April! She'd not talked to her at all! She was probably going crazy wondering. Ivy ran upstairs, grabbed her phone, and raced back down. She took another bite of soup while she dialed April's number.

"Hello?" April answered the unfamiliar number with a question in her voice, probably expecting a prospective renter for the cabins.

"Hey, it's me, Ivy. I cancelled my other phone because Elliott kept calling it, so I've got this prepaid deal for now." She waited for April to respond but heard only silence. "I'm sorry for getting angry earlier," Ivy added.

"Glad to know you're alive." April's voice was flat in response. Ivy knew she was still hurt over the way she left things.

"Sorry," Ivy said again. She would have to rely on grace from her friend and play on her sympathies, hoping that deep down April understood why she pushed her away and fled. "After you told me about Elliott, I just . . . ran. I couldn't put enough distance between us."

"So you drove until the road ran out?" There was a hint of April's humor.

Ivy envisioned herself doing that—just driving until the car dead-ended at the shore. "Something like that," she said with a smile.

"But really? Going back to them? Was that really smart or just salt on the wound?" April had stood beside her when everything went wrong, championed her right to follow her heart, dried her tears, done everything a best friend should do—even though the two had really just met.

"I know it's confusing. I'm confused too. I just know that there are some things I have to deal with here before I can face what's going on there. It's . . . unfinished business."

"As long as that unfinished business isn't named Michael." April wanted Ivy to be happy, but Elliott was still her cousin. "No, nothing like that." Was she lying? "It's with my sister, my mom. The way we left it from before. The wedding's brought it all back up again."

"So you're playing the role of dutiful daughter and loving sister and hoping that fixes it?"

"I guess." She thought about exactly what she was doing there. And the truth was, she didn't know. She was just taking the next step without knowing exactly what the destination was. Kind of like five years ago. Which wasn't very wise, considering. "I'm going to help out my aunt Leah too. You remember you met her?"

"You always did have a way with frosting." Though her responses weren't effusive, Ivy could feel her friend softening the longer they talked.

"Yeah." She grinned at the thought of having a job that didn't involve spreadsheets and contracts. "And I'm helping with the wedding stuff."

"Gonna carry her train for her?" April quipped. "Throw flower petals everywhere she walks?"

Ivy laughed. "I'm going to take care of the wishing tree."

"The wishing tree?"

"It's a tradition that's been in our family as long as anyone can remember. You put up a tree at the wedding, and people either send tags or write on them there. Everyone hangs their wishes on the tree, and then after the wedding the bride and groom take them with them into their new life." She couldn't keep the wistful sound out of her voice. Every woman in her family, it seemed, had their wishing tree story—except her.

April was silent on the other end.

"I know what you're thinking," she said to fill the silence. "I'm not the best person to be handling people's wishes for a happy marriage."

"I didn't say that, you did," April countered.

"You didn't have to."

"Actually, what I was thinking was that it might be too painful for you. And also, how insensitive it was of your mom and sister to make you deal with something so emotionally charged. They know what you're going through—"

"Well, actually . . ."

April's scream through the phone was so loud that Ivy had to hold the phone away from her ear. "You didn't tell them? What kind of person leaves her husband and doesn't let her family know?"

"The kind of person who doesn't want to see her family gloat," she said quietly. "I'm just too ashamed to tell them."

April was silent for a moment. "Okay, I get that, I do." Her voice softened as she spoke again. "I'm just sorry for all of it. If I could make it better for you, I would."

Ivy dragged her spoon through the bits of soggy cracker left in her soup bowl. "I'm glad you're there for me." She was past the hurt she'd felt over April defending Elliott—if that was even what she'd done. April had been put in an impossible position, and she'd done pretty well, considering. Whatever happened, Ivy knew her friend would be waiting there, on the other side of the gauntlet.

"Well, there's one thing I do have to tell you. Because if I didn't I wouldn't be the friend you think I am."

Ivy felt her whole body tense. "What now?" Her mind was already running through possibilities—April met the other woman, Elliott showed up at her house and confessed more awful stuff, he had already put the house on the market.

"He started a Twitter account."

She let out a sigh of relief. That was just his way of getting on her nerves. He knew she loved Twitter, and he'd made so much fun of it, of course he'd get on it just to show her he could, just to show up at a place she liked to hang out—even if it was just online. "You scared me for nothing. That's no big deal."

"Well, the way he's doing it is."

"What do you mean?" Her heart resumed its rapid pace.

"He's tweeting his apology to you. He said he can't get you to take his calls or respond to his emails, so he's tweeting them to you, hoping you'll have a change of heart and want to see what he has to say."

"Did he tell you all this?"

"Umm, no. It's all in his tweets."

"Then how do you know about it?"

"He started following my Mountain Stream Cabins account, so I went over to check it out." April took a deep breath and exhaled into the phone. "The stuff he's saying is actually kind of sweet. You really should take a peek."

"April, do not be fooled by this. It's just a ploy to get my attention or make people feel sorry for him. Don't fall for it!"

April ignored her. "If you want to check it out, his Twitter handle is—"

"Stop! I do not want to check it out! Do not tell me!" Now she was the one yelling into the phone.

April laughed good-naturedly. "Okay, okay. I won't

tell you. Just promise me that, maybe after you've calmed down, you'll think about looking at what he's said. You know some women never get an apology."

She didn't want to hear about other women or how grateful she should be for his apology. "I'll keep that in mind," she said. From outside she could hear her mom's car doors shutting, hear the chattering voices that meant Shea and Margot were back. "I'm going to go before my mom and sister get in here and start asking questions."

"Okay, well, it's @ElliottIdiot!" April called out, and Ivy couldn't pretend she hadn't heard it.

"Aargh! What did you do that for?" Ivy yelled into the phone over top of April's cackle.

"Love ya, mean it," April said good-bye their usual way, and was gone.

Ivy hung up the phone, grateful to hear someone say she loved her. That another person could say it, right out loud, with no reservations.

$$\mathcal{C}$$

Shea came back downstairs after storing her bags in her room, pausing at the foot of the stairs to consider Ivy, her hand resting on her hip.

"Why are you looking at me like that?" Ivy asked.

"Trying to decide if I should warn you Michael is coming over here or just let you be surprised."

Ivy closed her eyes for a moment, then rose from her seat at the island and calmly carried her bowl over to the sink, rinsing the bits of cracker and film of soup residue from the bowl before placing it into the dishwasher. No one could say she wasn't pulling her weight. All the while her heart was hammering erratically in her chest as she debated what to do. To run upstairs and change would make it seem like she cared. But she did care. The last time she'd seen Michael was five years ago. Her hair had been longer, her body eight pounds thinner, and her smile much wider. Nowadays she had to coax her smiles to the surface—and that certainly wasn't what she wanted Michael to see.

"What would you do?" she asked Shea, who had taken her seat at the island.

Shea looked her up and down. "Change. Definitely."

She nodded. "Point taken. When does he get here? And why exactly is he coming?"

Shea glanced at the kitchen clock. "Any minute. And he's going over some wedding stuff with us. He suggested coming over here so Mom could have input, and I didn't feel like I should say no." Shea gave her a look. "We can't let things get weird."

"I don't intend to." Granted she hadn't known Michael would be next door when she'd hastily packed her things and fled the mountains for the coast. But she had known somewhere in the recesses of her mind that she would eventually see him, that he would at the very least be at the wedding. And in a way, isn't that what she wanted all along? The chance to revisit the past, finish unfinished business, say "I'm sorry" face-to-face?

She thought about April's news about Elliott tweeting his apologies and let the thought fly right back out of her head. She couldn't deal with Elliott right now. She caught her reflection in the microwave door. She needed to take care of her appearance pronto.

"I'll be right back," she said, and scurried out of the room.

As she took the stairs two at a time, she heard Shea call after her, "I didn't expect you'd care that much!"

She fought the urge to try to explain things to Shea, as if she could, thinking instead about what she would wear to see the man who used to love her, the man whose heart she broke five years ago, the man who'd known her almost as long as her own family, and as well.

Eight

From downstairs Ivy could hear the front door opening and the low timbre of men's voices floating up to where she stood in front of the mirror, fussing with her hair and makeup like a teenager preparing for her first big date. She put down her mascara and studied her face. Her eyes were still the same shade of blue, though they had seen many things since she and Michael were last together. Her nose still tilted up a bit on the end, a quality Michael used to love to tease her about. She had the faintest hint of two lines forming between her eyes, though she was years away from real wrinkles, she hoped. Her hair was the same shade of blond, though a few highlights were now required to keep it that way.

She looked close to the same girl he once knew. But she was far from that girl. She wondered if, when he looked at her, he would sense the changes that lurked underneath the surface. Was she afraid that he would—or that he wouldn't? She turned away from the mirror with a sigh. It was time to find out.

She gripped the stair railing as she slowly made her way down, watching the three of them as they laughed and talked, unaware of her yet. There was a space on the couch beside Michael, a space she guessed was her space, saved all these years. She knew the three of them had felt her absence at first, but was it possible that in a way they still did? She wondered if perhaps in some ways they'd been waiting for this moment, waiting for her to come back and fill that empty space. She shook her head and smiled at herself. She was being ridiculous and melodramatic.

Michael turned and saw her, stopping whatever story he was telling in midsentence as the room went completely quiet. He stood, ever true to his Southern manners. "Ivy Copeland," he said.

She did not correct him for using the wrong last name. Reminding him she was married just didn't feel like the right thing to do at that moment. Instead she held her arms out. "It's me!" she tried to sing out, but her voice caught in her throat and came out sounding like a bird with laryngitis. She looked like a complete fool. So much for her poignant entrance.

He laughed and sat back down. "So it is." He patted the seat beside him. "Have a seat."

For just a moment she felt guilty. Was it right to sit next to Michael? She was still married, after all. And he was the man she almost married. What would Elliott think if he found out? But then she thought about what Elliott had done and plopped down next to Michael, squeezing his knee in what she hoped was just a friendly greeting, less overt than a hug, but more familiar than a handshake. Still, she noticed Shea's eyebrows go up.

"It's so good to see you again, Michael," she said.

He looked at her with his own version of Shea's reaction. "Yeah, you too." He studied her. "You cut your hair."

Her hand flew up to her locks, badly in need of a trim. "Yeah," she said, feeling self-conscious with his eyes on her, his gaze a mix of the familiar and strange.

He shrugged. "Makes you look older."

"I am older," she mumbled. She placed her hand back in her lap, trying to hide that her hands had started to shake.

She couldn't let on how rattled, how silly, how completely out of her comfort zone she felt at that moment. And she couldn't let on that she and Elliott were anything but happy. Instead she would pretend all was well, just like she had the last time she was with Michael. At some point she and Michael would probably have to talk about all of that, clear the air. But not tonight. Tonight she would listen and participate in the wedding discussions. And she would ignore the nagging feelings of déjà vu that sitting next to Michael and talking about weddings stirred up in her.

Shea broke in before things got too awkward. "Michael, tell us about the beach house rental you found. It sounds like it'll be a perfect place for the groomsmen to stay." Shea, Owen, and Michael continued their discussion of the house for the groomsmen, giving Ivy a chance to sneak the occasional look at Michael out of the corner of her eye. The laugh lines around his eyes were just a bit deeper, but his eyes were still the same shade of blue. He no longer had curly hair but had shaved it to a short buzz cut that made him look more rugged, tougher. When he smiled he still looked like he was laughing at something that was his own personal secret. This stranger was somehow still so familiar to her. She would bet that he was struggling with the exact same feelings she was having. At least, she realized, that's what she hoped.

As wrong as it was, as unfair as it was, she found that she wanted Michael to still want her. And yet, as they sat together on the couch, talking about the wedding that was not theirs, he was polite but not friendly, reserved instead of engaging. He was keeping her at arm's length, which was actually smart of him, considering all she had put him through. And yet, she wasn't used to him being smart where she was concerned, and she didn't like it one bit. She had expected him to be the Michael she left behind, not some new version of himself. The change in him was disconcerting.

She found it drew her to him. She always had been one to rise to a challenge. Maybe proving to Michael that she'd changed, that she wasn't what he thought, that he could trust her—and maybe even love her—again would be just the thing to help heal her broken heart. Maybe if she was with Michael, she wouldn't feel so alone.

She thought about her walk earlier, and her prayer asking God to help her not feel so alone. Maybe she felt so alone because she'd made a mistake and married the wrong guy. Maybe the one sitting beside her had been the right one all along, and God had led her back here to find him. She snuck another glance at him and ducked her head as the corners of her mouth turned up reflexively at the thought.

When she looked up, Shea was watching her, her brows knit together, the corners of her mouth turned down. Later she would have to explain all of this to her sister, but that was not a conversation she was looking forward to. Telling Shea how she felt about Michael would mean also telling her how she felt about Elliott. And telling her how she felt about Elliott would mean admitting that her family had been right all along.

She wasn't ready for that, and she doubted she ever would be. She would think about other things instead—focus on the past that she and Michael shared, and the meaning behind them being there together, both charged with helping two family members finally say "I do." Maybe—just maybe—in the united planning, there would come a new kind of unity. One that would change everything for her and Michael, one that would right old wrongs and heal new hurts. She would rise to this challenge, making her past somehow become her future, and the man she once thought was her future instead become part of her past. Maybe her pilgrimage was designed to lead her back to Michael.

After Michael and Owen had gone home, Ivy retreated to her bedroom and opened her laptop to log in to Twitter, her curiosity getting the better of her. She needed to put Elliott behind her, but she also wanted to find out what he was saying to her, about her, in a public forum.

She couldn't believe he'd resorted to Twitter as a means of reaching her. And yet, as she pulled up the handle April said he was using, she had to admit it was working. There was something about knowing that other people could see their private business that compelled her to look instead of ignore as she'd been doing. If his tweets were too much, she reasoned, she could always report him, get him shut down for using Twitter inappropriately. She had heard of that happening and she wasn't afraid to do it.

And yet, as she saw his photo pop up on his page, Ivy felt the familiar twinge his face always caused inside of her, ever since the night they'd met. It was a feeling she hadn't had in a while. With her busyness at work and the distance he'd put between them, her feelings for Elliott had been mostly nonexistent in the past few months. About the only feeling she'd felt at all had been anger. And yet, as she saw his face online, she felt . . . different. He'd always sparked something inside her—a combination of challenge and conclusion, the problem and the answer all in one appealing package. Once upon a time, she'd found the combination magical, intoxicating.

Under his profile picture was a short bio. He'd written: "Just a guy who messed up, trying to say 'I'm sorry' to the one he hurt. Since she won't talk to me, this is my only option. To those who listen, thank you. I hope one of you is her." She refused to let his sweet bio get under her skin. He was simply a man who didn't take no for an answer or know his own limits—which was actually the reason she left him, when you got right down to it.

Under the bio were his stats. He had a few followers already, which was strange considering that he had just started the account. She resisted the urge to click on the list and see what their names were, start stalking any women followers to see if they were communicating with him. She could just imagine the direct messages he'd get: "If she won't talk to you, honey, I will . . ." She harrumphed at the thought. Maybe he'd find some sympathy from them if he couldn't get any from her. Maybe that's what he was looking for.

She scrolled down to his first tweet, figuring she'd read them in order. It simply said, "You have no idea how sad I was to watch you drive away." She thought of him standing in their garage, asking her not to leave, as if he had a right to ask that. She pushed aside the image of him loading her suitcase for her, checking her tires.

The next tweet said, "I never thought you'd go back there. I never thought I'd be the greater of the two evils." He'd been the breaking point between her and her family, pushing her away from them with her choice to love him. He'd been the one who held her and promised he'd love her enough that she'd never feel the loss of her mother, her sister, her friends during those painful, strained months. Of course it had been a lie. Of course she'd missed the people she'd known and loved all her life, no matter how much he tried to love her to make up for it.

She had to admit that it had been unfair of her to ever expect him to, a lot to pin on one person. And yet she had to admit that she'd perhaps unconsciously held him responsible for the rift with her family, and resented him for it. That time in her life had been so tumultuous, and yet she'd chosen him over them. The anger boiled up in her again. And look how he'd thanked her.

She heard the sound of a throat clearing behind her.

Reflexively she slammed the laptop closed and twisted around to find Shea leaning in the doorway, her arms crossed.

Shea spoke up. "Did Mom put you up to that warm reception earlier? That was kind of . . . unexpected."

Shea's question flooded Ivy with relief. Shea had assumed that their mother had made her be nice to Michael, instead of her actually being interested in him. This would stave off any further conversation about the state of things with Elliott, buying her some needed time to sort things out.

She smiled. "Not in so many words," she said, not totally lying. Ivy was sure her mother *did* want her to be nice to Michael, even if she hadn't come out and asked her to be.

"You know, you don't have to sacrifice your marriage to make Mom happy," Shea said. "And you don't have to overcompensate with Michael now that you're back." She drummed her fingers on the wooden doorframe. "He's totally cool with things now. He's fine."

Shea thought Ivy was being nice to Michael because she felt guilty. She had no idea that Ivy was interested in him. Part of her longed to confide in her sister, just like when they were young. They would sit together and delve into the evening, analyzing the boys' every move, every word. Were they interested? How long would it last? Would they one day be bound by more than sisterhood and be married to cousins too? They used to be giddy, imagining their futures, entwined in this place and these people. It had all been so perfect, for a time.

And then she'd gone and ruined it.

"That's good," she told her sister, maintaining the safe distance they'd created since then instead of choosing to spill her guts. Things were okay with Shea, but there was a part of Ivy that still felt standoffish around her, guarded. She remembered the scathing letter Shea had written her, which came to the cabin she was staying in on April's property. Ivy still didn't know how she'd tracked her down there. She'd shared the letter with Elliott and he'd made her ceremonially burn it in the big fire pit on the property. Then he'd held her as she cried over all that she had lost, mourning her sister just as surely as if she had died. That wasn't a gap you closed in a few friendly conversations. Better to take cautious steps, build the bridge one thin plank at a time.

"I just thought I'd tell you that—while I appreciate you trying to make things okay—you don't have to try so hard." Shea studied her for a moment. Ivy wished she knew what was going on behind her eyes but didn't dare ask. "We're okay, here. All of us. It was hard for a while after you left, but over time, it got better."

"That's good," she said for the second time, her discomfort growing the more they talked. She changed the subject. "Oh, I talked to Dad. He said he's coming down here a few days before the wedding. He said to tell you he's sorry that it won't be sooner. He's just covered up with all this business stuff." Shea didn't care about the details that were tying him up. "But here's something weird. He's not bringing a date. I thought for sure he'd bring that woman he's been seeing. What's her name?"

Shea scanned the ceiling as she tried to recall. "Umm, Delores?"

Ivy laughed. "No, Delores worked in my office." The image of her dad dating Delores was truly comical. "Elliott and I had dinner with him and this one last winter." Since the divorce Simon had gone through a string of attractive older women, preferring the term *companion* to *girlfriend* whenever he referred to one of them. None of them ever lasted longer than four months.

Shea shrugged and smiled. "I have to admit I'm glad he's not bringing anyone. I've been kinda nervous about how that would make Mom feel."

Ivy nodded.

"So, it's all good, right? Everything's working out?" Shea was putting question marks at the end of her statements. Either she wanted to be reassured or she was giving Ivy an opening.

"Yeah, it's all good," Ivy responded. She hoped her face was as smooth and emotionless as she was willing it to be.

Shea looked like she was about to say more, but her eyes flickered to the closed laptop. "I'll let you get back to whatever you were doing." She gave a little wave and walked away, a familiar whiff of her perfume wafting through the room, reminding Ivy of summer nights riding in a yellow Jeep with the top off, the warm air rushing past as they sang along to the Dave Matthews Band at the top of their lungs, thinking things would never change as only the young can do.

Nine

Monday morning Ivy woke with one purpose: to send out the tags to Shea's wishing tree. She would do the job she'd been assigned to do perfectly, because she could. And, in the face of everything else going on, taking care of something and checking it off a list felt like the perfect activity.

She walked downstairs, poured herself some coffee, added her mother's plain half-and-half (not the same as her hazelnut creamer from home, but beggars couldn't be choosers), and walked over to inspect the sad little tree.

When she'd set it down, one of the branches had listed farther over, causing a gap down the middle. There were hardly any rocks left in the bottom of the pot to anchor it down, which was why it wasn't standing. And upon further inspection she saw a crack in the pot itself. She shook her head and stood back up, taking a sip of coffee while she thought about what she needed to restore it. Her mom came over and stood beside her, silently observing the tree too.

"I think it's the Charlie Brown version of a wishing tree," Ivy quipped.

Margot raised her eyebrows, no doubt recalling all the Christmases she'd sat with her daughters as they watched the *Charlie Brown Christmas* show. "Remember what Charlie Brown did with that tree."

Ivy smiled and shook her head. "That was the magic of television."

"That's what you need to learn, Ivy, my darling. That was the magic of love. You show that tree a little love and you'll see what it can be."

"Mom, it'd be better to just scrap the thing. I was just online last night, and you can actually buy a ready-made wishing tree. They even color coordinate the tags and everything."

Her mother laughed and sashayed out of the room. "Now, Ivy, surely you know me well enough to know what my answer to that will be." She stopped and turned to look at Ivy. "Don't you give up." She winked and disappeared into her bedroom, no doubt to get ready for another day of running wedding errands with Shea.

Ivy grabbed a sheet of notepaper from the pad her mother kept by the phone and the fuzzy, color-coordinated pen that apparently came with the notepad, shaking her head at how her mom still loved anything with some bling to it. Gripping the pen, she started writing a list of what she would need to fix that tree: rocks, a new pot, tags, ribbons to hang the tags. Shea's wedding colors were blue and white, so she would get white tags with a pretty blue toile ribbon if she could find it. Even though it might involve driving all the way to Myrtle Beach to do so. She remembered her aunt sometimes used ribbon in her cake decorating and resolved to make the bakery her first stop. She would love it if Aunt Leah could save her from running around on a wild-goose chase.

"Hey, Mom!" she called in the direction of her mother's room. She waited but there was no response.

As she walked closer to the room, she could hear her mom talking on the phone. Suddenly she was thirteen years old, reduced to spying on her mom just to get a glimpse into her interior life. She stood outside the door, out of sight, and listened to her mom, trying to figure out who she was talking to by what she was saying.

"I'd like that too," Margot said. Then she giggled.

Her mother? Giggling? She leaned forward.

"Of course I remember that." Another giggle.

She sounded like a teenage girl.

"Are you still planning on arriving when you said? I've got that date circled on my calendar." A pause. "Yes. Circled. In red." The giggle had changed to this seductive purr that made Ivy cringe. Ewww. That was her mother talking.

"I guess I will see you then. Can't wait." Realizing Margot was hanging up with her mysterious beau, Ivy backtracked to the kitchen, her heart racing at the idea of Margot catching her listening. That was most certainly not a conversation she would want Ivy to overhear. And just who was she talking to?

Later, if she could find the right moment, she would ask Shea if mom had been seeing anyone. It was so odd considering the two of them had just talked about how nice it would be for her dad and mom to not be at the wedding with other people. But maybe Simon deserved to have to watch Margot with someone else and eat his heart out while he did. Margot was turning out to be a strong woman, which meant perhaps Ivy could as well.

She glanced down at the list she had made and saw Leah's name where she had written it across the top. First Leah and her new employee, Lester. Now her mom and some mystery man. She could remember when her mom and Leah swore off men forever, saying they'd had love and could never expect to have it again. What was going on around here?

She ran upstairs to shower and dress and get her errands taken care of. No sense worrying about her mother's love life—strange as that sounded. She had her own issues to deal with without dwelling on someone else's. And from the sound of things, Margot was holding her own.

∽

There was a yellow Jeep Wrangler parked outside the bakery when she got there. Her heart started pounding inside her chest just at the sight of it. The image that had filled her mind the night before returned: driving down Main Street with Michael, the radio blaring Dave Matthews as they sang at the top of their lungs, her turning around to smile at Shea in the backseat with Owen, feeling like the world was indeed their oyster. That life would always stay just this good. She'd been fifteen years old, and her boyfriend owned a car. And not just any car—a very cool Jeep Wrangler. If only the girls back at her high school could see this. That next fall she'd papered her locker with snapshots from that magical summer when everything changed.

And then everything changed again. And nothing was the same. And here she was. She looked over at the Jeep. As much as it looked like his, there was no way it was. He would've sold that thing years ago, gotten a much more sensible, grown-up car. For all she knew, it was Lester's car. She smiled at a new image that filled her mind: Leah and Lester driving down Main Street, her hair blowing in the wind, singing Beatles songs at the top of their lungs. Maybe her mother and whoever her secret love was would be in the backseat. Ivy sighed and got out of the car.

This time Lester wasn't manning the counter. Her aunt was there, packaging up a gorgeous birthday cake. This one was a daring black and white, for a fortieth birthday, no doubt. "Looks good," Ivy said.

"Yeah, don't know that I would've chosen it, but it's not my birthday."

"Looks like it's for an office."

"Yes, I have to get it delivered today. Lester's out already doing some deliveries."

Ivy's gaze lit on the binder displaying photos of wedding cakes. "I take it the wedding rush has started?"

"When has it ever stopped? Our wedding business— phew! You wouldn't believe how much it's grown."

"Still making the bride and groom come in and bake it together?"

Leah gave her a look. "What do you think?"

Leah had this crazy idea years ago that she would only make a wedding cake for a couple if they came in and baked the actual cake with her. And so, all throughout the wedding season, you found Leah walking nervous brides and clumsy grooms through baking what was usually just the base of the cake. But it was enough to give them a good idea of the work that went into the cake. She had a saying, "You don't get to taste the sweetness if you don't put in the work." It didn't take a genius to figure out she was talking about a whole lot more than just cake. Leah believed that brides put too much focus on the wedding and not enough on what came after. This was her way of getting a few minutes with them, to help them remember what they were doing—and why. It was a bold move, but it had worked for her. If anything, the practice only made her services more desirable, her cakes more meaningful. When a bride or groom fed their other half that first bite of cake, they knew what it was they held in their hands.

Needless to say, Elliott and Ivy had never baked a wedding cake with Aunt Leah. "Ya know, Leah, they should do a study of all the couples who bake cakes with you. I bet they have a lower divorce rate than the national average."

Leah put her hands on her hips. "That's a good idea. I'll put Lester right on it." She cackled, slapping her hands together.

"So what's the deal with Lester?"

Leah turned back to securing the cake for its journey. "What do you mean, 'deal'?"

"You've never mentioned him when we talk. Just seems like someone you woulda mentioned."

"Why? He's an employee. That's all. I hired him to do deliveries initially. But it's gotten to where he does all kinda stuff. Helps clean up. Waits on customers. I've even been known to have him help me with some of the baking. He's right good at making those cheese biscuits you love so much."

Ivy raised one eyebrow, something she once practiced for weeks to master. "And you're sure that's all he is? Just an employee?"

Leah stopped messing with the cake. "You girls and your fascination with love. It doesn't always have to be about love." She looked back at the cake, but not before Ivy saw two distinct circles of color spreading across her cheeks.

"It sure seemed like more than your typical employer-employee relationship when I was in here last time. If you ask me, he likes you. And you like him, Le Le." Ivy raised her eyebrows at Leah, who ignored the reference to Lester's nickname for her.

Finished with her packing, Leah pushed the cake farther down the counter and rested her elbows. "Of course he likes me. I gave him a job. A purpose. That's all." She quickly changed the subject. "Now, what about you? When's that husband of yours getting here?"

Great. She'd walked right into that one. "Oh, he's real busy with work. He can't just come at the drop of a hat. It's a six-hour drive, you know."

"But he is coming to the wedding, isn't he? I want to dance with that handsome man." She rubbed her hands together with a devilish glint in her eyes.

Ivy felt panic rise in her chest. She had no idea where she and Elliott would be in a few weeks' time. As it stood now, she really didn't think it would ever be any better between them. And what about Michael? How would it look if she and Michael were the ones dancing at her sister's wedding while her husband was nowhere around? She would eventually have to come clean about the situation. But not now.

"Sure, sure. He'll come a little closer to time."

"That's a relief. I haven't gotten to dance with him since that great party y'all had in Asheville. Now that was some night." Leah did a little pivot and twirl, being silly. Ivy winced a little at the memory of that night—of all the promise it held in spite of everything, of how grateful she'd been to Leah for showing up, the sole representative of her family.

"What was some night?" *Michael.*

Ivy and Leah turned to see the owner of the yellow Jeep Wrangler standing in the kitchen doorway, a goofy grin on his face, looking much more at ease than he had Saturday night. Leah and Michael were both smiling at her expectantly.

"Speaking of nights," Leah jumped in to save her, "this one said the four of you had a little reunion the other night." She nodded in Michael's direction and waited for Ivy to affirm her comment. But Ivy's mind was spinning. It was all too close, too real, too much. She was back at the bakery she'd helped to start, standing near the boy who used to pick her up after work, with wedding cakes all around her, symbolizing her greatest failure—and possibly her greatest regret.

"Yeah," she managed. "It was . . . fun. All of us together again."

A big smile filled her aunt's face. "It does this heart good to think of you four back together again. Just like old times!"

Ivy thought she saw a hurt look cross Michael's face.

Like her, he knew they were nowhere near old times. The old times between them weren't strained or awkward or forced. And the hurt she saw on his face now? Well, there was no denying she'd put it there. She'd ruined all of that.

She wanted to blurt out "I'm sorry!" right there in the middle of the bakery. Instead she just said, "Yeah, old times," and tried to smile in a way that looked convincing. From the look on his face, Michael was doing the same. It warmed her heart to know that, to see him trying. She was learning to take what she could. And today this moment of recognition was it.

Ten

She returned from Leah's shop with a lovely ribbon that was close enough to what she'd had in mind and didn't require a long drive. She'd also run by Walmart in Shallotte and picked up some tags, a rubber stamp that said "Wish" on it, and a large bag of blue glass marbles. She hoped they'd be strong enough to hold the tree in place in the pot. The one thing she hadn't been able to find was a pot to replace the cracked one. She was sitting on the floor, letting the blue marbles run through her fingers, thinking that a white or silver pot would look best, when Shea plopped down beside her.

"I take it this is going to be my wishing tree?"

Ivy looked over at her. "I'm not so sure you're supposed to see it till it's finished. Isn't that like the groom seeing the bride in her dress before the big day?"

Shea studied the assortment of items Ivy had spread out

in front of her on the floor, then gave the Charlie Brown tree a once-over. "No offense, but I don't feel like I've seen anything."

Ivy smirked at her. "Touché."

Shea lay her hand on Ivy's forearm. "I'm sure it'll be just beautiful when you're done, though."

Ivy froze, welcoming the unfamiliar sensation of her sister's hand on her arm, as if the ice was breaking between them just by the warmth of her touch. She held her breath for just a moment before answering, knowing that when she did, Shea would move her hand away. She wanted to say something touching, something sweet, in response. Instead she went to her default and gave her a snarky answer. "Yeah, we'll see."

Shea stood up and stretched out her legs. "I'm going to go for a walk. Wanna come with me?"

Ivy gestured to the mess on the floor. "And leave all this?"

Shea waved her hand, dismissing the mess. "It'll be here when you get back. Come on. Let's get some exercise." She hooked her hand under Ivy's armpit and started pulling.

"Ow! You're hurting me!" Ivy said, but she was laughing as she said it. Even getting manhandled by Shea felt good after years of polite distance and awkward conversations. You had to love someone to fight with them.

She shuffled off to find her flip-flops. Shea preoccupied herself with pulling her hair into a high ponytail that was so tight it tugged at the corners of her eyes. "You just gave yourself a face-lift," Ivy said. Shea glanced in the mirror hanging in the entryway, laughed, and pulled the elastic back down a bit. A loosened strand fell onto her forehead, and Ivy resisted the urge to reach out and tuck it behind her ear like she once would have. She looked at her little sister. "Ready to go?"

"Yep! Follow me!" Shea led the way out the door, down the steps, across the yard, and onto 40th Street, walking faster than Ivy would've thought. She had to hustle to match Shea's pace.

"Should I have put on my running shoes?" she asked. "You said a walk. This might qualify as a run."

"I said we were getting our exercise." Shea had an intent look on her face and was moving her arms in time with her fast steps. She gave Ivy a sideways glance. "You're not the one who has to fit into your wedding dress in a couple of weeks."

The two were halfway down the street when Shea slowed and stared at a house with scaffolding covering the front of it. It was the McCoys' place. Shea made a visor with her hand and scanned the front of the house, then peered around the edge. She shrugged her shoulders and kept going. "What happened to Mrs. McCoy?" Ivy asked. It hardly looked like the same place.

Shea resumed her fast pace, and Ivy kicked herself into gear to keep up. "She died a few years back." Shea said it like Ivy should know. Mrs. McCoy used to make them cookies and have them over for tea parties. She and her husband were empty nesters so they loved entertaining the children on the street each summer. She and Shea and Michael and Owen figured that out pretty quickly and, consequently, found any excuse to go over there. Ivy felt a little pang at the thought of being so removed from things around here that she missed the death of someone who had once been a big part of her life.

"Wow, sorry to hear that" was all she said in response.

"Michael bought the house, and he's the one fixing it up. Sometimes Owen helps him. I was checking to see if they were here."

"So how did Michael manage to get the house?"

"Not really sure how it all happened. I expect he made an offer to the McCoy children. You'd have to ask him. I mean, if you're willing to talk to him."

"I'm willing to talk to him. In fact, I saw him at the bakery, and we talked just fine. I'd like to be . . . friends with Michael." She used the word *friend* for lack of a better one, but the truth was she couldn't imagine being friends with Michael, not with everything that had passed between them. But she couldn't go into that with Shea, not yet. She couldn't share her feelings about Michael without sharing her feelings about Elliott. And she just didn't think she could say that out loud. Not without a lot of tears and incoherent blubbering. She and her sister were making strides, but they weren't at a bare-your-soul point.

Shea slowed down and looked at Ivy. "You and Michael cannot be friends." She started walking again.

Ivy, huffing and puffing, tried to get back in lockstep with Shea. "What does that mean? We're adults. Surely we can work at being friends. Especially since we've got to be around each other for the next few weeks. What would you have us be? Enemies?"

"I just think that you should think about it. That's all. I mean, what about from Elliott's perspective? Would you want him being all buddy-buddy with some girl he almost married? Wouldn't that weird you out?"

If you only knew, Ivy wanted to say. "Let me worry about Elliott. This isn't about Elliott. It's about trying to salvage something I lost." She didn't just mean what she lost with Michael. She meant what she lost with all of them. "I–I made a hard choice five years ago. I followed my heart and it hurt a lot of people. I see now how things maybe could've been different." *Like I could've not done what I did at all,* she didn't say either. "So now I'm back here and I'm trying to put things right. If that can even be done."

Shea kept walking in silence. Ivy knew her sister was mulling over what she had just said. Finally she spoke. "Just don't expect too much. Michael's in a good place. A really good place. I'm not sure he wants what you're talking about. Friendship."

The way Shea said it, it sounded like a dirty word.

"So you don't think it's possible for me to put things right?"

"I think it's always possible to put things right. As long as you don't expect them to be the way they were."

The two women walked on in silence. Ivy wondered what Shea was thinking—if she was angry with Ivy still or had already resolved to move forward with this new—different—relationship. Perhaps that was why Shea could so easily touch her, ask her to go on a walk, talk to her about things that didn't lie on the surface within easy reach. Somehow her younger sister had gotten wiser in the time they'd spent apart. She snuck a look at the set of her jaw, the intensity of her gaze, the rhythm of her blonde ponytail swaying back and forth with each step. Her little sister had grown up. It seemed she could take some lessons from her.

When they reached the Sunset Beach pier, Shea looked at her. "Wanna turn back?"

Ivy, panting, agreed that was the best idea. As they made their way back where they came from, Ivy remembered the strange conversation she'd overheard Margot having. "Hey, do you know if Mom's seeing someone?"

Shea laughed. "Someone as in, like, a man?"

"Yes, that was the general idea."

"Uh, no."

"You've never seen her talking to a man? Not at church or at a store or anywhere? Has she met anyone new in all the wedding plans?"

"Ivy, no. Mom talks to Dad about money for my wedding, which is never pleasant. And sometimes she talks to Lester at the bakery. And, of course, occasionally Owen and Michael when they come over." Shea thought about it for a moment. "No. There's no one else."

"Then Mom has a secret admirer."

"What?" Shea shrieked so loud that a hovering seagull darted away, scared.

"I heard her on the phone this morning talking to someone. She was giggling like a lovesick teenager. And then she used—oh, this is gross to even say—but she used this kind of, I don't know, sexy voice."

As if it was possible, Shea started walking faster. "I don't think so. Maybe you misunderstood. Maybe she was just being friendly. What you're saying just doesn't even sound like our mother. Some things have changed since you've been gone, but trust me, Margot is still Margot. She doesn't like to get too excited. She never musses her hair. She is always proper. And she's not capable of flirting." Shea's voice got quieter. "And besides, she's done with men. You remember."

They both remembered that weird fall they'd come back to Sunset, missing a week of school before they were told they were going to live there "for now" and go to high school there, away from all their friends and activities and the comforts of home. Shea and Ivy had loved the beach house for vacations but never desired to live there full-time. But for that year, while their parents decided to divorce and fought over the details, that's exactly what they did. The two girls lived on the fairly deserted island with their mother, who stayed in bed listening to Carly Simon a lot. The fact that Michael and Owen came down often to fish in the off-season was the only thing that made that year bearable. But even then, things started to change with her and Michael. Ivy had watched her parents split up, and something inside of her had split too, making her half of the whole she had once been. Sometimes she felt like the rest of her life had been a search for the half that had gone missing.

"Yeah, I wouldn't have believed it either if I hadn't heard it with my own ears."

"Leave it to Margot to create some drama just in time for my wedding," Shea said with an emphatic sigh.

"Just keep your ears open and your eyes peeled. She's up to something."

Shea shook her head. "As if I don't have enough to think about without trying to figure out who my mother's secret lover is."

Ivy started to sing an old song, "This Guy's in Love with You." But instead she changed the words. "Our mom's in

love. Our mom's in love with who?" Shea pushed her playfully, started to giggle, and then broke into a full-on run.
Ivy did her best to chase her sister but found that Shea was
now hard to catch.

∽

After they returned home, the two of them parked themselves at the kitchen table and began assembling the tags to
go out. It took them the rest of the afternoon and into the
night, but they stamped, ribboned, and addressed the tags
to all of the guests, creating a stack of envelopes ready to go
out in the morning's mail.

"I'm still not sure it's right to let you help me with this,"
Ivy said. "Mom put me in charge of the wishing tree. You've
got a lot of other things you could be doing."

Shea elbowed her. "Let me decide that. It's okay to need
help, Ivy."

Margot came in often, checking on their progress and
making little digs about how Shea had refused to help her
with the same project when she'd mentioned it. The first
time they saw her, they both had to stifle their laughter.
"What are you two up to?" Margot asked.

"Oh, *we're* not up to anything, Mother," Shea said.
"What are *you* up to?"

"Why, nothing at all. I just came in here to get a Diet Coke."

"Why are you drinking a diet drink, Mother?" Shea
kept on. "Need to watch your girlish figure?"

"Shealee Montgomery Copeland, sometimes I don't
know what goes on inside of that head of yours." Margot

looked at Ivy. "It's a good thing you're here to keep her in line or she just might not live long enough to see that altar."

Ivy, meanwhile, was struggling not to crack up laughing. "Yeah. Good thing I'm here," she managed with a straight face.

Margot wiggled her fingers with her free hand. The other gripped her Diet Coke in a silver can. "See you girls later."

Once Margot was out of earshot, Shea said, "Just run along back there and call your mysterious beau," which was enough to set Ivy off into the fit of giggles she'd been holding back since Margot had entered the room. She'd forgotten how nice it was to do life with a sister, someone who knew the whole you, and not just the part that you chose to show the people who came into your adult life. She thought of her choice to forsake all of this and wondered yet again what she'd been thinking five years ago.

$$\circ$$

After they called it a night, Ivy shut her bedroom door and got out her laptop, opening to Twitter and entering Elliott's handle. This whole thing was like a train wreck—she didn't want to look but she couldn't turn away either. This man was talking to her in a public forum. She wasn't ready to contact him—which is what would be required to ask him to stop—but she couldn't ignore it altogether. Quite simply, the curiosity was killing her.

She gazed down at the Twitter account. Apparently, other people were drawn to it too. His following was growing rapidly. One tweet by some guy she'd never heard of said, "@ElliottIdiot Way to show the ladies that men are capable of apologizing." He'd included a link to a song by Timbaland called "Apologize," which made Ivy laugh in spite of herself.

She scrolled down to the last one she'd read, then started reading again. He was tweeting several times a day, it looked like, random thoughts about the two of them interspersed with pleas for her to contact him. She read the tweets as if she were reading words written by a stranger, as if this were someone else's husband. She wished she could feel something. But the jolt of finding out the truth about him had been like an electric current that short-circuited her ability to feel much of anything at all.

The only surge of emotion she was feeling these days was whenever she was around Michael. She thought about when she'd spotted his Jeep parked outside the bakery. She'd told herself it couldn't be his, but deep inside she'd wanted it to be. And when she and Shea had walked by the McCoy house on the way back from their walk, she'd hoped he would be there. She bit her lip. In some ways it felt like that first summer when they'd become more than childish pals. How she'd lived for him to notice her, to tease her, to say something laced with meaning. That had been before her parents split, that one perfect summer she always went back to in her mind—when everything seemed filled with joy and she still believed that the kind of love she wanted was possible.

Of course, then she'd landed Michael and things started moving faster and faster until she hadn't even known what she wanted. The one thing she had known was she didn't want to end up like her mother, heartbroken and alone. *So much for that life goal.*

She kept reading the tweets until she got to the last one. It said, "Drove by the ski lifts. Remembered our nighttime ride."

She smiled reflexively over that one. Almost as if she'd watched it in some romantic movie instead of lived it. Was it only five years ago she'd taken that ski trip alone?

She shut the laptop and looked around the room that was hers but not hers. She'd gone a long way only to end up back where she started. She crossed the room and picked up an old framed photo of her and Michael, Shea and Owen, the four of them together. They were all wearing T-shirts and sunglasses, their faces tan, their smiles white and wide. They all looked so happy. She peered closer at the picture. "Were you happy?" she asked her younger self. "And if you were, why didn't you know it?"

Eleven

The next morning Ivy was up and out early, dropping the bundle of envelopes at the post office before heading to the bakery to help Leah. She watched the man carry the bag away, sending the tags off to their destinations, hopefully to return bearing wishes for Shea and Owen. Wishes for the life—the marriage—Ivy herself had once wished for. It was all too ironic for words. But she didn't dare deny her sister a chance at happiness just because she'd missed out. Making this wishing tree happen was one small way to say she was sorry for the mistakes of her past.

She caught herself looking for the yellow Jeep again as she pulled into the bakery parking lot, then shook her head at how silly she was being. She might as well get into a time machine and travel back to her teenage years for how she was acting. She grabbed the bag of assorted things Margot had thrust into her hands as she left, and headed inside to find Lester at the counter.

"Hi, Lester, good to see you again," she said.

He nodded. "Yeah, you too."

She held up the bag. "Leah back there? I've got some stuff for her from Margot."

"How is Margot?" Lester asked.

"Um, fine?"

"That's good, that's good. Please tell her I said hello when you see her, if you would."

"Um, sure. I will." She headed into the kitchen, where she could hear the radio playing and Leah, as always, humming along softly.

"Why was Lester asking after Mom?" Ivy asked without preamble, dropping the bag on the work area Leah was using. She pointed at it. "That's from Mom."

"Good morning to you too, Ivy." Leah made a face at her. "And if you must know, Lester is a nice person. Just because he asks after someone does not imply anything. Why? Are you trying to pair him off with your mother now? And move that bag out of my way, please." She shooed the bag off the table, and Ivy, frowning, moved it over to a crowded countertop.

Ignoring her insinuations about Lester, Leah instructed her to roll out the dough for a batch of cinnamon rolls. Ivy was rusty at first, but the feel of the rolling pin working against the elastic dough came back to her quickly. Leah stopped long enough to watch and comment. "Good job. I knew you'd get back in the swing of things."

Ivy wished that a few minutes working with dough was all she needed to get back in the swing of things. Instead she kept her attention focused on what she was doing, finding the physical activity good for stress relief. She could feel the tensions about Elliott start to ease, moving out of her body via her shoulder and arm muscles. She imagined the burning sensation she felt from the exertion was the stress, burning away. She listened to the radio along with Leah, and they worked in companionable silence for a time.

"So, I was wondering the other night about you and Elliott," Leah said, interrupting Ivy's reverie.

With her head down so Leah couldn't see, Ivy closed her eyes for a brief moment and took a deep breath. "Oh? What about?"

"I couldn't remember how you met him. I mean, I know it was on that ski trip you went on, but I was hoping you'd tell me the rest while we work." Leah laughed. "Ain't got nothing else to do."

Inside Ivy was panicking. She used to love the story of how she and Elliott met, used to tell it to anyone who would listen. But now of all times? That was the last thing she wanted to talk about, and she certainly didn't want Leah or anyone else to see the shame she carried over what Elliott had done. April wasn't the only one with a broken picker.

She knew Leah was just trying to be nice, trying to take an interest when the rest of the family never had, maybe trying to shed some light on her romance since everyone was making a big deal over Shea's. But her timing couldn't have been worse. She exhaled and looked up to see Leah's expectant face, watching her.

"It'll make the time go faster, you'll see," Leah said, nodding.

"I'm sure it will," Ivy responded. She thought about it for a moment, allowing the memory to come back full force instead of shooing it to the corners of her mind like she usually did. As her relationship with Elliott had started to deteriorate, she'd all but stopped thinking of their love story, focusing instead on fueling her anger. If she thought about what they'd had, she'd have to think about what she'd lost.

She glanced over at Leah, who had turned her attention back to the intricate lace pattern she was creating on a wedding cake that would go out later that week. White on white, it was quite possibly the most beautiful cake Ivy had ever seen.

"You're right," she began. "I did meet him on that ski trip." She decided she would tell it like the story was about two other people, people she used to know a long time ago who had faded away over time.

She took a deep breath and began. "If you remember, Shea and I were supposed to go with Dad. But then he had to cancel because he had some business thing come up."

"It's always business with your father," Leah observed.

"You're right about that," Ivy agreed, though she felt bad for her father, who had always worked so hard. She'd never understood that until she started working for him. "So when Dad cancelled, we thought the trip would get cancelled. But then Shea came up with this brilliant plan that we'd just go on our own. I was just out of college and she was in college, so we figured, why not just go together?" Sometimes she wondered if things would've turned out like they did if Shea had gone with her.

"And then Shea got sick." Aunt Leah seemed to be reading her mind.

She rolled her eyes. "And then Shea got the chicken pox. Who gets chicken pox at twenty years old?" She could still see Shea, red-spotted and clawing at her skin like a mad-woman, crying over missing the trip. Her mom had made her wear gloves so she didn't scar her skin. But Ivy could still see that one little scar beside her nose, a reminder of the way things don't turn out as planned.

"I bet you thought the trip was over for sure then," Aunt Leah said.

"Of course. Who goes skiing alone? So I called Dad to tell him. And he said, 'Now why would you let that stop you?' And he proceeded to talk me into going on the trip alone."

She thought for a moment about that day, how she'd called Michael and run the idea by him. He'd actually agreed with her dad. He'd said she should see it as a per-sonal adventure. "It'll be like climbing Everest. Only you won't have to leave the state," he'd joked. Funny how nearly everyone in her life at that time had been all for it. Except for Margot, of course. She'd thought it was risky for a young woman to travel alone and lectured Ivy about precautions all the way out to the car the day she left.

But she hadn't warned her about what to do when a handsome stranger talked to her in the lodge restaurant.

"So you went." Leah's comment interrupted her reverie.

"Yeah, sorry." She smiled ruefully. "I went. Drove by myself. Checked in by myself. Skied by myself. And I was proud of myself. But lonely. I was going to just get room ser-vice that first night, but I wanted to be around people. So I had dinner in the lodge, sitting by myself, naturally."

Leah looked up from the cake, sensing what came next.

She loved a good love story as much as the next person. "And you met Elliott."

She nodded, unable to keep the smile from filling her face as she remembered seeing him that first time. "He was working there, helping set up their computer reservation system. He'd been there awhile at that point, gotten to know the employees. He was having his dinner at the bar, cutting up with the bartender. But he kept looking over at me." She remembered how she'd tried to do things with her left hand, so he would see her engagement ring. Still, that hadn't stopped him from coming over to her table when she finished eating. She hadn't known if that made him a snake or just a determined suitor.

Leah snorted with laughter. "I've seen him. You'd have had to have been blind not to look back."

She smiled. He was good-looking. But more than that. He had been unfamiliar. Intriguing. For the record, it would've never gone further if he hadn't initiated things. But then he walked over, pulled out the chair opposite her, and said, "I believe this seat is taken." And for some reason, it hadn't seemed like a line. It had seemed like that seat was taken, had always been meant for him. And as they talked that night, she'd felt less and less like he was a stranger and more and more like he was someone she'd known forever.

They'd covered emotional ground in the course of that night that she hadn't known was possible, Ivy telling him things she'd never told a soul. Later she would tell Shea that Michael knew her history, but Elliott knew her heart. Shea, angry by then, had scoffed at that, dismissed it as the silly ramblings of someone with a bad case of infatuation. But how else could she explain it to someone who didn't understand what happened between them that night? It was like . . . magic, to quote Tom Hanks in *Sleepless in Seattle*. She continued her story, breezing through the details of him approaching her in the restaurant. There were some things she didn't want to get into with her aunt. There were some things that hurt so much to remember, she couldn't speak them aloud. One of the things that disappointed her the most was the height from which they had fallen. For a time, they had flown.

"So did you know he was different right away?" Leah asked.

"Of course. But it took me a long time to admit that to myself—much less anyone else. I kept telling myself this was completely *other* from my real life. That none of it counted because it wasn't reality."

"And did you think of Michael?"

Her eyes filled with unexpected tears at the thought of how much she hurt Michael. "All the time," she managed. So much for maintaining an emotional distance from the story.

"Done!" Leah pronounced suddenly, stepping aside so Ivy could admire her handiwork.

Ivy walked closer so she could get a good look. "It's beautiful," she breathed. Leah couldn't make an ugly cake if she tried, but this one was particularly spectacular. As Ivy studied it, she couldn't help but think that it looked just like a cake she might've chosen for her and Michael's wedding, had it happened.

Leah called Lester in to snap photos of it for the bakery website. (Elliott had designed the site in a failed effort to get in good with the family, back when he still tried.) Somewhere in all the excitement over the cake and packaging it up for delivery, her story ended. She left off with her and Elliott still sitting at that table in the lodge restaurant, talking long after the restaurant closed, the staff making little jokes as they left them there and Elliott promised he'd lock up. In the wee hours he'd made them coffee so they could keep talking. But she didn't tell Leah any of that. She just thought about it as she finished her shift and drove back to 40th Street, her thoughts a mixture of the beginning of her and Elliott and the ending of her and Michael.

But she was getting ahead of herself. And the story was over. That was, if she could stop thinking about it.

∽

After work she stopped at a garden center to buy a new pot for the wishing tree. Back home, she was standing over the pot, trying to make the branches stand up, when her phone rang. April. "I was just thinking about you earlier," she said to her best friend, who felt very far away at that moment.

"Look, I know I said I wouldn't bother you," April said. "But have you looked at his tweets today? I checked and I see you're still not following him."

"Nor will I ever follow him. Feel free to tell him that." She poured in some more marbles to try to shore up one side. She would neither affirm nor deny that she had looked at his tweets.

"Well, you ought to go check out what's happening over there. People are starting to respond. Like, a lot of people."

She sat down at the table and put her head down with a sigh, suddenly overcome with exhaustion. She either needed to nap or take one of Shea's power walks. "Okay," she mumbled.

"What are you doing?"

"Working on the wishing tree."

April laughed. "Feel qualified to be in charge of wishes yet?"

Ivy looked over at the tree, which had listed to one side again. "I'm feeling less and less qualified with each passing day."

"Talk to your ex yet?"

"Briefly."

"And?"

"And . . . it's complicated. He's my childhood, my past. We share a lot."

"Does he see it that way?"

"He's . . . understandably guarded."

This time it was April's turn to sigh. "Why do I get the feeling that you're trying to talk him out of being guarded?"

She laughed. "Because you know me."

"You're my best friend. Elliott's my cousin. He screwed up. You left. Understand I love you both and I'm torn. He's sorry, though, Ivy. You're really going to turn away from someone who wants forgiveness?"

"I can forgive him without letting him back into my life." She said it, but even as she looked around the house she had run back to, she thought about the way she'd needed to make things right with her family. She wasn't sure the two could be mutually exclusive like she said. Sometimes to forgive is to let someone back into your life. She'd not started feeling forgiven by her family—or feeling like forgiving them—until she'd been in their midst these past few days. But she didn't say any of that to April.

"Just read his tweets. At least then I know you're listening somehow. I mean, what he's doing for you? I'd give anything to have someone stick his neck out for me like that."

"Okay," Ivy said again. She knew that April was still hurting over the pastor's speedy departure to Michigan, how easily he'd given up. And for just a moment, she wondered if Elliott's tenacity was saying more than she was hearing.

"And one more thing," April added. "Just remember what you used to say: Michael's your past, but Elliott's your future."

She had no comeback for that, except that that might've been true once. But she wasn't sure it was true anymore. She hung up the phone and thought about going to check his account like April wanted. But then Margot and Shea walked in arguing over the "hideous flowers" Shea had picked out for the wedding, and Ivy got caught up in the argument. She had to admit it was easier to listen to them than to deal with her own stuff. As long as wedding plans were swirling around her, she could stay distracted. She could ignore Elliott and his plan to get her back, leaving her more time to focus on Michael. Going back to where she started to determine how she got to where she was.

༄

It was no coincidence that her walk that afternoon took her by the house Michael was restoring. She tried to look nonchalant as she passed, but secretly she was praying he would see her and call her name. But she walked all the way by, and there was no sign of him. Just her luck.

She continued on, thinking about Mrs. McCoy and her tea parties, feeling sad that the old woman had died without her knowing. That fall after her parents split, Mrs. McCoy had been one of the few neighbors still there after the summer crowds left. Ivy and Shea rode their bikes endlessly up and down the street, killing time and trying to stay out of the house so they didn't hear Margot crying. With each loop around the island, Ivy became more resolved that men couldn't be trusted. Maybe not even Michael. An anger against men—him included—began to burn in her heart. How dare they hurt women like that? How dare they walk away without a backward glance? The pure love she'd once held for her father was tainted by this mistrust that had seeped in, chemicals leaching into the ground water.

Sometimes Mrs. McCoy was in her yard, watering plants, when the girls rode by. She would wave them over and offer them lemonade. Mrs. McCoy made the real thing, squeezing the lemons as Shea and Ivy sat at her table and watched. She always wanted to know if the lemonade was good enough, sweet enough, cold enough, and they would give her a thumbs-up or thumbs-down accordingly. Once when she and Michael walked by Mrs. McCoy's house holding hands, the old woman caught her eye and gave her the thumbs-up sign with a coy little smile. Ivy had walked away wondering if Mrs. McCoy was right about Michael. What had happened between her parents had caused her to question everything.

She thought that meeting Elliott had ended her questions,

that it was him she'd been looking for, his absence she'd been feeling until the moment he took the seat across from her. But it turned out that the questions were only hibernating, awakened by Elliott's distance, mobilized by his confession. She'd been holding her breath, waiting for him to be like all men, waiting for him to show his true colors. When he had, it had almost been a relief.

Still, she didn't know what to do about those tweets of his. He didn't appear to be chasing skirts in her absence, based on how much he was tweeting and what he was tweeting. She had to admit that he seemed to be truly sorry and truly trying to change. This morning when she checked Twitter, he'd said he was going to see the counselor at their church. Men who just wanted to chase skirts didn't do that, did they?

And yet, she saw comments from women who were following him, women who thought he was wonderful and that she was stupid and weren't afraid to say so. Something in her seethed as she read the words—and not just because they were calling her stupid without even hearing her side. The mere thought of him being followed by women—even if he didn't initiate it—was enough to bring all the trust issues right back up. What if he was secretly communicating with one or more of them? What if he was going to find someone who responded to him in the way he was looking for while she ignored him? She didn't want to admit it, but that thought scared her. Deep down, she liked him tweeting to her. She liked the thought of him pining away, filled with remorse. Part of her just wanted to freeze him like that for a long, long time. Keep him lonely and miserable as punishment.

The yellow Jeep caught her attention as she headed back toward home. She saw movement on the scaffolding and her heart quickened. She looked for the blond hair that meant it was Michael up there, hope propelling her forward. As she got closer, she saw the blond hair, the height, the stance that told her it was him.

"Hey!" she called out impulsively. "Whatcha doin'?"

He turned around to see who was calling him, his brows furrowed as he squinted into the sun. She expected a big smile to fill his face when he recognized her. Instead he merely said, "Oh, hey, Ivy," and turned back around to keep working.

Undeterred, she crossed the yard and paused beside the scaffolding, looking up at him and the blue, cloudless sky beyond. "Whatcha doin'?" she repeated.

"Working," he said. He sounded tired. Or just unhappy she was there. She hoped it wasn't the latter.

"Oh, well, don't let me keep you from your work. I was just on a walk. I've been going on these long walks to figure out life, and stuff. Ever do that?" In an effort to create a conversation, she was making herself sound like an idiot.

"Not lately," he said. He continued to pull siding off the house, the wood making cracking and splintering noises of resistance. He had pieces of wood in his hair. She resisted the urge to climb up there and pull them out. She could still remember how soft his hair was, how it would tickle her nose when she whispered in his ear. "I love you," she would say. And for a time, she meant it.

He pulled another piece of siding off the house, speaking over the noise. "As you can see, I've got quite a bit of work to do. So I don't have time to get into some discussion right now." He swept his arm out to indicate the rest of the house and the many, many boards that needed to be removed. He was right, he had a lot of work to do.

"You could teach me how to do that, and I could help you."

His back was to her, so she couldn't see his reaction. She wanted him to sound happy that she asked. She wanted him to welcome her presence. Even if she had to get dirty and sweaty and do manual labor, she'd find a way to spend time with him, to work her way into the conversation they'd needed to have for five years. Not that he was acting like he wanted that to happen.

He glanced back down at her and—there! She saw it!—a flicker of a smile crossed his face. "You're hardly the construction-worker type," he observed. She knew he was taking in her designer denim shorts paired with a T-shirt with the name of another designer proudly scripted across the front. She hadn't just dressed for walking; she'd dressed for an encounter with him.

"You might be surprised," she said. Her tone was flirtatious, promising. She was teasing him and she suspected he knew it. He remembered that tone just as well as she did. She only felt a little bit guilty for using it with someone besides Elliott. She wasn't the one who'd broken their vows. And a tiny bit of flirting never hurt anyone.

He shrugged. "I won't turn down help." It wasn't begging. It wasn't even interest. But it was an opening. A tiny crack in the door that she could use her feminine wiles to throw wide open if she played it smart. She reminded herself that this was not a game.

"Okay, I have to be at the bakery tomorrow morning,

but I can come tomorrow afternoon if you'd like?" She sounded too eager. She needed to dial it down a bit. Men liked a challenge and all.

He gazed down at her with those blue eyes she used to hope their kids would get, a more brilliant blue than hers. He crossed his arms so that his biceps bulged and his pecs showed through the threadbare T-shirt he had on. Had Michael always been this . . . buff? Maybe it was the manual labor. She shivered in spite of the sweat trickling down her back.

"Sure. Tomorrow would be fine. I'll see you then."

She smiled up at him for all she was worth, knowing that he used to love her smile. Said he found his tomorrows there. And she'd known he wasn't just being cheesy. He'd meant it. "Great! I'll see you tomorrow."

She turned and walked away. She knew he wasn't watching her go like he used to. And that was okay. Everything had to start, or restart, somewhere.

Twelve

The next morning Ivy and Leah worked on cupcakes to stock the cases for the customers off the street who wandered in craving something sweet. Today they were making Oreo and red velvet and lemon meringue and Ivy's favorite, caramel. She bit back a smile as she thought about Psalm 84:5, which still often came to mind. It was taking God's strength not to just sit down with a spoon in front of the container of caramel icing.

The bakery was truly a happy place to be, and Ivy knew Leah had intended for that to be the case. When she'd made recent improvements in the store, Leah had had the floor painted blue and the walls yellow, boasting that the colors represented the sunrise and the ocean. Her aunt had wisely chosen a location with lots of natural light, perfect for aiding her vision as she labored over the more intricate cakes.

She'd set up a work center right in front of a large window that faced the parking lot, and it was common for a group of tourists out enjoying an afternoon to stop and watch her, a crowd gathering in front of the window. More often than not, that led to the people becoming customers, unable to resist the temptation of butter and sugar and flour, reasoning they were on vacation after all. What could it hurt?

It didn't take long for Leah to bring up their last conversation—cajoling her to finish her story about Elliott. "I want to know what happens!" she insisted.

"But you know what happened," Ivy retorted good-naturedly. When it was clear Leah wasn't going to give up, Ivy told her an abbreviated version, relaying the story like a journalist instead of a romance writer. She could tell that Leah wanted the dirt, but Ivy wasn't willing to go there, racing instead through the short version of the story she didn't want to tell. She just couldn't talk about what had happened that night, or where it had led. She'd told Leah that he'd asked her out when they parted, that she'd accepted in spite of her reservations about Michael, and that doing so set the dominoes in motion that led to everything else. But there were parts she still thought of even as she left the bakery and drove home to meet Michael, memories that came to her without her consent or permission.

Elliott had walked her to her room sometime in the wee hours, the sun's first streaks making their way across the dark sky. She hadn't felt self-conscious about what she'd done until they were in the elevator headed to her hotel room, Elliott staring at her in a way that told her she might have just dove into the deep end headfirst. And he wasn't going to be the one to throw her a lifeline. She bit her lip and looked away from the intensity of his stare, wondering what she was going to do if he tried to kiss her at her door. There was something between them—there was no denying that—but at that point, she was telling herself they could keep things under control. It was like hoping to put out a wildfire with a garden hose. But she hadn't known that yet. Not really.

She'd avoided his gaze as they made their way down the hall. At the door she made a production of getting out her key card, swiping it a few times until she got the green light that would permit her to slip through the door and flee. Suddenly she just wanted the distance that would allow them both some perspective. What had happened between them that night was magical but not realistic. Apart, they could both arrive at that conclusion, but together there was no chance of that. She spun her engagement ring around on her finger, pressing the pad of her thumb down on the prongs that held the diamond in place so hard they made indentations in her skin, the pain a penance.

She looked up at him as she held the door with her foot. "I had a nice time," she said. It hurt to look at him, to think that this could possibly be the last time she would see him. Cinderella was home from the ball; the magic was over.

He laughed. "A nice time?" He crossed his arms and smirked at her. "Isn't that an understatement?"

"Look, I . . ." She spun the ring faster. "There's someone else." She'd avoided saying that all night as they talked about everything from where they grew up to their favorite foods to memories of their grandparents to dreams for the future. Everything but Michael, even though he was at the edge of every word she said.

Elliott gestured to her left hand, the ring she was spinning round her finger faster and faster. "I'm not blind." He dropped his hands to his sides, the affront gone, his posture vulnerable, open. She could walk right into his arms, and they would go around her, a reflex. And she would fit there. "Besides, girls like you always come with complications." He shrugged.

"Girls like me?" Now she was the one to cross her arms, the door weighing more heavily on her foot by the minute. But she didn't want the moment to end, the inevitable to come any faster than it had to. She was, she realized, anxious to leave the door open, in a manner of speaking.

"Pretty girls. Smart girls. Together girls." The cocky grin came back. "Hot girls."

She'd been with Michael her whole dating life, belonged to him in such a way that she'd been closed off to the advances of other men, turning away when they tried to catch her eye, making terse comments if they tried to talk to her, taking her leave if anyone made it past her first line of defense. She'd been true to Michael in every sense of the word, and consequently she'd never let any man know her well enough to pay her compliments like Elliott had. She'd heard from her family she was pretty, and of course from Michael, but they didn't count. From Elliott, unsolicited, it felt brand new. It felt amazing. She glowed under the weight of his appreciative gaze. "Thank you," she managed.

He reached out and traced his fingertip across her cheek, making her shudder, her skin burning in the path he had traced. "Didn't mean to embarrass you," he said, his voice husky, thick with something she recognized as desire.

"It's okay. I just—I mean, I—" She held up her hands. "I have no idea what I'm doing. I never do things like this."

He rested his palm against her face, his fingers caressing her hair. "I bet you say that to all the boys." A teasing smile filled his face.

Exasperated, she argued. "I don't! I swear!"

"Would you believe me if I said I never do either?"

"Huh! No, I wouldn't believe you."

He shrugged. "Ask around. You'll find out. I've never done this." He looked into her eyes and removed his hand, leaving her cheek exposed, cold. "Never wanted to. Never felt . . . drawn to someone. Like I was to you."

"Me either," she confessed. She looked down at the carpet, black with tiny tan stripes. She needed to go, while she was still in the place of being able to explain all this away, dismiss it as a fluke. But if he kissed her . . .

"I should really go." She faked a yawn. "I'm really tired and I was hoping to hit the slopes today, not sleep the day away."

Instead of arguing, he looked around the hall, as if realizing where he was. "Yeah, and I've got to be at work in a few hours."

Her hand flew to her mouth. "Oh, gosh! I'm so sorry! You stayed up all night and now you have to work!"

He reached out and pulled her hand from her mouth, squeezed it. "It's fine. I wouldn't have wanted to spend last night any other way. I can sleep anytime. And I know this is all rather fast and I'm being awfully bold, but . . ." His voice trailed off. Their night was ending, but it was obvious neither of them wanted that.

Unwittingly, her eyes filled with tears at the thought of what came next. She was scaring herself with the depth of her emotions. She couldn't remember the last time she cried at the thought of parting from Michael. "Look, I'm gonna go. This isn't ever going to be easy, so I'm just going to rip the Band-Aid off. Okay?" She looked at him, not afraid to show him the tears in her eyes.

"I'll see you later," he said, his face serious.

She laughed. "Is that your way of avoiding the inevitable?"

He pressed his lips into a line and shook his head. "Nope. Just stating the obvious."

"So you think we're going to see each other again?" Her heart soared at the thought, then plummeted with guilt over what a terrible person she was to do this to Michael.

"I think any two people who can't tear themselves away from each other after staying up all night talking are destined to see each other again."

"I don't believe in destiny." She'd said that too quick and his face showed it.

"Then I guess that's my charge—to prove to you that some things are just meant to be." He reached for her hand and tapped on her ring. "Even when there are obstacles in the way. I'm sorry for whoever he is, but I can't ignore what's been happening between us. I hope you won't either." He leaned down and kissed her on the cheek.

He turned and ambled away as she stood in the hall and watched him until he disappeared into the elevator, resisting the urge to chase after him. Only after he was gone did she go inside her room, flinging herself on the bed and letting the tears she'd been holding back flow into the hotel pillow, her mascara leaving angry black smudges on the pristine white pillows. She'd never met anyone who made her feel so crazy. The feeling was like nothing she'd ever experienced and everything she'd never known she'd wanted. She'd fallen asleep as the sky filled with light, wondering how she was going to make these feelings go away and how she was ever going to forget Elliott Marshall and go on with the life she had planned.

Ivy left the bakery at noon. Back home, she parked her car in the driveway and strolled over to the mailbox out of some old force of habit. She grabbed the bundle of mail inside and wandered up the walkway, absently sorting it. One envelope caught her attention. Someone had already responded to her request for wishes for the wishing tree. She ripped into the envelope with the excitement of a child, extracting the tag and a note from the sender.

Stepping into the house, she examined the tag, finding a Bible verse scrawled in some old woman's arthritic handwriting, a friend of Owen's family who was apparently so on top of things she'd turned around and sent the tag back the very next day. Along with the tag was a note bearing her regrets for the wedding. She'd written that her husband was terminally ill and she was caring for him in his final days. She said that she wished Shea and Owen the same happiness she'd had with her husband for over fifty years.

Ivy's eyes filled with tears and she hurried up to her room before anyone saw her crying over a wishing tree tag. That would raise some eyebrows.

She sank down on the bed, still clutching the tag and note. The words swam in front of her. She wasn't prepared for how hard it would be to read the wishes. She and Elliott, despite her former hopes, would never celebrate their fiftieth. They'd never grow old together. In hindsight they hadn't had what it took to go the distance. Her family had been right. She'd made a mistake, and based on how Michael had responded to her, she could no longer count on him as her backup plan either. She stared up at the ceiling. She'd made a mess of things and now she had to face it, alone.

She turned the wishing tree tag around and around in her hands, studying the verse, "Let marriage be held in honor by all," Hebrews 13:4. This woman had obviously had the kind of marriage that was held in honor. It was hard to think that, at one point, she and Elliott had believed in that too. They'd planned to take on the world together, no need for anyone else. That was how she'd let go of her family so easily. As long as she'd had Elliott, she'd had all she needed, often quoting another Bible verse, the one about leaving and cleaving. She'd done that in spades, for a time. But she couldn't ignore the nagging feeling that she hadn't honored her marriage. Not really. She'd put it last—after her work and her longing for her family and the million little stresses that became their life together. She'd started out so strong, so resolved. And as the resolve had faded, so had their love.

She sat up. No sense mulling over her disaster of a marriage. Nothing she could do about it now. So she left the room, carrying the tag down to put it on the tree. Shea would whoop and holler when she saw the first tag, yell for their mom to come see, and thank Ivy for making it happen. Ivy couldn't wait for that moment, her single victory for the day, but a significant one. She couldn't put her marriage back together, but she could have a relationship with her family again.

She propped up the note where Shea would see it, her thoughts wandering back to Michael standing on that scaffolding looking tanned and toned, his face familiar yet mysterious. She looked forward to working with him today. She might even manage a relationship with him again, if she was lucky.

She stepped back and studied the tree with its lone tag, imagined it full at the wedding, guests stopping to admire it between dances. Then she imagined dancing with Michael, laughing as his arms held her in that easy way of his, secure without being suffocating, loving without letting go. She'd had it good once upon a time. Just maybe she could have it good again.

Thirteen

She showed up that afternoon, as promised, dressed in clothes that had belonged to her before she left—clothes that hadn't been worth taking with her when she moved to Asheville, for obvious reasons. She'd tried to make the work clothes look cute but opted instead for looking efficient—someone who'd come to get some work done, to actually help. Michael stopped working long enough to give her instructions, but that was about all. He'd either lost his social skills in the last five years or he was still pretty mad at her. She had to hand it to him, he was giving her a chance, not avoiding her altogether as he'd probably been tempted to do. With a little work and determination, she could fix things between them.

She climbed the scaffolding next to Michael's and looked at the row of boards she was charged with pulling away. "No," Michael said as she was deciding how much time this was going to take. "You move down there." He pointed at the last scaffolding, the farthest away from him. "We'll work from the outside in."

Okay, so with a *lot* of work and determination, she could fix things between them. With a sigh she hoped he heard, she hopped down and walked to the other end of the house, scaling that scaffolding. When she looked back at Michael, he had his earbuds in his ear and was bobbing his head in time to some music she couldn't hear. She hadn't thought to bring her iPod, foolishly thinking they'd spend the day catching up, mending fences even as they mended the house.

She shook her head, reached for a board, and began to pull, surprised at how easily it gave way. How something that looked so sturdy could really be falling apart. It reminded her of Elliott's last tweet: "When you left, it all came tumbling down."

Her mind wandered as she worked, thinking about what he'd been tweeting and how she shouldn't even be looking if she really didn't want to hear from him. She mainly wished he'd stop retweeting the things other people were tweeting about him. The women saying that he sounded sincere and she, Ivy, should give him the chance to explain. The ones who said they'd give anything to hear what he was saying from their husbands, that many women never got an apology or so much as a backward glance, that she, Ivy, didn't know what she had.

She snuck a glance at Michael. Maybe there was some truth to that. There had been before.

There were also men tweeting to him. Telling him that he shouldn't grovel, that he should look for another woman—one who would appreciate him. Some were complimentary, saying that he had inspired them to reach out to women they loved and make amends, or try to. Whatever they all had to say, there was one thing that was certain, with each passing day her husband was picking up followers like a snowball racing down a mountain, growing in size and momentum. He was causing quite a stir in the Internet world. But he still wasn't getting what he wanted. She wondered if all this attention was a good substitute, if he could be happy with reaching everyone but her.

She wished Michael would take off his earbuds and turn to talk to her. She wanted to ask him questions. Things like "What have you been doing for the last five years?" "Are you seeing anyone?" "Why'd you decide to renovate the McCoys' house?" "Are you happy for Shea and Owen?" And even: "Do you wish it was us?"

Instead he never looked at her, flint-faced as he pulled the boards off and tossed them into the now-cluttered yard.

A little later, he climbed onto the next scaffolding, a bit closer to her. "That's more like it," she said aloud, assuming he couldn't hear her with those earbuds in his ears. "What?" he asked her.

She looked over at him, shocked. He must've turned his music off.

"Oh, nothing. I just had a board that wouldn't come off. I got it off. I said, 'That's more like it' because I got it off. Wasn't talking to you." She turned back to her work, grimacing dramatically as she did.

"You're not moving very fast over there," he shouted.

"I'm a girl. And I work for free. You can't fire a volunteer."

"Yeah, yeah." He laughed. "Stupid me, I thought having you here would actually speed things up."

She stopped and crossed her arms for emphasis, staring at him until he stopped working and looked back at her. "What?" he asked.

"Maybe I should go home, then. If I'm no help at all." Her hands and arms hurt from pulling and she had a few splinters. She was dirty, she was hot, and she was tired from getting up early to work at the bakery. She didn't need to be there at all, and that was becoming more and more apparent.

"No, stay." He said it halfheartedly before he turned back to his work. "But I'll have two-thirds of the house done before you have your little third down there done." He looked so smug she wanted to shimmy over there and hit him upside the head like she used to do when they were little and got in fights. Though the physical brawls stopped when they grew up, the feelings behind them never did. In part they had always acted like siblings, or cousins. So familiar with each other, they were family by default. That's why the decision she'd made five years ago had had such far-reaching ramifications.

In some ways it had been like cutting off a body part. A useful part, something she'd once relied on and had to learn to do without, still reaching for the missing limb out of habit, still feeling the phantom pain even though she knew it was gone. Elliott had been her therapy, her rehab, helping her learn a whole new way of life apart from them all, letting her lean on him as she took those first halting steps away. And then he'd betrayed her, let her fall. And now she was discovering that the limb really was . . . gone.

She spun around angrily, knocking over a barrel she'd been stuffing the rotten boards into. The barrel started to fall over the side and she reached for it, realizing as her hands flew out that there was nothing for her to grab hold of. She screamed as her hands flailed, then blessedly grabbed the side of the scaffolding. Though it wobbled dramatically, she stayed put. The barrel, however, slid over the side of the scaffolding and landed in the yard, spilling the boards within it.

She looked over, panting, to find Michael watching with a horrified expression on his face. She was gripping the rail of the scaffold with white knuckles, her eyes wide with fear as they locked on his. And there, for just a moment, was that trace of concern that she'd hoped to see the whole trip. But then he grinned and flashed her four fingers.

The signal was an old joke between them that had started when they were kids. That school year he'd learned roman numerals and had discovered that the roman numeral for four was IV. From then on, he'd called her, simply, "Four." When she entered her gawky, clumsy adolescent stage, and he'd taken up golf, he'd learned that *fore* meant an out-of-control golf ball might hit someone else. He'd then changed her nickname from "Four" to "Fore," meaning "You better stay out of her way or you might get hurt." Everyone got a good laugh out of it. And to this day, if she did something clumsy, she could hear his voice saying "Fore" to her.

She smiled back, her heart filled with the rich memories of their shared past. He could act mad, or distant, or past their past, but there was no way he could be. It was too much to get over, too much to ignore. She would find a way to tell him that, to make him understand.

There on the scaffolding, she took a bow and he clapped. When she turned back, she was smiling and feeling more hopeful, in spite of her brush with serious injury.

They worked steadily into the afternoon. After making a spectacle of herself, she got serious and got into a rhythm, enjoying the release of yanking the boards out with violence. She felt powerful, in control, a force to be reckoned with. Her hands were a bloody mess, she stunk from sweat, and she was sure she looked a sight. But she put all of that out of her mind and just focused on the satisfaction that came from tearing something apart.

When she climbed down the scaffolding and looked at the house laid bare, she saw a resemblance to her own life.

Michael came down and stood beside her silently as they both surveyed the house. "Looks pretty bad," he finally said.

"I'll say. We tore it up good." She couldn't keep the pride out of her voice. He had no idea what she was thinking, what this exercise had really meant to her.

"Well, sometimes you have to destroy something in order to restore it," he said. "Want something to drink inside?" He nodded toward the house, and she, struck dumb by his words, nodded her answer before following him into the house, the place where she once had tea parties and drank lemonade and dreamed of a future that looked so different from the one she was living.

~

She gazed around as they entered the kitchen. Not a thing had changed. Everything was as she had remembered it:

pictures on the wall, furniture, everything. Hadn't the McCoy kids wanted any of it?

Michael handed her a bottle of water from the cooler, and she pressed it against her cheek before opening it, the icy water dripping onto her face with refreshing coolness. "Ah," she said. "Perfect."

The expression on his face was one of amusement. "You're supposed to drink it," he said, using his best "duh" voice. She remembered it well from their childhood.

"I'm getting to that." She rolled the bottle across each cheek and down her neck. He turned away to look out the window. "It's just so hot," she continued talking as if he were listening. "If it's this hot in June, what is it going to be in August?"

"Dunno" was his only response.

She rolled her eyes. So much for progress. She cracked open the water and took a long sip, the water cooling her from the inside out.

He turned from the window. "You'll be gone by August anyway. I'm sure that it's cooler where you're going. So no worries."

She knew a veiled dig when she heard one. This was his way of bringing up their situation without seeming to, his way of pointing out that she was married to someone else, living somewhere else, bringing up the situation just so she knew he remembered. Yet never really saying any of that.

"I remember now that being passive-aggressive was your specialty." She closed her eyes. She hadn't meant to blurt that out. She could hear her mother instructing her when she was younger: *Just because you think it doesn't mean you have to say it.* She should've learned her lesson.

He whirled around, anger flashing in his eyes. "What's that supposed to mean?" he yelled.

This wasn't the man she knew five years ago. That man was sweet, soft-spoken, agreeable. The worst thing he ever did was subtly manipulate her into what he wanted. But she could hardly remember him raising his voice to her. Even at the end, even when she betrayed him like she did. "I'm sorry," she said. "I shouldn't have said that. Really. I was way out of line."

He came to stand behind her and laid one hand on her shoulder. For a few seconds neither of them spoke. "Don't be sorry. I just—I wasn't—" He stopped, then said, "I don't understand what's going on."

She shrugged. "Maybe I just want to fix things between us. Make them like they once were."

He took a step back, his hand falling as he did. "Things can never be like they once were."

She put her water down and took a seat, resting her head on her hands. "I didn't mean like that. I meant like before before. When we were friends and not . . . involved."

He gave her a sad little smile. "Fore, we were always involved. It just took us awhile to realize it." He turned away, back to the window. "I've got some stuff to do outside," he said. "You're welcome to stay as long as you like." Without waiting for her reply, he walked out the back door and left her in the house alone.

The brief flash of anger was gone and the nice guy was back. And yet, she knew there was more to be said to each other, that conversation they'd never had hanging in the air between them. But he'd made it clear he was closed for business. She'd just have to be waiting outside the door when he hung the Open sign.

She walked outside and searched around the house until she found him in the back, messing with the railing to the deck. "Say you'll have dinner with me," she said to his back.

It was better than saying it to his face.

He continued to tinker with the railing as she waited for his response, watching his back muscles flex underneath his T-shirt. "I know you heard me," she said.

He stood and faced her, his face red. "I can't do that, Ivy." He pointed to the ring she had on. "You're not free to have dinner with me." He turned away from her. "But I guess you forget that pretty easy, Fore."

She sucked in her breath, reeling just as sure as if he had punched her in the stomach. It wasn't that she didn't deserve it—she more than did. It was just that she'd never expected him to say it. In her absence, Michael had gotten some . . . fight in him.

"If you'll have dinner with me," she continued, never easily deterred and dang it, he should know that. "I'll explain everything to you. What I'm doing here. Why I want to talk to you. Everything."

From the look on his face, she knew she was close to a sale. She had her father's blood in her, after all. He just needed one more little push. "Stuff I haven't even told my family," she admitted.

She watched his face. *Ding, ding, ding, ding. We have a winner.* He always did love being the first to know something. "So, will you? Have dinner with me?"

"I guess it can't hurt." He sighed.

"Okay, good. Fireside in Calabash?" While others gravitated to the many seafood places, they always went to Fireside for Italian, a little place that didn't look like much from the outside but served some great food. She could tell it hurt him a little to remember those many dinners together. But he recovered quickly and nodded.

"Thursday? Six?" she said.

He nodded again, then turned back to the railing. Conversation over. She said good-bye and headed home, happy to have something to look forward to, glad she'd given herself enough time to practice what she was going to say.

Fourteen

In her dream she was in a tree, sitting out on a limb, reading a book. Below her she could hear voices calling to her— her mother's, April's, Shea's, and two male voices, voices that touched different places inside her, elicited different responses. Instead of responding to any of the voices, she'd just kept reading. But when someone knocked on her door and jarred her from the dream state, she woke up wishing she could go back, to see who finally got her attention.

"What?" she called sleepily from her bed.

"You decent?" It was Shea.

"Yeah, come in." She sat up in bed and rubbed her eyes, blinking to bring Shea into focus as she buzzed into the room, a force of barely contained energy that seemed to gain power the closer they got to the wedding.

She hopped onto Ivy's bed, joining her without asking

permission just like she used to when they were kids. "So, Mom's 'not feeling well' today and says she can't take me wedding dress shopping."

Ivy's eyes widened. She'd assumed the dress was already bought. With the big day looming, Shea would have no choice than to buy the dress off the rack. Shea read her thoughts. "Don't freak out. I'm going to Wilmington and I'm going to find my dress today. They'll alter it and then it'll be ready in time." She shrugged. "With us agreeing to this televised thing, there was no way around it." She looked down at her hands. "It'll be fine."

There was something in the way she said it that told her Shea was not being entirely truthful about her feelings. But the distance between them kept her from delving into what was really going on. "So, do you want me to go with you?" Ivy asked.

Shea turned to her. "Will you? Do you have to work at the bakery today?"

Ivy shook her head. "I'm pretty sure Leah can survive without me." Shopping with Shea would be a good distraction. It would keep her from making some lame excuse to try and see Michael. She needed to play it cool until their date-that-he-would-never-call-a-date.

"Okay, great. I really didn't want to be a loser shopping for a wedding dress alone."

"Why not wait till Mom is feeling better? Seems to me that this is the kind of stuff she'd live for."

"She says she doesn't feel well, but I can't shake the feeling that she's lying. If you ask me, I think she got a better offer from her secret admirer."

Ivy giggled. "Maybe we should follow her."

"Or set up a stakeout!" Shea agreed, her eyes dancing at the thought of catching their mother.

"No, we're going to go find you a killer wedding dress. Let Mom sort out her own stuff." She rose from the bed, wearing a nightgown that Elliott had bought her as a joke. He called it her spinster gown, cotton plaid that looked like a nightshirt a man would wear in the 1800s. It was her favorite thing to sleep in, a fact that chagrined Elliott. She closed her eyes. Enough about Elliott.

Shea was watching her again, her expression curious, as if she were trying to read Ivy's private thoughts. No chance there. "See you after my shower?" Ivy asked.

"Sure thing," Shea said. "I'm going to go work on the seating chart for the reception, make Margot happy."

"She's got a lot to be happy about, from the sound of things," Ivy quipped. Shea cracked up laughing and left the room making kissing noises.

Ivy parked in front of the wedding shop in Wilmington, wondering if perhaps they should've gone to Myrtle Beach, or driven farther to Raleigh. So far they'd tried on a fair amount of dresses, but none of them was "the dress." If she'd heard about the trip secondhand, she'd have thought that Shea was being too picky, too dramatic, too Shea. But she'd been there to see it herself. There'd never been that "wow" moment when she emerged from the dressing room.

Ivy had expected to feel a wild range of emotions when

Shea came out donned in the dress she would marry Owen in—happiness, jealousy, uncertainty, guilt. Instead she'd sat outside several dressing rooms feeling void of any emotion save boredom. She never wanted to see silk, tulle, or lace trim again.

The elation she'd felt when she set off with her sister for a day of shopping had quickly diminished, a slow leak that neither of them could seem to find and plug. By the time they reached this last shop, they were both nearly flat. Ivy had tried making a few *Sleepless in Seattle* jokes, realizing when Shea barely managed a smile in return that that was something she shared with April, not Shea. And even reminiscing about Coral and Oceana, the mermaids they once pretended to be, hadn't roused a smile.

Ivy could feel herself giving up as she opened the car door and followed Shea inside with a dejected sigh. She just wanted to get home and go out with Michael. He would listen to how the day had gone, help her dissect what was obviously bugging her sister, and why Shea's mood could so quickly affect hers.

As she'd done in all the other stores, Ivy started pulling random dresses from the rack in Shea's size or close to it, all but ignoring the helpful salesgirl who hovered around them hoping for a sale. *Don't get your hopes up*, she thought silently. "Here," she said, piling the yards of fabric into Shea's arms. "Go." She pointed in the direction of the dressing room, and Shea stalked away without a word.

Things had gotten progressively tense each time they left a store with empty arms. Ivy feared that this last store would also leave them empty-handed. The closest they'd come was an ultra-simple white dress, one that looked more like a prom dress than a wedding gown. While it had been pretty on Shea, it wasn't what she wanted to wear on this one important day. She'd put it on hold at the other shop and—barring a miracle here—they would be headed back to buy it before driving back to Sunset.

Ivy smiled and shook her head politely at the salesgirl, who offered her coffee or soda while she waited. She knew this batch of dresses was also a no-go when Shea didn't even emerge from the dressing room to get her opinion. Ivy yawned from boredom, wishing she'd brought a book to read or something. If she still had her smartphone she could at least get online. Stupid, cheap pay-as-you-go phone had no bells and whistles. It also had no phone calls. She'd not given the number to anyone except her mom, dad, Leah, Shea, and April. She couldn't believe there'd once been a time when her phone was never out of her reach. Elliott used to beg her to put it down, to put it up, to leave it behind just once when they went out. But she never did. He had to have been shocked when she turned off her cell phone service entirely. She thought of him, wondered what he was doing at that moment, realized she hadn't checked his tweets this morning, as she usually did, in an effort to hurry up and get shopping with Shea.

She heard crying coming from the dressing room and looked around to see if anyone else could hear. Slowly she got up and quietly moved to stand outside the door. "Shea? Are you okay?" she whispered.

"Just go, Ivy."

She looked around the small bridal shop. There was

nowhere to go. "Okay, I guess I'll just go sit back down then."

"No, I mean just *go*. Go back to Sunset. Or back to Asheville. Or wherever you belong." Shea's voice had gone from weepy to angry.

She stood still for a moment, grateful that the salesgirl had honed in on some other unsuspecting bride—one who looked much happier to be there. She kept speaking in a whisper to Shea, hoping it would persuade her to do the same. "Shea, I'm not sure what's wrong but I'd like to help. That's what I'm here for."

Shea yanked open the dressing room door, completely clothed. Behind her, dresses were tossed willy-nilly around the tiny room. If Shea would let her in, she'd hang them all back up properly. "You've already done plenty, don't you think?" Shea spat out.

Ivy drew back just as surely as if Shea had slapped her, uncertain as to what had provoked this outburst. One minute they were united in finding her a dress (their standards had slipped from the beginning of the day—now it was just a suitable dress instead of the perfect one), the next minute they were as divided as they'd been before Ivy came back. She'd expected the cool reception from her sister when she arrived at Sunset, but she thought they'd made progress in the last few days, united over the wishing tree, their mother's mysterious phone call, even their reunion with the guys the other night. This anger of Shea's was out of the blue, but from the sound of things, she had decided to be angry all over again about Ivy's own wedding that never happened. She just couldn't figure out how not being able to find a wedding dress provoked it.

"I can't leave you, Shea. I'm your ride home."

Shea swiped at her eyes, smearing mascara and making her look even crazier. "I've already called Owen. He's coming to get me. We're going to hang out here for a little while. Get a break from home." She said the word *home* like it was a bad word. Ivy had once felt that way about it, so *that* she understood.

She backed up, stooping beside the chair she'd been sitting in to retrieve her purse. "Okay, then, I guess I'll go. If you're sure."

Shea crossed her arms. "I'm sure. I just can't talk to you about this right now. Please just go."

Ivy looked at her sister, trying to figure out what had just happened, how things could've gone from good to bad to really bad in the course of a day. Hadn't she been sitting on the bed with her sister just this morning, giggling? "Can I ask what I did to upset you?"

Shea shook her head and looked away. "That's the problem. You don't even know."

"I'm sorry I don't. I really don't."

Shea turned away and began grabbing mounds of white fabric to put away. "Then we have nothing more to say to each other."

Ivy stood for a moment and watched Shea busy herself with hanging the dresses. When it was apparent that she'd meant what she said, Ivy turned and fled the shop, wondering why she'd come back to Sunset, the tears falling as she realized she had nowhere else to go.

She drove back to Sunset with the windows open, even if running the air-conditioning made more sense. She wanted the wind whipping her hair, the breeze in her face, the ocean scent following her all the way down Highway 17. She wanted the wind to blow all her troubles away.

A few minutes into the drive, she stopped trying to figure out what had set Shea off, reducing her to tears and dress throwing and dismissing her entirely. She wrote it off to a severe case of wedding stress, but something kept nagging at her that it was more than that—that the scene with Shea had much deeper roots than her wedding plans, roots she'd have to reach down deep to pull up. She pressed harder on the gas pedal, willing herself back to the beach house, where she'd do her best to put the day behind her.

As she drove she thought about Elliott and Michael, and how she thought she'd made that choice long ago. Once and done. Yet now she was back here again, geographically and emotionally. And both men were in her life again. And her certain decision . . . wasn't so certain anymore. Her thoughts took her back to her ski trip, to when Elliott had called her hotel room that next day. She'd come in from late-afternoon skiing to find the message light blinking on the hotel phone, her heart beating wildly in her chest as she dialed the number to access the message. Michael would've called her cell phone. It had to be Elliott. She'd found she wanted desperately for it to be Elliott calling and, as she heard his voice, felt guilty for thinking it. This would become the roller coaster that was the next few days for her—wanting, then feeling bad for wanting, then wanting again.

He'd taken her out that night, riding beside her on the ski lift in the darkness, snuggling to stay warm as they climbed higher and higher. She remembered thinking how ironic it was that she was finding love on the other side of the state—the opposite of where she'd come from, beach to mountains, warm to cold. The winter stars shone around them, their breath coming out in puffs of white air as they talked, continuing that all-night conversation they'd begun the night before. They'd had so much to say then, never running out of words, never guessing they'd one day become a couple who stopped talking altogether, communicating in as few words as possible. He'd tweeted about that night, that starry winter ride through the cold air. And she'd felt—for just a moment—the pang of loss, which is, she supposed, what he wanted. He wanted to remind her of what they had.

But the point was, they didn't have it anymore. She was resolute in her commitment to keep her distance from Elliott, to not get tangled up in the emotions of the situation but to take things one step at a time. And the first step was deciding where to go after the wedding. Should she move in with her father for a time? He was the least likely to gloat or hover, and he could help her find a job. Or maybe she should go back to Asheville and beg April to let her live in one of the cabins while she figured out what her next step was.

She swallowed, taking in what she'd just decided. Not one of those possibilities included Elliott.

Red flashing lights behind her jarred her from her runaway thoughts. She looked down at her speedometer. It seemed that her thoughts weren't the only thing running away with her. Her foot had gotten heavier along with her thoughts, and she was going 85 in a 65-mile-an-hour zone. With a sigh she pulled over, fighting back the tears as she waited for the police officer to approach her car. This day just kept getting better and better.

She rolled down the window, and as she opened her mouth, the pent-up tears began to flow. "I am so s–s–s sorry," she sobbed. "I had no idea I was going that fast. I'm just a mess. My sister's mad at me and my husband is cheating on me and I think I married the wrong guy and now I don't even know where to l–l–l live." She stopped talking, realizing the policeman had backed up a few steps, adjusting his hat.

"Wait right here, ma'am" was all he said before he scurried away, back to the safety of his car.

As she waited, she flipped down the driver's-side mirror and took a good look at herself. She looked haggard, her nose and eyes red and running, her face splotchy. In a word, she was a mess. And she'd made a fool of herself in front of that cop. She glanced in the rearview mirror and saw him talking on his radio. He was probably asking for the men in white to come and cart her off before she did something far worse than speed. It wasn't a half-bad idea.

After what seemed like an hour, he came back to the car. While she waited, she'd composed herself, dried her tears, and put on some lip gloss, which always made things seem better, something Margot had taught her. She greeted him with her most serene smile. "Sorry about that earlier," she said. "I shouldn't have said all that."

He shuffled nervously, looking at her like she had a

loaded gun pointed at him. But to a male confronted with a female's wild emotional ramblings, it might've seemed like the same thing. "No problem, ma'am." He fiddled with his clipboard and handed her a piece of paper. "Seeing as how you had some . . . external circumstances going on, I've just written you a warning. You have a good driving record, so I'm sure this is just a one-time occurrence."

"Oh, yes, sir, you can count on that." Her heart lifted. The last thing she wanted was for Elliott to find out from their insurance agent that she'd gotten a speeding ticket and think that it was because she was upset about him—even if that were true. "I don't speed. I'm a law-abiding citizen." *Law-abiding citizen? What was this, the Old West?*

"Well, just make sure you keep it that way," the officer said. He reached up and adjusted his hat, shifting uncomfortably again as they looked at each other for a moment. He had on sunglasses, and she found herself wishing she could see his eyes. "And, ma'am?" he asked. "I'd just like to say that these things usually work themselves out."

She chuckled at his feeble attempt to reassure her. "I'm sure you're right. I'm probably just overreacting."

"Well, best of luck to you," the officer said. He turned to go and she called out after him. "Thank you!" She waved as she pulled away from the side of the road, merging into the traffic and keeping her eye on the speedometer as she made her way home, whatever that word meant anymore.

Fifteen

When she got home, she found the house empty. Wandering into the kitchen, she discovered a note from her mother saying she was feeling better and had gone out for dinner with friends. Ivy sighed, relieved she wouldn't have to face her mother yet. She dreaded her questions about how the day had gone with Shea.

Her eyes fell on the stack of mail on the counter. From the looks of things, more tags had arrived. She was surprised by people's prompt responses, the heartfelt notes from those who couldn't make it, glad for the chance to send their wishes ahead for the happy couple.

She thought of Shea, crying in the dressing room, forcing her out, turning away from the progress they'd made in the past few days. What did Ivy wish for her sister? A happy wedding? A life that turned out differently from her own? She tore into the first envelope, unsure of the answer.

The tag bore a wish for Shea and Owen to never have to be apart, and to long for each other when they did. She rolled her eyes and shoved it back in the envelope, gathering the stack and dumping them unceremoniously on Shea's bed upstairs. Shea could go through them on her own. Ivy wasn't interested in reading anymore—she was upset with Shea for earlier, and she didn't like the reminders the wishes triggered. She'd once thought that she and Elliott would never be apart, would long for each other when they had to be. What couple who enters marriage doesn't believe that? If you didn't, you wouldn't go through with it.

She turned and walked out of the room. The wishes people were sending were nothing more than a collection of pipe dreams.

And yet, as she went into her room and closed the door, she couldn't escape the memory of what had happened after that first date with Elliott, after their nighttime ride high above the snow-covered landscape, the hills glowing blue in the moonlight. She couldn't forget, no matter how hard she tried, what it felt like to have someone she couldn't bear to be away from for even an hour, someone she longed for when she was apart from him. Someone who incited feelings within her that she'd never felt before. Alone in her hotel room that night, she'd taken off her engagement ring, stared down at her naked finger, and wondered what it all meant.

When they'd said good-bye at the end of her trip, Elliott had taken her into his arms and held her for a very long time. "Follow your heart," he'd whispered. "Whatever it tells you when you get home, listen to that." She'd scoffed internally at this. She wasn't the type to live life that way. And yet she wanted to.

But back home she could feel her heart closing up again, slipping into the robotic mode that was her typical MO. She kept busy, did what was expected, and—except for when she snuck in a call to Elliott—barely listened to her heart. She didn't trust her heart, remembering that fall when her mother lay crying in bed. Listening to your heart led you down a dead-end road, and left you there alone. Better to be smart and cautious. Michael, she'd told herself more than once after she got home, was the safer bet. She didn't know Elliott at all. The time she'd spent with him was entirely other from real life and best forgotten.

And yet, deep inside, her heart kept speaking, beating out daily reminders of this man who'd captured her in a way she couldn't deny. She would look at Michael across the table as they planned their wedding and exchange a smile, all the while thinking of Elliott, remembering something he'd said, the way he'd finish her sentences, the feel of his hand on her cheek.

After a while she could no longer deny that this was more than a passing thing. Elliott had stayed with her. The question was whether he would stay with her forever. And then he'd called her and asked her to come back, said he couldn't stop thinking about her either. And she'd known that, eventually, she'd have a choice to make. Ignoring it wouldn't make it go away.

Five years after she made her choice, she looked at the clock and checked the mirror. She looked like she felt—the stresses of the day visible on her face. If she hurried, she could get a shower before Michael picked her up for their dinner. Even though she knew he was only coming under duress, she hoped that he'd come around as they spent time together. Somehow, some way, she had to show him that she'd made a mistake all those years ago. Following her heart had gotten her nowhere, just as she'd feared it would. "I was wrong," she said aloud in the silent room, watching her mouth form the words. She hoped she got the chance to tell Michael that.

It seemed no time had passed as she grabbed the roll bar of the Jeep and pulled herself into the passenger seat, a move that she'd performed countless times in her life. It was like riding a bike—you never forgot. As the Jeep rumbled to life and headed away from her house, her hair blowing in the warm evening air, she felt even more déjà vu. A smile filled her face and she did her best to forget what had happened that day—Shea, the cop, the weird dream that began her day, and the wishing tree tag bringing back memories of a time best forgotten. She liked this image, this moment, sitting beside Michael, moving forward, as it should be. She said a little prayer that the evening would go well, that her words would come out right and he would understand just how sorry she was.

They were quiet as they drove to Calabash, her stomach rumbling as she realized how long it had been since she'd eaten. She thought of the angel hair pasta with shrimp dish she used to always order at Fireside. She hoped they hadn't changed the menu.

She glanced over at Michael's profile, the same intense expression he'd always had on his face as he drove. And yet, she couldn't reach out and lace her fingers with his as he rested his hand on the gearshift, the act as natural as breathing.

Michael found a parking place beside the restaurant, got out, and headed for the door without getting her door for her like he used to. She opened her door and hopped out resolutely, understanding that this was the way things had to be. She'd hurt him. She'd rejected him. She'd given him back that engagement ring in the worst possible way. And she deserved even more anger than he was showing.

As the hostess showed them to their table, she knew she didn't even deserve this much. What Michael was showing her was grace. She remembered learning in church that grace was always undeserved. As she looked into his eyes once they were seated, grace was what she saw looking back at her.

"Thank you," she breathed.

He blinked at her. "I haven't done anything."

She knew him well enough to know he was doing his best to remain casual, to act as if this were just another dinner, that she was just another woman. She looked around the restaurant, finding it unchanged. She hoped he'd never brought other women there—but what right did she have to hope that? This had been "their place" and yet there was no "their" anymore.

"I just want you to know, I never brought Elliott here," she said.

He shrugged. "Okay." The look he gave her was hard to gauge.

"I mean, I've just always thought of this as . . . our place. It seemed . . . wrong. To bring him here."

He chuckled and shook his head, looking down at his menu. "You really beat all, you know that?"

"Why? What did I say?"

"You offer that up like it's some sort of equalizer. 'I know I ended things between us, but hey, at least I never brought the guy I dumped you for to our place.'" He held out his index finger in front of her face. "Here's the gold star you're obviously gunning for."

She studied him for a moment, took in the blankness of his face, the anger behind his eyes. This was going to be harder than she'd thought. She pushed his hand away. "I don't want a gold star. I want to . . . talk over things."

"You mean since you didn't five years ago?"

She did her best to meet his gaze instead of look away in embarrassment. "Yes."

He leaned back, lacing his fingers behind his head as he stared at her. The waiter placed waters in front of them, said he'd bring back some bread while they looked over the menu, and disappeared. They were quiet as they scanned the familiar menu. Her favorite was still there. She smiled as if she'd run into an old friend.

"Lemme guess," he said. "The angel hair with shrimp."

She nodded, a flicker of what once was passing between them, the acknowledgment of what they'd shared before Elliott came along.

He blinked, and the moment disappeared as he leaned forward on his elbows. "So, are you going to make good on your promise to tell me why you're really here, back in Sunset?"

She paused. She'd sort of forgotten that desperate promise. And yet, telling him why she was there was part of her explanation, part of admitting she'd been wrong. She exhaled loudly and held his gaze. "Sure."

The waiter slid the rolls in front of them, and she watched as Michael reached for one and dipped it into the olive oil and herbs in a dish beside the bread basket. She thought for a moment about how to put the situation into words. She thought about Elliott that day as she pulled out of the garage, how sad he'd looked as he watched her go, the moment when she lost sight of him as her car got farther away—and closer to Sunset, to Michael, to this moment. Inexplicably, she felt a little sad. It was five years ago all over: choosing one meant losing the other. She would make the right choice this time.

"Elliott cheated on me," she blurted out. She took a sip of water as if the admission made her thirsty when really she just wanted something to do under his gaze. She rested her head on her hand and forced herself to look back at him. "I left him," she finished, watching his reaction, willing him to say the right thing.

He pressed his palms on the table and stared at his hands for a moment. "I'm sorry to hear that," he said. This time he was the one to take a long drink of water.

"Are you?"

He shrugged. "Sure. That's terrible. I'm sure that was tough."

"It just happened. I mean, I just found out. I'm not sure when it happened. Or who it was. I . . . didn't really give him a chance to fill in the details."

"And what does he think of your reaction?"

"He doesn't really get a vote. He put me in a pretty impossible situation." She slid the menu out of the way, her eyes flickering over to where the waiter was watching them for a signal they were ready to order.

"Does he know you're here?"

"Yeah."

A smile flickered across his face. "I bet he hates that." He had the look of a man who was enjoying the taste of revenge. He licked a bit of olive oil from the corner of his mouth and she thought of kissing him after other dates to this restaurant, how he'd tasted like Italy itself to her. She didn't bother to hide her smile.

"I hope he does." For some reason, she felt comfortable reaching across the table, resting her hand on his forearm, smoothing down the hair like she used to do. "But that's not what I came to say."

Under her hand she could feel the muscles in his arm tense. She took the hint and put her hand back on her side of the table, pretending to need to unroll her silverware at that moment. She looked up and caught the waiter's eye, imploring him to rescue her from this awkward moment. To her relief, he crossed the restaurant to take their orders.

When the waiter was gone, Michael fixed his gaze on her. "So what did you come here to say, if not to tell me that your husband is cheating on you?"

"I came to say that I was sorry. And that I was wrong."

"Wrong?" She could tell her admission was not what he'd expected. Maybe he would see that she had changed, or was changing. Maybe if he saw that, he'd want to see more.

"To do what I did. To you." She paused, her eyes filling with tears. "To us." Her hand went to her fork, pressing the tines into the red-and-white-vinyl tablecloth, leaving four little hole prints behind. She blinked the tears away and looked back at him. "Sorry. I'm . . . just really confused right now."

"Confused?"

"About what happened five years ago. About why I did what I did." She swallowed and put the fork down. "Why I broke your heart to be with some guy I barely knew."

Michael reached for another roll and tore it in two. "He was your soul mate. That's what you said." He didn't meet her eyes as he dropped the torn roll back into the basket. "You said in your letter that you couldn't bear to be away from him. That's why you left here—to be with him." He pushed the basket away and looked up, his gaze piercing her. "And now you leave him to come back to me? Is that what this is all about?"

"I didn't come back here to see you," she answered, a hint of anger cropping up. He was enjoying his smug position a bit too much. "I didn't even know you were here. I thought you'd be with your family in Raleigh. And then once I found out you were here, I thought maybe . . . we could . . ." She fumbled for the right words to describe the many thoughts that had been racing through her head about him—words that didn't make her sound crazy.

"Pick up where we left off?" He sat up straighter in his

chair, the expression on his face as he looked at her so confident and assured that she wanted to hit him.

"No. I know that's not possible," she lied. Did she really know that? "I do realize a lot has happened." She paused to think. "I just hoped we could . . . be friends again." She ignored the way her heart stuttered over the use of the word *friend.*

"We stopped being friends when we were fifteen years old." His words penetrated her heart, reminding her of that summer when everything changed, when he got out of the car that bright June day and she saw a different Michael, one that captured her imagination that whole summer as she'd schemed how to get him to notice her the way she'd noticed him. He'd been a bit slow on the uptake, but eventually he'd come around.

"I hope you don't mean that," she said.

The waiter materialized again, setting plates of steaming food in front of them. Her stomach rumbled in response to the scent of garlic and tomatoes and olive oil and pasta. She eyed the perfectly curled shrimp dotting the top of the dish and reached for her knife and fork. Maybe she could manage a few bites after all.

Michael bowed his head and silently prayed, but she found herself wishing she could hear what he said to God, what he would thank Him for. Instead she did the same, her silent prayer filled with thanks for reuniting her with this dish—and with him. When he finished praying he attacked his food, scooping large bites into his mouth. At least that hadn't changed.

They made small talk for a while, catching up on their

jobs, his family, and the whereabouts of mutual friends. Ivy carefully avoided asking about his dating life—she didn't need to know, really, since Shea had given her the basic outline. As he talked about his renovation work, she snuck glances at him, smiling at the red sauce on his chin, resisting the urge to reach across the table and wipe it off like she once would've.

Instead she ate about half of her meal, then signaled the waiter for a box. When she looked back, he was smiling.

"You and your boxes," he said.

It was as if he was glad to see that not everything about her had changed. They couldn't retrieve everything they had had together, but maybe they could find enough to hold on to.

Sixteen

"Mind if we stop by the house on the way back?" Michael asked as they got back into the Jeep. "I've got to check on this stain I tried on the deck this afternoon. I wanted to see if I need to get more of it in the morning. It might need another coat."

She rested her box of food on her lap and nodded. "I don't have anywhere else to be," she said, hoping he would take that as she meant it—that the evening by no means had to end. The sun hadn't even set yet. The last thing she wanted to do was spend an uncomfortable evening with her mother and sister, dancing around what happened in the bridal store. The more time she spent with Michael, the less time she had to spend at home.

They sped past the ocean and she noticed the tide was out. If everything went well, they could go for a walk at sunset, one of their favorite things to do. Well, one of the things they used to love to do.

He pulled into the drive of Mrs. McCoy's house, the house that was now his. He got out, then turned and leaned into the Jeep. As he did, a breeze kicked up and she caught a whiff of his cologne. He always did smell good, strong and clean, not wimpy like some men. She looked into his eyes, noting how blue they were. Elliott's were so dark brown you couldn't tell the pupils from the irises. It was hard not to compare them.

"If you want to come in, you can. I won't be long," he said.

"Sure." She sprang from the seat, eager to be alone with him—away from attentive waiters and the watchful eyes of her family. Maybe they would stay up talking late into the night. Maybe she'd make her sister *really* worry.

Michael's cell phone rang from inside his pocket. He pulled it out and studied it. "Owen," he said to her and answered it. She listened to the one-sided conversation.

"Yeah." (Silence.)

"Yeah." (A glance over at her. More silence.)

"Of course not." (Silence.)

"Shut up, O." Owen's laughter was so loud, she could hear it coming through the phone.

"Yeah. At the house." (A longer stretch of silence.)

"Huh, no need to worry about that." (A frown followed by another glance at her.)

"Yeah, later, man." He hung up and resumed his trek around to the back entrance, since the front entrance was covered by the scaffolding. She followed along glumly, thinking that she knew what Owen had been saying to

Michael, and what Michael had assured him of. Owen was cautioning him to be careful, and Michael was telling him that it wasn't a problem. She pouted a little at the thought of not even being a temptation.

Inside the house you couldn't tell that the major renovation was going on outside. Everything pretty much looked like she remembered it. The same 1970s furniture. The same lighthouse figurines cluttering the surfaces. The same smell even—part old-lady perfume, part mothballs. "What are you going to do with all this stuff?" she asked just to make conversation.

He shrugged. "Get rid of it I guess." He smirked. "Why? You want it?"

Her eyes flickered over to the cabinet where Mrs. McCoy kept the teapot she used for their tea parties. "Maybe some of it." She scanned the room again.

"Be right back," Michael said, and walked outside.

Ivy crossed the dining room and opened the cabinet door, hoping that the teapot was still there. Ah yes. She breathed a sigh of relief when she spotted the white china teapot, painted with pink-and-blue flowers. She reached out and touched it, running her fingers along the surface. Pulling her hand away, she found a thick layer of dust coating her fingers. She pulled the teapot out and decided to wash it off.

She was drying it when Michael walked back in. He stopped short when he saw her. "Where did you find that?" he asked.

She pointed at the cabinet. "Where Mrs. McCoy always kept it," she said. "It was dirty, so I decided to wash it."

He stood and watched her, his eyes following the

movements of the towel across the surface. Finally he spoke. "You and Shea were always coming over here."

"Yep," she said. She walked over to the table and set the teapot down, dry and shiny. She sat down too and looked over at him, an invitation. Amazingly, he didn't argue, didn't say that he should get her home, didn't walk back outside and make some lame excuse so he could keep his distance. He simply took the seat beside her, resting his hands on his thighs as he stared at her.

"You look like you did back then. When Owen and I would come over here to get you, to talk you into coming outside with us." He smiled. "And to steal those cookies Mrs. McCoy always served."

"Scones," she said. "They weren't cookies, they were scones."

"Whatever. They were good."

Mrs. McCoy used to make the best cinnamon scones. Ivy had tried many others since then, but none tasted as good as hers. Of course she kept that little bit of information from her aunt Leah. "She always made sure that you and Owen got your share." As she said it, she could picture the two towheaded boys with impish smiles leaving a trail of scone crumbs as they dashed back outside, shooed away as she and Shea yelled in outrage, "No boys allowed!" She suspected that Mr. McCoy put them up to it. He wanted a scone too.

"Those were good times," he said.

She nodded, her mind playing a reel of memories from this kitchen, this street, this beach. Someone had long ago erected a basketball goal on the street and there were often neighbors involved in an informal game, pausing whenever a car drove by. Sometimes she and Shea played against Owen and Michael even though they never won "The best," she agreed. "I was sorry they had to end."

He leaned back in his chair and sighed. "They didn't have to end."

He was referencing her decision to marry Elliott. But that wasn't what she meant. For her, the magic of Sunset ended long before then. She looked over at him, wondering how to explain that. She pictured herself on that bike, circling the island in large, aimless loops, trying to make sense of this new life she found herself in, unable to escape the sadness that had gripped them all.

"Do you remember when we decided to get married?" she asked.

His wrinkled forehead told her she had shocked him. "What a question," he said.

"Well, do you? Do you remember actually deciding to get married?" She looked away from his penetrating gaze. "Or did it get decided for us somehow?"

He glared at her. "Is that what you think?"

She glared back. "Sure. Remember how my mother and your mother started planning our wedding, right in front of us? We had only been dating three months, for pete's sake!"

She could see their two families gathered that last summer her dad was there, all laughing and talking at once, the adults sipping cocktails while the kids calculated how long they had to be there before they could slip away. They were having dinner out on the deck. Her mother had looked over at Michael and Ivy, holding hands, and with a knowing smile on her face, remarked about when they would get married. As Ivy stood silently, gripping Michael's hand a bit tighter, his mother and hers had started planning their wedding. She watched while her life got decided for her—when they would get engaged (their senior year of college), where the wedding would be held (on the beach, of course), and where they would live (near his family, since his job would be working for his father), but still close enough for plenty of visits to Sunset, just a "hop, skip, and jump away," as Michael's mother always said.

"So what?" Michael asked. "I thought girls liked that sort of thing."

"Well, not me. I didn't."

"Well, *sorry*," he said in exaggerated fashion.

She sighed and tried again. "What I'm trying to get at is the fact that everything was so decided. You all thought you knew what my future would be—should be. I didn't like my future being so certain."

"I did," he said softly.

There, too, she saw the difference between them. He wanted the safe path, the certain future. Go to college a few years. Work for his dad. Marry his childhood sweetheart. He needed—craved—that kind of stability. But something in her always longed for more, something different. More excitement. More challenge. But she couldn't tell him that, so she changed the subject.

"It didn't help either when my parents divorced."

He nodded slowly. "I always suspected that was part of it. You changed after their divorce. I thought you'd eventually get over it, but . . ."

"I'm not sure I ever did," she admitted. "It shook up my whole view of men. So I ran away from it—from you."

"Out of the frying pan into the fire."

"It appears that way, yes." She smiled grimly at his offer of backhanded sympathy. "Did I tell you Elliott's been tweeting to me? I cut off my old email address and phone service. I just wasn't ready to talk to him, or hear from him. I guess he thinks if he yells his apologies to the whole Twitter universe, I'll come running back."

"At least he's sorry. That's something. Don't you want to work on it?" He examined her closely, too closely for her liking.

"Eventually." She waved her hand airily. Not wanting to go into detail, she rose and busied herself with putting the teapot back in the cabinet and closing the door. "I've had quite a day and I'm getting pretty tired, so I think I'll just walk home," she said.

"Suit yourself," he said. Then added, in that new Michael way he had, "You always do."

She smiled at him with just one side of her mouth. "Maybe this trip I'll prove to you just how wrong you are about me."

Before he could respond, she turned and walked out the door.

Seventeen

Shea was nowhere to be found the next morning. Ivy couldn't help but wonder what had happened after she left the bridal store. Perhaps Shea had ended up finding a dress without her. Perhaps Owen had calmed her down with his sweet, sensible ways. Perhaps the two of them had eaten dinner and Shea had restored her sense of humor over crab cakes at Elijah's. Perhaps—and this was a reach—her sister had forgiven her.

She sat for a long time at the island sipping coffee, wondering if either her mother or sister would happen by. At one point she thought she heard her mother on the phone, the girlish giggle she'd heard before wafting through the house. She frowned into her coffee, thinking that today she would mention her mother's secret conversations to Leah, press her to tell her what she knew. One thing she'd learned about her mother long ago, there was precious little she didn't tell Leah.

That had once been true of her and Shea.

Her mother entered the room just as Ivy was about to go upstairs and shower. Ivy set her cup down on the island, empty except for a fraction of an inch of milky coffee in the bottom of the cup. She watched Margot bustle around the kitchen, intent on making the single piece of wheat toast she ate each morning, whistling as she buttered the bread and slid it into the toaster oven. In her head, Ivy rehearsed different ways to bring up what happened with Shea. She wondered if her mother even knew.

"Good morning, Mom," she ventured.

"Good morning, Ivy," Margot replied, her voice preoccupied. She even nearly burned her toast. Ivy suspected the phone conversation she had heard was what was tying up her thoughts—and inspiring her whistling.

"Were you on the phone back there?" she tried. "I thought maybe you were talking to Shea."

"Shea is with Owen and no—I was not talking to her." Margot smiled. "I was taking care of some wedding business." She looked over at Ivy meaningfully. "Nothing for you to worry about."

Ivy took the hint and dropped the subject but didn't leave the room yet either, even though she needed to shower and get to the bakery. In her head, she practiced broaching the subject of what had happened with Shea. She wondered if her mother knew and was just pretending not to, or if Shea hadn't confided in her. Perhaps there hadn't been time, or perhaps Shea didn't want to open up to Margot either.

Ivy had definitely sensed tension between the two of them, but she had chalked it up to wedding stress. Maybe it was more than that.

"So, Shea and I didn't find a dress yesterday," she said.

Her mother looked up, her blue eyes locking with Ivy's over the top of her glasses. "I heard about that," Margot said. She returned to eating her toast standing up, the bread crunching loudly as she bit into it.

"Shea got really . . . upset. At me."

Margot nodded. "Heard about that too."

"She made me leave her there. Called Owen to come get her."

"Shea's been . . . kind of emotional lately."

"About the wedding?"

"Of course that's a big part of it." Her mother put her toast on a plate and looked out the large bank of windows, studying the marsh as if she'd never seen it before. "I think that she's also trying to make sense of your return. Seeing Michael the way you have been." The tone of her mother's voice was suspicious, as if Ivy were there to cheat on Elliott. When really it was the other way around.

Ivy got defensive. "I'm just resolving things, Mom. The wedding gave me a good reason to come back and . . . face up to what happened five years ago."

Margot held up her hand. "I understand that. Better than you know. But Shea . . ." She looked back out at the marsh again as she searched for the right words. She turned back to Ivy. "Shea's a bit of an idealist. She hasn't been married yet. She thinks that things should go a certain way." She raised her eyebrows. "And there's no convincing her otherwise." A smile flickered across her face. "Better to let her find out for herself, kind of like someone else I know."

Ivy swallowed. Her mother's inflection was deserved and even expected. She'd refused to listen to anyone in the family when they warned her against moving to Asheville, against pursuing a relationship with Elliott. "He's a stranger," Margot had said. Then later, "Whatever you're running from will eventually find you in Asheville just like it found you here." Her mother had been right on both counts—but you couldn't have told her that then. Then she believed she knew all she needed to know about Elliott. And she believed that happiness waited for her in Asheville—a happiness she'd never known at Sunset Beach. Somewhere amid the mountain peaks and artsy atmosphere of her new home, she'd find the kind of life she'd always wanted.

But she'd never been able to stop missing Sunset. When she looked at the mountain peaks, she wanted to see the vast ocean. When she gathered with new friends for dinner, she wanted to gather with people who'd known her all her life. It wasn't that she didn't like her life in Asheville—she'd been quite happy there. It was that she'd wanted all of this too. She wanted her future to include her past. Part of being back at Sunset was figuring out if the two could mutually coexist.

"Shea wants to wear my wedding dress," her mother said, her tone turning businesslike. She took Ivy's coffee cup, rinsed it, then popped it into the dishwasher. "I've begged her to let it go. That's why I sent you out shopping with her yesterday. I had hoped that either she would find something she liked or she'd find the courage to ask you about the dress." Her mother eyed Ivy, gauging her reaction. That wedding dress was a sore subject, and they both knew it. "Since she found neither a replacement nor the courage to ask you, I told her that I would ask you. She's . . . afraid to bring it up with you. She knew it would make you uncomfortable."

"Is that why she got so angry yesterday? She's mad that I have your wedding dress?"

Margot walked around and sat beside Ivy at the island, resting her hand on Ivy's knee. "She's just . . . mad. I don't really totally understand why, and I suspect that the two of you will, at some point, have to talk about it before either of you can move on." Her mother squeezed her knee. "I think you coming back here to help out with your sister's wedding was very brave. It's something that I never thought I'd have again—both my girls, together, planning a wedding. It's so wonderful that we're all together." Margot's smile was radiant. She looked every bit like the mother of the bride.

Ivy resisted the urge to point out that they weren't exactly all together—her father was conspicuously absent, and she and Shea weren't speaking. "It is nice, us back together," she agreed dutifully. In her mind she was already trying to remember where she'd stored that wedding dress. Was it the attic? Or the back of her closet?

She stood up and patted her mom's shoulder. "I'll see if Elliott can find the dress," she lied. In truth, she'd ask April to ask Elliott. "But now I'd better get to the bakery," she said. "I told Leah I'd help her get ready for a cake tasting for a prospective bride and groom."

Her mom snickered. "It's all hands on deck for that one.

Apparently the mother of the bride is quite a case. Very demanding. Very particular." Margot smiled. "Don't even say what you're thinking." She winked at Ivy, a small acknowledgment that she might be a wee bit over-controlling with Shea's wedding too.

Ivy smiled. Then she left her mother and headed upstairs. Closing her bedroom door, she dialed the number that was as familiar to her as her own. When April answered she said, "I need your help," instead of hello.

April teased, "What now?" as though she was put out by Ivy's request. But they both knew different. They both knew April would do whatever Ivy needed. That was just the kind of friend she was. And as expected, April promised she would do exactly what Ivy asked. Ivy hung up the phone, happy that there was one person in her life she could count on.

As she showered and dressed, her thoughts drifted back to the first time she met April, on her second trip to the mountains—a trip she'd told her family and Michael was for a job interview but was really to see Elliott, who'd she'd kept up with daily since her solo ski trip. Their attraction had only grown as they communicated via daily email and phone calls. She'd even found herself being less careful about keeping it from Michael. It was almost like she wanted to be caught, wanted to confess to him what was going on. The problem was even she wasn't sure what that was.

So when Elliott begged her to come back for a second visit, she agreed. The trip, she was certain, would help her find out what really existed between her and Elliott. She would either resolve to love him or leave him behind.

Though she knew the right answer, she found herself hoping for the wrong one. In the weeks leading up to her departure, she'd found it hard to look Michael in the eye.

Being a gentleman, Elliott had arranged for her to stay with his cousin, a girl named April who he promised was "a lot of fun—the sister I never had." Desperate for the time with him, she readily agreed, though she doubted she'd warm to his cousin. When she arrived at April's cabin that first evening, she asked April one simple question, "What do I need to know about your cousin?" And that had been all it took. Three hours and many mugs of coffee later, the two young women had become friends.

By the end of the trip, April had grown to feel like family. Which had been good, considering what came next. It had been April Ivy ran to after the big blowup with her family, April who made her more coffee and offered her listening ear as Ivy sorted through what it meant to leave everything she'd believed about her certain future to pursue an unknown, uncertain one. The one thing she'd needed to know back then was that Elliott would be in that future. The rest would take care of itself, she'd believed. What a fool she'd been.

Her thoughts stayed with her as she finished getting ready and drove to the bakery. Pushing them aside, she breezed through the display area into the kitchen, where she could hear Leah singing along to her oldies station on the little radio she kept back there. She thought about Leah's line of questions the last time she'd been there, pressing her to tell the details of her love story with Elliott. She hadn't wanted to talk about it and hoped that Leah didn't ask her this time to continue her story.

She was relieved to find Leah busy setting up the cake tasting for the bride and her mother, too distracted to ask questions. She waved Ivy over and started throwing out instructions. The two worked in companionable, welcome silence, with no mention of Elliott's name. Ivy cubed the cakes, mounding the samples on plates: red velvet, magnolia vanilla, chocolate fudge, caramel, and lemon. Leah spooned a variety of frostings into retro-colored bowls with colorful spoons for scooping out dollops onto the cake cubes: buttercream, white wedding, and whipped, and the fillings: cream cheese, and raspberry. She was glad they didn't have time to talk, but she couldn't keep the love songs that Leah played from bringing up memories of times shared between her and her husband. Much as she tried to push Elliott to the back of her mind, he had a way of elbowing his way back up to the front. She couldn't help but think that he would love knowing that.

When they were done setting up the table, they took stock of their work, making sure every detail was attended to in preparation for the tasting. The idea was that the customers would build their own custom cake with Leah's subtle, expert guidance. Ivy's favorite combination was the chocolate fudge topped with whipped-cream icing, a combination Leah's customers had dubbed the Ho Ho Wedding Cake. But Leah's bestseller was the lemon paired with a raspberry filling and topped with the white wedding icing, a combination that had been dubbed by satisfied customers as the Pink Lemonade Cake because it really did taste like pink lemonade. No matter what customers chose, they were always satisfied. Leah made sure of that.

They stood back and complimented each other on a job well done. Leah wiped her hands on an apron that looked like it belonged in an exhibit about the American home-maker, circa 1950. Bright red cherries dotted blue fabric, with a rickrack trim circling the edges. Ivy wished she had her camera—she'd snap a picture. She felt a little pang at the thought of who she'd show it to first. Elliott had always liked Leah, his respect for her growing when she'd defied the rest of the family and come to the party April threw them after they got married. If she showed him that pic-ture, he'd laugh. He'd say, "That's so Leah." Because it was. She tamped down the pang of missing him, focusing on the work to distract her. Satisfied that the display was ready—and ahead of schedule at that—Leah walked over to the computer across the room and turned it on. "Come over here," she directed Ivy. "I've got something that a young person like you should be interested in."

Ivy blanched as the homepage for Twitter filled the com-puter screen, her heart racing as Leah watched it load with a smile. Her background was hot pink with cupcakes peek-ing out from behind the text boxes. She watched as Leah sat down and typed in a tweet about a tasting being ready, listing off the choices the customers would be sampling. She turned proudly to Ivy. "Lester says this is the way to get in touch with new clients." She pointed proudly to the num-ber of followers. "Look how many people are following me already!" Leah had only a couple dozen followers, but from the look on her face, it might as well have been millions.

She rested her hand on her aunt's shoulder. "You are so cutting edge, Aunt Leah." She could feel her heart resuming its normal pace. She'd been so worried Leah was going to show her Elliott's tweets, tell her to reconsider or something inane like that. Instead she was just happy about her own foray into social media. Ivy exhaled her relief.

"You spend much time on Twitter?" Leah asked. "It's so addictive." She turned her attention back to the screen, scrolling through her news feed as she half-paid attention to Ivy's response.

"I did some," Ivy lied. "But just for business. You know, real estate connections and that type of thing. Now that I'm not doing that anymore . . ." She let her voice trail off intentionally so that Leah would assume she had lost all interest in Twitter when in fact she'd been on just that morning, checking on Elliott because she couldn't resist knowing what he was saying and, more and more, who was following him and what *they* were saying. It seemed a lot of women wanted to hear the kind of apology he was issuing, wanted to be pursued the way he was pursuing her.

"Oh, well, that's too bad," Leah responded. "I could've followed you!" Leah closed out of the Twitter screen and turned to face Ivy. "Let's go taste some cake." She rubbed her hands together and grinned, easily mustering the enthusiasm necessary to ooh and aah over her own cakes. *That must be what it feels like to do what you love*, April thought as she followed Leah out to greet the potential clients. She had only truly followed her heart one time, and that hadn't turned out to be her best decision. Not by a long shot.

She watched as Leah greeted the bride and her mother, wondering why some people could make a go of things that mattered, and others—like her—fell flat on their faces. She thought of Michael's face last night, the push me–pull you nature of how things were between them, a mixture of hope and despair battling in her heart. She had to figure out how to put things right with Michael, and forget Elliott Marshall ever existed.

Eighteen

The weekend passed without any heart-to-heart between Ivy and Shea. Ivy had tried to talk with her, but Shea dodged the deeper problems, declaring she was perfectly happy with the simple dress she'd found. Not wanting to add to her sister's stress, Ivy didn't press the issue. And when Shea didn't bring up their mother's dress, she didn't either.

The family was hitting warp speed in this last week before the big day. All the hubbub created a needed distraction, but more and more, Ivy wondered what she would do after Owen and Shea waved good-bye and rode away like Cinderella and her Prince Charming. Without the excuse of the wedding, she had no more reason to be there. Eventually she'd have to tell the truth, or go back to Asheville and perpetuate the myth that was her life.

April had said there was a small unrented cabin she could

live in for the summer if she wanted it, but that prospect felt like repeating the past. The longer she stayed at Sunset, the more she wanted to spend the summer there. And the longer she was around Michael, the more time she wanted to spend with him. At church on Sunday they had actually chatted like the old friends they were, the tensions slowly melting away as they found common ground in their dual duties of helping with the wedding. He did a good job of keeping things on the surface, focused on Shea and Owen, but she had hopes that it would become more.

On the Wednesday before the wedding, she checked Twitter as she was in the habit of doing each day, accessing Elliott's handle and scrolling through both his tweets and the comments that mentioned him, an odd form of torture. She had to hand it to him, he wasn't giving up. But she couldn't ignore the fact that something very well could've sprung up between him and one of these women who told him what he wanted to hear.

She scrolled through the tweets. His messages had gone from yearning and apologetic to more serious. Some of his tweets spoke of what he was learning from his counselor. Thankfully he kept his revelations general enough that no one reading could guess at the exact nature of his offense. She didn't need the whole anonymous Twitterverse to know she'd been cheated on. He claimed he was dealing with his issues, that he was willing to work on their relationship, that he would take full responsibility for his actions. Of course she'd be a fool to believe his empty promises. His other tweets mentioned their past—the promises they made to each other, the memories they shared, the faith they tried to follow. Try as she might to divorce herself from her feelings as she read his allusions to the love they used to have, the pain crept in, her heart clinching at his words.

∽

One thing she was glad for, Elliott had been kind enough to never address her directly, never let his followers know who she was. He'd protected her anonymity, shielding her from his followers who sometimes sounded like they were out for blood because she wouldn't forgive him. "How can this woman resist you?" one woman had written. Another had written, "You say the things I never got to hear. Your wife should count her blessings, not your transgressions."

These women just didn't understand. There was so much more to the story.

She closed out of his account, then checked her Twitter account just in case there was anything she needed to see there. She saw she had a direct message from a Twitter handle she didn't recognize and clicked on it. A thumbnail photo came up of a very attractive woman. Her name was Vivienne White, and her bio said that she was a reporter for the same major network that was covering Shea's wedding.

Ivy read the message from @VivReports with a lump forming in her throat: "Are you the wife of @ElliottIdiot? If so, I'd like to hear your side for the story I am developing about the response to his tweets."

She closed Twitter and shut her laptop a bit too forcefully. She didn't want to talk to reporters about her husband's public apologies or the women who loved what he had to say. She didn't want to dissect his infidelity on national television or in any way draw attention to who she was or where she was or what her side of the story was. And how in the world did this woman figure out who she was anyway?

She walked over to the window of her room and peered out. A news truck was parked on the street, getting ready to take shots of Shea and Owen that would be used in the footage they would air before the wedding was broadcast. As she watched, Shea bounded out of the house to meet Owen as he came up the stairs to fetch her, throwing herself into his arms and laughing as she nearly knocked him down. They were disgustingly cute together. The TV photographer jumped out of his truck, snapping photos as he did, catching the touching moment on film.

Ivy took a moment to listen, making sure the house was really empty. Her mother had gone out earlier, claiming a coffee date with friends, but Ivy suspected she was off to meet her secret love. She had looked too nice when she left the house. With both her mom and Shea out of the house, Ivy could place a call without anyone hearing. After hearing from the reporter, she knew she couldn't avoid it any longer, and the truth was, she'd already gone much longer than she'd thought she would.

She went downstairs and drank a cup of coffee for fortification. Then she dialed the number, her fingers expertly moving over the keys after years of practice, then pressed the phone to her ear and listened to it ring. Her heart raced as she tried to think of what to say. The last time Elliott had made her this nervous, he was standing too close to her in the hallway of her hotel that first night. She closed her eyes.

He answered on the fourth ring, breathless. It was all she could do not to ask why he was out of breath, insinuate that he was with someone, and hang up the phone. But acting that way would only make it sound like she was jealous. That was *not* the attitude she wanted to project.

"Hello," she said.

"Ivy." He breathed her name, relief evident in his voice. This didn't sound like a man who was with someone else at that moment. "You called."

"Well, not for any other reason except to tell you that I was contacted by a reporter wanting my side of your ridiculous Twitter . . ." She couldn't think of what to call what he was doing. "Have you heard from her?"

He was quiet for a moment. "Yeah. She contacted me. We've talked."

"I don't want you pursuing this, Elliott," she said. "You claim to care about me. To be sorry. Then prove it by putting a stop to this. I don't want this woman snooping around me or my family. If she's found out who I am, then what's to stop her from finding out where I am?"

She waited for him to say something in response, but he was quiet.

"Are you there?" she asked. She knew he was there. She could hear him breathing.

"I'm just trying to think of what to say to you now that you're finally talking to me. I mean you cut me out of your life. You cancelled your phone, your email, blocked me from your Facebook. I had no way to communicate with you. And I had to tell you how sorry I was."

"Well, you've made your point, so you can stop now."

"I can only stop if I've convinced you to come home and give me another chance."

She laughed out loud, unable to keep it inside. "Fat chance of that." He was crazy if he thought she'd make the same mistake twice.

"So you're saying you're never coming back?"

"Well, of course I'll have to come for the rest of my things at some point. But no, as far as living in that house with you, I do not intend to come back."

His voice was quiet. "I see."

"Do you see, Elliott? Do you see what you did?"

His response was instant. "Of course I do. That's what I've been trying to tell you these past few weeks. I know you've seen at least some of what I've written. April told me you knew about it and were reading some of the tweets."

April and her big mouth. She shook her head. She'd never admit that she'd read every single one, even going so far as to read the comments from women who were following him. He didn't need to know that; it would only give him false hope that she really cared. "I've read some of it. I think it's ridiculous. But what do I know? You obviously have plenty of female fans who think what you have to say is great." Now she just sounded jealous and bitter. She switched tactics. "But none of that matters. What matters is you and I figuring out how to amicably part ways. I know you're sorry. Maybe you can apply what you've learned to your next relationship."

That sounded much more grown-up. She was about to congratulate herself when he said, "I don't want another relationship. I want *our* relationship."

An ironic little laugh escaped her lips. "Forgive me if I don't want to run right back to our relationship. You might want to make it out to be something great, but I remember, Elliott. I remember all the nights you refused to come to bed with me. All the nights we sat on the couch and stared like zombies at the TV so we didn't have to talk. All the meals you ate in front of the computer while I ate alone. That doesn't sound like something I'd ever go back to. It's not just that you cheated on me."

She expected him to argue in response. Instead he just said, "You're right. I didn't know how to do this marriage thing. When you got all busy and the romance was gone, I didn't know what to do, so I pulled away." He sighed. "You know what I've been doing? I've been getting to know you again. Through social media, if you can imagine that. I see what you love on Pinterest and what you read on Goodreads and how you spent your days on Twitter. And you know what? I'm falling in love with you all over again." She could hear the smile in his voice. "I forgot how much I liked you. What an interesting person you are."

She looked over at the wishing tree, growing fuller each day, the tags hanging from the branches bearing wishes for a marriage that might or might not live up to its expectations. She and Elliott hadn't had a wishing tree, but they'd had wishes. Wishes to be different from her parents. Wishes to be good to each other. Wishes to bring out the best in each other. Wishes to grow old together, their own branches intertwining in such a way that made it impossible to tell just whose branch was whose. She supposed every couple started off with wishes such as these, but sadly, very few saw theirs realized.

The back door opened, and the tags on the wishing tree fluttered in the breeze that came in with the open door. Ivy looked over to see her mother coming into the kitchen.

"I've got to go," she said quietly into the phone. "Just call off that reporter. And stop tweeting about us. It's not going to change anything." She hung up the phone without waiting for his response and got up to greet her mother, who was wearing a bemused expression on her face. Ivy looked back at the tree and noticed that one of the tags had fallen to the ground.

"Did you have a good morning, Mom?" she asked as she walked over to pick up the tag and replace it.

"Hmm?" Margot asked, taking the sponge from its perch on the kitchen sink and beginning to absently wipe down the pristine kitchen counters.

"Your morning?" Ivy asked again. "How'd it go?"

Margot waved the sponge in the air. "Oh, fine. Nothing special."

"Coulda fooled me," Ivy quipped. She looked down at the tag in her hand. "May you always find the space in your hearts to forgive each other," it said. Ivy nearly threw the tag in the trash. That was not what she wanted to hear at that moment. She hastily replaced it on the tree and went back to the kitchen.

"Are you going to tell me your secret, Mom?" she asked.

"What secret?" Margot asked, looking shocked. She returned the sponge to the sink and dried her hands. When she tried to leave the kitchen to escape to her bedroom, Ivy blocked her way.

"Something's going on with you that has nothing to do with this wedding and I know it. I wish you'd just tell me."

Margot cocked her head for a moment, studying Ivy's face. "You mean like your telling me what's really going on with you?" she asked.

Ivy inhaled sharply, her mother's response lodging in her solar plexus. Margot drove the point home. "Ivy, I'm your mother. It's pretty hard to pull one over on me. I know there's more going on than you've let on. I just figured you'd talk about it when you were ready." Margot crossed her arms as Ivy had done. "I'd like to think you can do the same for me."

Ivy blinked at her a few times. "Okay," she managed. "I guess I can do that."

Her mother nodded. "Good." She started to go to her bedroom but stopped and looked back at Ivy. "I really would like to hear what's going on with you, when you're ready to talk about it."

Ivy nodded, wondering when that would be. "And I'd like to know who your mystery man is," she joked back.

Margot didn't answer, but Ivy saw the smile that played at the corners of her lips as she retreated from the room. She was glad her mother was happy. It gave Ivy hope that she could be too—that even after a disastrous marriage, healing could come.

She headed upstairs to shower and go to work, even as Elliott's words about not knowing how to do marriage repeated in her mind. She couldn't shake the feeling that he didn't just blame himself for that one. And the truth was, neither did she.

Nineteen

Ivy arrived at the bakery ready to help set things up for Owen and Shea, who were coming in to bake their wedding cake, Leah's custom for her brides and grooms. It took a bit of maneuvering to honor health codes and match up Leah's schedule with the busy couples, but in most cases, she found a way to make it work. What they didn't know was that they rarely ate the cake they made. Leah was such a perfectionist, she almost never served what the novices created. But they felt more invested in what they fed each other on their special day, and that was what mattered. As Leah always said, they knew the hard work that had to happen to taste the sweetness. More than once, Ivy thought that perhaps she should've pushed harder for her and Elliott to participate in this tradition. Of course at that point they weren't up for coming anywhere near Sunset.

She shook her head and continued setting up the ingredients like Leah had instructed. Since a camera crew was going to be filming a portion of their baking session, Leah wanted everything more streamlined. Leah was always efficient about her bakery. Even the timing of today's baking affair was calculated so that the cakes could be frozen in advance of the wedding. Cakes that had been frozen first were easier to ice and transport, a trick Leah had learned through practice.

"I don't know how I get myself into these things," Leah grumbled good-naturedly as she bustled around the store, making sure everything was ready for the cameras.

"Your store is going to be famous, Aunt Leah," Ivy said, attempting to sound normal and not at all flustered by her conversation with Elliott and the direct message from the reporter, not to mention her mother's admission that she knew there was more going on than she was saying. She'd been so convinced she could fool everyone.

Leah, dressed in a chef's hat and apron, looked like she'd stepped right out of a French cooking school. But when she opened her mouth, her Southern accent gave her away. "You hush your mouth. I can hardly keep up with wedding cake orders as it is. I don't need to be famous unless you're volunteering to leave that husband of yours and come down here and help me full-time."

Her heart pounding, Ivy managed to match Leah's lighthearted response with one of her own. "You just never know, Aunt Leah," she said, turning her attention to measuring the flour while she waited for her heart to slow down. "I might have to swoop in and save you in your hour of need."

"Well, if there was anyone I'd trust to help me with this bakery, it's you. You always did have a knack for cakes."

She thought of the last cake she'd taken to the office, the one for Delores's birthday. Her employees had always adored her cakes, going on and on about how much they loved being the benefactors of her weekend baking projects. She'd loved baking as a hobby but never considered it as a real job. Yet just look at how successful the bakery had become. Built on reputation and word of mouth, Aunt Leah's wedding cakes were known for destination weddings all over the area and recommended by several different popular wedding venues. Leah was right, she didn't need the publicity they were about to get. Maybe Ivy would have to stay. Maybe that could be her excuse.

She looked up to see Shea and Owen entering the bakery, cameras already rolling as Shea clapped her hands together and announced she was ready to bake a cake, looking every bit like she was made for the spotlight. Ivy remembered the strained look she'd given her when she'd first asked her about the wedding being televised. From the looks of things, she'd gotten past all of that. Shea looked at Ivy and winked, her happiness filling the bakery along with the camera crew. Ivy gave the cameraman her best smile too, acting for all the world like this moment was the only thing that mattered in her life.

∽

Ivy ducked out when it became clear that Leah had everything under control at the bakery, escaping the lights and cameramen that had taken over every available space. The bakery was a good size but certainly not spacious enough to hold all those people comfortably. The heat of the lights, the overly enthusiastic producer, and Shea's bubbly exclamations just became too much after a while. When Leah gave her the nod that told her it was fine to make her exit, she gratefully took the opening and slipped away.

Back home, she made herself some lunch, then curled up and read one of the paperback novels her mom kept stashed all over the house. She was relieved to find that she could still escape into a good story, forgetting what was happening in hers.

Later she took her customary walk on the beach. During the time she'd been here, the weather had grown steadily warmer. Today she found herself stepping frequently into the water to cool off, wishing she had worn her swimsuit so she could take a quick dip.

Her phone rang in her pocket, and she fished it out. She saw Michael's number on the display of her cheap phone and smiled as she answered. Maybe he wanted to see her again.

"Hey, where are you?" he asked. He sounded impatient, and worried.

"Um, walking on the beach?" she answered, wondering why his voice sounded funny.

"I don't guess Shea's with you?"

"No, she's at the bakery. Today was the day she and Owen were supposed to make their cake together. You shoulda seen the entourage they showed up—"

"I know all about that." Michael cut her off. "Shea

freaked out at the bakery today. She took off and no one can find her."

Ivy couldn't help but ask, "Did she freak out on camera?" That would make for good ratings.

Michael sighed. "I don't really know. I don't think so. I just know she freaked and took off, and everyone is trying to find her."

"Except me. I was out here oblivious." She couldn't ignore the nagging feeling that no one had thought to call her until now. After several years of not being part of their daily lives, she had become an afterthought.

"You might want to go home and help your parents look for her."

"My parents? My dad's here?"

"Yeah, apparently. Owen said he talked to your dad, and I got the feeling he was at your house."

The last time she'd seen her dad in that house had been that last summer they'd spent there as a family. Leave it to Shea to create a drama that would draw him back in. "Then I guess I'll head that direction," she said. Before she hung up, she thanked him for calling, pushing aside the hurt over the fact that it wasn't her family that reached out, taking comfort that Michael had.

She turned and headed back toward home, the now familiar landmarks telling her how close she was: the cluster of three sea-oat bushes, the mound of rocks that resembled an altar, and the sign for the 40th Street public access. She climbed the steps and made her way down the boardwalk, through the wide jungle of sea oats and sand dunes that separated the houses from the ocean, the boards weathered to the color of the sand, creating a nearly monochromatic landscape. She felt the boards beneath her bare feet, tan from her many long walks, the toenails painted with a nail polish she'd swiped from Shea, just like when they were kids. The color was Petal Pink, a bright attention-getting shade she'd never have chosen for herself. But her pink toes had grown on her.

As she approached the house, she saw cars and news vans gathered. Some were parked on the narrow street, nearly blocking the road. Some had pulled onto the grass, something that would surely send her mother into orbit. She could feel her frustration mounting at the thought of these strangers crowding into her personal space. She wondered again why Owen had okayed this, remembering the strain on Shea's face when his decision came up. She wondered if the stress had finally gotten to her. Ivy had seen indicators of it when she had a meltdown in the dressing room. But she had blamed herself for that, reasoning that Shea had been upset about their mother's wedding dress.

She entered the house to find the living room and kitchen filled with assorted people, most notably her dad and mom, standing together, so close their shoulders were touching. They looked at her like they'd forgotten she was there. "Shea's missing," Margot said.

Ivy crossed the room and took her mother's shaky hands in her own, squeezing gently. "Mom, she's not kidnapped. She just needed a sanity break." She surveyed the room. "Anyone would."

"I know, I know. I told her and Owen not to agree to this nonsense, but they didn't listen. A wedding is stressful enough without adding this." She made a sweep of her arm to indicate the people all milling around, waiting no doubt for Shea to show back up so they could film part two of her breakdown. Somehow her family had become stars of a reality TV show. One she had no desire to star in.

An attractive woman bustled toward them, sipping coffee from a mug that was from their kitchen. Leave it to Margot to provide Southern hospitality even to unwelcome guests. The woman had long dark hair caught back in a clip, her face radiating a kind of light that was obviously meant for the camera. *A commanding presence* were the words that came to mind as the woman turned her smile on Ivy. Juggling the coffee cup, she extended her hand. "Hello, I'm Vivienne White. And you must be Shea's sister."

"Oh yes. Vivienne, this is my other daughter, Ivy."

Vivienne's brow furrowed slightly as she looked from Margot to Ivy and back again. "Ivy. What an interesting name. So strange that I just heard it earlier, when I was doing some background on a smaller story I'm following."

At about the same time that the lightbulb went on in Vivienne's head, it went on in Ivy's as she placed Vivienne's name: @VivReports. The reporter who was trying to interview her was standing in her beach house, drinking her mother's coffee.

The front door opened, providing a welcome distraction. Michael entered the room and walked quickly over to Margot. "No sign of her in the usual spots. Owen and I've been all over."

Ivy watched Vivienne watching all of them, her eyes dancing at the unfolding drama. If possible, she seemed to have perked up even more when Michael arrived. Obviously she wasn't blind. Ivy felt jealousy rise up inside her. She moved a step closer to Michael. "Want me to go look with you?" she asked, doing her best to pretend that the reporter wasn't standing there.

Michael's gaze flickered over Vivienne as he noticed they weren't alone. Vivienne took the opportunity to extend her hand and introduce herself. She sure was pushy. The two exchanged brief introductions, and Ivy noted gleefully, Michael showed no interest as he shook Vivienne's hand quickly.

He turned back to Ivy. "Maybe you can think of somewhere she could be that we haven't thought of. You might be Ivy Marshall now, but you still think like a Copeland, whether you admit it or not. Come on." He waved Ivy along.

She started to follow him when she felt a hand on her shoulder. She turned back to see Vivienne's red nails gripping her T-shirt.

"Marshall?" she asked. "Are you Ivy Marshall?"

With her heart pounding she looked at her parents, then over at Michael, who had stopped at the front door and was looking back to see where she was. Then she glanced briefly at the woman who could blow the lid off everything she'd kept from her family. She gave a brief nod and, seeing how Vivienne's fingers had relaxed their grip, took the opportunity to dash away before she had to say anything else.

She'd deal with Vivienne later.

∾

"What was that all about?" Michael asked as they jumped into the yellow Jeep and drove down 40th to Main. Michael took the left-hand turn a little too sharply and Ivy fell into him. She had to force herself to sit back up. She wanted to stay where she was, bury her head in his shirt, and hide there awhile, in the safety that was Michael. She thought about the way Vivienne's face had looked when he entered the room. To her he had always been "just Michael"— someone as familiar to her as her own reflection. But to other women—strangers—he was a handsome man with broad shoulders and strong arms. How could she have forgotten that?

As they approached the pier, she signaled for him to pull over. The sun was setting and the warm air was turning slightly cooler as it did. She wished she'd grabbed a light jacket on their way out, but of course there hadn't been time in her rush to get away from Vivienne. Michael parked the car in the pier parking lot and turned to face her. "You not gonna tell me?" he asked.

She shivered slightly and Michael reached behind him in the Jeep, pulling out a blanket he kept back there and tossing it over her. "You okay?"

The concerned look on his face brought the tears she'd been holding back to her eyes. She buried her face in the blanket that smelled like him. "I will be." She breathed him in, thinking of summer nights on this very beach when she was his and he was hers and life was much less complicated. How she wanted to go back.

She raised her eyes to see that he was looking at her, studying her. "That reporter you just met?" she asked.

He nodded. "The pretty one?"

She narrowed her eyes at him. "You didn't have to point that out."

"You'd kinda have to be blind not to notice," he said.

"Whatever. She's covering this story *and* another one." She paused, exhaled. "And they both concern me. And I'm pretty sure she just figured that out back there."

"What?" His laugh was incredulous, as if no one would be covering one story that involved her, much less two.

"Remember how I told you that Elliott was tweeting his apology to me when I wouldn't respond to him?"

Michael nodded. "Have you responded?"

"No, but a lot of other people have. He's got quite a following that grows exponentially every day. Women clamoring to hear what he's going to say next. All these rejected women who never got to hear their husbands or boyfriends apologize, so they're, like, living vicariously through Elliott or something. It's weird."

"And this reporter is wanting to do a story on that?"

Ivy shrugged. "I guess. She contacted me just this morning via Twitter, not knowing she'd meet me in person later today. Weird, huh?"

"Weird," Michael agreed.

"You can say that again."

He couldn't let that one go. "Weird," he said and gave her a smile that nearly melted away all the anxiety she was feeling. He put his hand on her knee, squeezing it slightly, like a brother might.

She wanted to move past the friendship he was trying to create. Soar right over that and land on the other side, in a world of love and passion she had been missing so much lately. She put her hand over his and leaned toward him.

He abruptly pulled his hand away and turned his head. "We should go find Shea," he said, his voice steady and matter-of-fact.

"Shea's a big girl. She'll show up when she's ready." She couldn't keep the disappointed snark out of her tone.

"It means a lot to Owen."

"This means a lot to me," she said.

"Why?" he asked. He took his large hands and placed them on her shoulders, pushing her away gently. "Why are you doing this, Ivy? Didn't you do enough five years ago? What's your goal this time? To finish me off?"

She looked at him, incredulous. "Is that what you think? That this is some sort of game for me? That what happened five years ago meant nothing to me?"

"Oh no, I know it meant everything to you. He meant everything to you. You gave everything up for him." He extended his arm, sweeping it in an arc to indicate the whole place—Sunset, the beach house, her family, him.

"It was a mistake," she said quietly. "I made a mistake. That's what I've been wanting to say all this time. Ever since I got here."

"When did you decide it was a mistake, though, Ivy? Was it before you found out he was cheating on you, or after?"

She flinched at the ugliness of his words, how cutting they were. "Why does it matter?" she managed, not wanting to answer him.

He fixed her with that blue gaze of his. "Because I won't be someone's consolation prize. Not even yours."

"I'm not asking you to be. I'm just . . ." She sighed. "I don't even know what I'm asking."

His laughter was laced with irony. "And here we are again. Ivy doesn't know what she wants."

Her voice was quiet. "I want you."

"Do you know why I bought the McCoy house?" His response was not what she was expecting.

"Because it was a good bargain?" She sighed and leaned back against her seat.

He shook his head and raised his eyes to meet hers. "It was the final step in a long process."

"Process?"

He didn't blink as he spoke. "The process of getting over you."

Her heart skipped a beat. "Oh," she said, so quiet she doubted he even heard her. She tried not to let his words about getting over her sink in.

"Last summer I was driving around here, thinking about us, about how I was doing well and moving ahead and how—finally—it didn't hurt so much. I could think about building a life apart from you, with someone else. And I turned the corner and saw the For Sale sign in the yard, and I just . . . knew."

"Knew what?"

"That I had to buy this house, and restore it. It was . . . symbolic." He sat up a little taller.

She nodded, pretending to understand, sensing that if she asked too many questions, he would close back up tighter than a clam shell. "Do you want to know why?" He gave her a devilish grin, letting her know he already knew she did. Teasing her came natural, even now. "It was in that kitchen that I first knew I was in love with you."

She blinked at him, her heart hammering in her chest, thrilled at the admission, yet searching her memory banks for a significant exchange between the two of them that had taken place in that kitchen. She came up empty. The only memories she had of that kitchen involved Mrs. McCoy's tea parties and homemade lemonade.

He chuckled to himself. "I don't expect you to know what I'm talking about. It's something insignificant, nothing you ever knew about. Something I kept to myself."

"I guess we both kept some things to ourselves," she observed, thinking of the things she still hadn't said to him.

He nodded and continued. "One day Owen and I went there looking for you and Shea. We were going crabbing and we wanted you guys to come with us. Your mom said to look for you there. So we did. You were thirteen years old, sitting at the table with Mrs. McCoy and Shea, and you were all laughing at something. And I remembered I stood watching you for a moment before you noticed I was there, and I was just so—" He rolled his eyes heavenward. "This sounds cheesy, but it's true, I was captivated by you. You were so beautiful and it was like you didn't even know it. You were just so . . . you. And I knew I couldn't change that and I couldn't control it. But at thirteen years old I didn't want to. I just wanted you to be you—whatever that was— for as long as you'd let me be a witness to it."

She swallowed, trying to gather herself after his unexpected revelation. She found it hard to look at him, dropping her eyes to the gearshift and his hand resting there. Finally, she asked a question. "We were thirteen? But we didn't . . ."

He laughed. "Get together for two years? Yeah, it took me that long to get up the nerve."

She smiled, grateful at the humor breaking up the tension. "And here I thought I was the one who orchestrated us getting together all this time. That summer we were fifteen, I made it my goal to get you to notice me."

"Oh, I noticed."

"Well, you did a good job hiding it."

They both laughed and she noticed her breathing was becoming easier, her heart returning to its normal rhythm, the laughter an equalizer. This was turning out far better than she had hoped.

He moved his hand from the gearshift to rest on top of hers, his touch warm and clearly meant to just be friendly. "I know what happened. Why you broke it off," he said.

"You do?" She wasn't sure *she* completely knew what happened between them or why they broke up beyond Elliott coming into her life, sweeping her off her feet, convincing her that the life she craved waited in the mountains.

He nodded, his eyes intent. "Somehow, after we got together, I stopped seeing that girl at the table. I forgot that I didn't want to control who you were . . . and I started trying to manipulate who you became. Because who you became affected who I became, and that scared me. It was my fear that led to us doing what was expected of us, going along with the plans our families made for us." He moved his hand away again. "I think I knew you didn't want the wedding they were planning, didn't want the life they signed us up for. And yet it was a life I knew, a life that felt safe."

Tears filled her eyes. So he *did* understand. "Meanwhile I was learning that nothing in life is safe."

"Your parents' marriage breaking up really did a number on you. And there was nothing I could do to change that."

She pressed her lips together, nodding. "When I looked at you, I just saw something else I couldn't count on. I figured that everything we knew about each other was bogus, that even people you think you can count on are bound to disappoint you in the end."

"It sounds like a lesson you're learning all over again."

She shrugged. "I think that's just life—you know? One disappointment after another. I ran to Elliott because he was so different from what I knew. And I think I thought if I went after something different, then maybe my life would turn out different. That one of these days I'd find someone who would stick—who would be there no matter what."

"You never really gave me that chance."

She held up her hands. "No, I guess I didn't."

They sat silently for a while, each thinking over all that had been said. Ivy felt a range of emotions—thrilled at the admissions Michael had made, anxious over what would happen now, relieved at having said some of what she wanted to say to him. "So what do we do now?"

He shook his head. "We find Shea? We get through this wedding?"

A sense of bravery rose up in her, enabling her to ask a question of her own. "We see if there's something still there for us?"

His reaction was immediate. He shook his head. "No. I meant what I said. Restoring this house—and then selling it—is the final step in a long process for me. A process I never want to go through again. I want to make a fresh start, one that enables me to take what I've learned from this experience and make a new life. Something different." He winked, using her own words against her.

"I think you and I talking over all of this is good. And I get that you need to address some of this stuff with me. I think we both need that. For closure, even if that does sound like psychobabble." He grinned, signaling that their heart-to-heart was over. He gave a quick squeeze to her left hand, the one still bearing her wedding ring. "You need to figure things out with your husband," he said. "Betrayal is devastating if you let yourself really feel it. I know that better than anyone."

She wanted to say something in response, her stomach hurting over the thought of what she'd done to him. But he continued before she could find the words. "You need to let yourself feel that betrayal—really face it—before you can go on. Admit to yourself how alone you feel. Take it down to the base level—just you and God—then rebuild from there."

He turned from her, gripping the steering wheel as he stared straight ahead. They were silent as the minutes passed. The night sky deepened to a dark gray, and the stars came out as she waited. She looked above her at the expanse, thinking of the night she and Elliott had ridden the chairlift in the dark and stared at a winter sky that looked much like this early summer one.

He turned the key in the ignition. "Let's go back. Maybe

they've found her by now." He backed out of the parking space and went back the way they'd just come. And as he did, a tear trickled from the corner of her eye and made its way down her face before falling onto the upholstery of his Jeep, a part of her remaining with him. There was so much that had remained with him, and that was what she had to make him understand.

Twenty

The production crew had given up and gone back wherever they had come from by the time Michael dropped her off and drove away without another word. She stood in the front yard and watched his taillights disappear, wondering where he was going and wishing she could go wherever it was. She tiptoed up the front steps and into the house, running into Owen as she stepped into the dark, quiet house.

"Oooph," he grunted, rubbing his shoulder. "Watch where you're going, Ivy."

"How was I supposed to know you were going to be standing in my living room?"

"Oh, so it's your living room now. That was quick."

She shook her head, refusing to let him get her riled. "You know what I mean."

"Was that Michael dropping you off?"

"Yeah, we were looking for Shea."

"I drove past the Jeep and saw the two of you talking in it earlier. Didn't look like you were looking very hard to me."

"We figured she'd be back by now."

Owen exhaled loudly. "Nope, I was just giving up and going home." As much as he could get under her skin, she felt sorry for the guy.

"She'll show. Knowing Shea, she's watching the house right now, just waiting for everyone to leave so she can come home and sleep. Margot always taught us 'everything looks better in the morning!'"

She reached for the lamp and clicked it on, casting Owen's dismal face in bright light.

"Not everything always looks better in the morning, Ivy," he said. He brushed past her and was about to throw open the front door when he stopped and turned to her. "You have no right to do what you're doing with my cousin. He's a nice guy and he doesn't deserve to be yanked around just because you're bored."

Her mouth opened and closed and opened again as she cast about for something to say. "I—I'm not bored."

"You're some bored housewife who lost her job and is jealous of her sister, so you're trying to see if you can create some drama of your own. Just be honest."

She crossed her arms and threw her foot out to widen her stance. "First of all, I'm no housewife. I've been running a company until a few weeks ago. And second of all, I don't need to create drama, I have plenty of it already, thank you very much." She clamped her mouth shut before she spilled the beans about the reporter she'd met earlier.

"Then why can't you just leave the poor guy alone? He was doing so good. Then you show up and you're all 'Oh, Michael, I'll help you fix up your house.' 'Oh, Michael, let's go to our favorite little restaurant.' 'Oh, Michael, let me help you find Shea.' That's the last thing he needs."

"Why don't you let him decide that for himself?"

"Why don't you go back to your husband?"

"I will. As soon as your stupid wedding is over. I was invited here, I will remind you."

"Well, that invitation didn't include confusing my cousin over his feelings for you."

Her heart skipped a few beats. "Michael's confused?" she blurted, hating the hopeful note in her voice. He'd sounded so resolute and certain in the Jeep, his heart as closed as his hand, fisted on the gearshift as they talked.

"Yeah. Of course. The girl he almost marries comes back into his life and starts basically throwing herself at him. I'd say that would confuse most anyone."

"Do you think he wants things to . . . work out between us?"

Owen frowned and opened the front door. "Look, Michael's over you. He just doesn't like this game you're playing. And neither do I. So cool it, okay? And if you see your sister, tell her to call me ASAP." He shut the door behind him with a bit too much force and from the porch she could hear him say, "*Women*" in a disgusted tone.

She paced around the room, trying to make sense of what Owen had revealed about Michael. Things weren't as cut-and-dried as he had made them sound. He was at least a little bit interested in her, no matter how much of a fight he put up. She couldn't repress the smile that filled her face and was glad she was completely alone so she didn't have to.

To distract herself from too much thinking about Michael, she got busy opening the wishing tree tags that had arrived that day. She'd found herself looking forward to seeing what was on each one. Some were cute: "May you always remember the three magic words: 'You're right, dear.'" Some were spiritual, containing verses or quotes by Christian writers. Some were sad, paying homage to a lost wife or husband and wishing Owen and Shea what the author once had. But all were poignant in their own way. Even the one by the six-year-old girl who had written that she was the one who should be marrying Owen, if only he'd wait. Shea would have a good laugh over that one.

One of the new ones said, "I wish for you to be surrounded by your family and friends always, even as you create a new family and become each other's best friend." She turned that one over in her hand, the sentiment taking her back in time to the moment she realized she wasn't going to be surrounded by family and friends if she married Elliott. She'd broken the engagement with Michael, accepted a ring from Elliott, and told her parents, only to be greeted with icy disapproval and a distance that was about more than the miles between Sunset and Asheville. "If you do this," her mother had said, "understand that we will not support it."

Ivy had tried to take in what her mother was saying. "You're saying you won't come? To my wedding?" Her voice had risen at the end of each question, giving away the panic she felt at the thought of having to choose between this man she'd fallen head over heels in love with and her family. Why would anyone ask her to choose? But the lines were drawn. Michael and her family fell inside one, and she and Elliott fell inside the other. The only person willing to cross the lines was Leah, which Ivy appreciated. But it hardly healed her hurting heart.

"Can I at least still wear your dress? Grandmama's dress?" she'd asked, gripping the phone and wishing that Elliott were there to comfort her. The dress had been passed from bride to bride in their family, with tradition dictating that the older daughter wear it just like she wore the name Ivella Margaret.

There'd been a pause that stretched out like saltwater taffy being pulled, thinning across the distance. Then quietly her mother had said, "I guess. I'll send it to you."

And she'd at least made good on that promise. But when the dress arrived, it only served to make Ivy sad every time she looked at it. She didn't know what made her sadder—that she'd received it from the hands of the UPS man or that she'd be wearing it in front of a group of total strangers. Granted they were now her friends, but really they were Elliott's friends. In the end she'd packed up the dress, shoved it to the back of her closet, and convinced Elliott to get married in front of a justice of the peace on a Thursday afternoon. April had thrown them a lovely party later, held on the cabin grounds. Ivy had sent invitations to all of her family, but only Leah showed up, making apologies and excuses for the rest of them, telling Ivy what a good choice she'd made with Elliott, even if there was a hitch in her voice as she said it. All the while one word seemed to hang in the air: Michael.

Though no one said it, she knew she'd done the unforgivable in breaking Michael's heart when she broke their engagement. And in such a cowardly way. It was no wonder he wanted nothing to do with her now.

A flash of white on the back deck startled her, and she dropped the tag she was holding. She bent down to pick it up, scanning the view from the den windows to see what was out there. She saw a form sitting on one of the deck chairs, head down, the blonde hair glowing almost white in the moonlight, giving away who it was. Ivy placed the tag on the tree and went to her sister, crossing the room soundlessly and sliding open the door as quietly as possible. The last thing she wanted was for Margot to hear and decide to join them. This was a conversation she needed to have with Shea alone.

As Ivy approached, Shea lifted her head and gave Ivy a weak smile before looking away. "Just don't start in on me," she said.

"I'm not one to throw stones," Ivy responded. She sat down on the deck chair next to Shea's, resting her hands on her knees as she decided what to say next. "I thought coming here would be a help to you, but I've probably just added to your stress," she admitted. "I'm sorry."

She heard Shea sniffle and tried to look at her face, but she kept it down. Shea raised her hand and wiped her eyes, her voice strained and cracking as she spoke. "We ruined the cake," she said, and began to cry in earnest, the utterance enough to launch a fresh wave of tears. Ivy waited patiently while she got control of her emotions. Any other time the ruined cake would've been funny, a family story to laugh about for years to come. But for some reason, to

Shea this ruined cake had become a commentary on her and Owen as a couple.

"I bet Aunt Leah sees that happen all the time," Ivy offered. "I bet plenty of couples ruin their cakes. I know for a fact that Aunt Leah bakes the cake that actually gets served for most of them."

Shea looked up and Ivy thought that her words had helped. But her hope was short-lived. "But we were supposed to be different," Shea wailed.

Ivy rested her hand on Shea's shoulder tentatively, ready for her to move away at any moment. Ever since the strange meltdown in the dressing room, she'd been walking on eggshells around her sister, hesitant to tackle their emotional garbage in the emotion-wrought days before the wedding. Maybe it had been a mistake to come, but now that she was here, she really did long to make things right with her sister. "You are different, Shea. You and Owen are this amazing couple that other people want to be like. I mean, look at what's happened. The *Have a Good Day USA* people are filming your wedding!"

"Don't remind me," Shea mumbled. "The cameras were right there filming the whole debacle."

Ivy couldn't resist lobbing a joke into the situation. "Wow, Shea, debacle, that's quite a word."

Shea cut her eyes over at Ivy, giving her a small grin in reward. "I'm full of surprises."

"You always were," Ivy agreed. She waited a moment to see if Shea would say any more, but she kept silent, lost in whatever thoughts had tangled her up and made her run.

"Where were you today?" Ivy ventured, hoping it was a

safe question, hoping that if she asked the right one, while treading lightly enough, she would draw her sister out. She missed the days when she and Shea used to tell each other everything.

"I went for a walk," Shea said, then sniffled again. But at least the tears had stopped flowing.

"That was quite a walk."

"I walked to Ocean Isle at low tide. Remember how we used to say we were going to do that one day?"

"Yeah, every time Mom and Dad backed the station wagon out of the drive at the end of the summer to head back to Charlotte, we always said, 'Next year.'"

"Well, I decided today was the day. So I walked across, then I walked back. Then I just sat at the end of the island for a while, thinking." She held out her arms. "I even got sunburned."

Ivy felt a mixture of emotions as Shea described her day—pain at the thought of her sister doing that without her, loss of the life she'd once had, and regret over what she'd given up five years ago. She should've walked to Ocean Isle with her sister. She should've married Michael. She should've tried harder to restore things with Shea. Instead she'd given up, assigned blame to other people, and isolated herself. In that moment, in her heart, she felt more than heard a nudging voice telling her that she was doing the same thing all over again—this time with Elliott.

She ignored the voice, focusing on Shea instead of her own problems. This wasn't about her. She looked at her sister, thought of her in that dressing room, demanding that she leave. "What did you have to think about?" she asked.

"Oh, you know, the typical stuff brides think about: lifelong commitment, whether I made the right choice, if I have something blue for the 'something blue' category." Shea grinned. "Stuff like that."

Ivy went for the easiest point. "I thought you were wearing Grandmama's blue hairpin in your hair?"

Shea nodded. "Yeah, I am." She laughed a little, knowing that Ivy was hesitant to touch what she had revealed. Shea elbowed her. "Go ahead and ask me about the rest of it."

"Are you really having cold feet? You?"

Shea sat up straighter. "Why not me?"

Ivy shrugged. "Because you're . . . Shea. And Owen. You go together. You're the most likely to . . ."

"To what?"

Ivy laughed. "I don't know. Be together forever. Ride off into the sunset. Have 2.5 children and a house with a white picket fence. All of it."

"Then I guess you'd be surprised to know that I think the reason Owen proposed to me on national TV was because he was betting I wouldn't say no if there were cameras filming the whole thing."

Ivy thought of that moment in her living room alone, watching Shea live every little girl's dream on live television. How envious she'd been. How alone she'd felt watching it with no one to share the moment. How far away from her family she'd seemed. She'd never once considered that her sister wouldn't want what Owen was offering.

Shea continued. "Haven't you ever stopped to think about why Owen and I aren't married by now?"

Ivy sat in stunned silence, backtracking over all the thoughts she'd had about her sister and Owen in the years that had lapsed since she left. She'd always seen them as the perfect couple, her sister stepping into the role she'd walked away from, their wedding inevitable and certain. She'd always thought it was a matter of timing, of finding that perfect timing. She'd thought that Shea was waiting because it was the right thing to do, never because getting married to Owen might be wrong for her.

"Are you going to call it off?" she asked, glancing over her shoulder just in case. Her heart was racing—a mixture of dread at the thought of another wedding being called off and excitement at the thought that she wouldn't be the only one.

Her heart slowed as she saw Shea start to shake her head. "No. I decided not to." She turned to face Ivy. "Am I crazy to go through with it?" Her eyes begged Ivy to offer her assurance. Even in the dark Ivy could see evidence of the tears she'd shed throughout the day.

Ivy thought of her anger at Elliott, her fear of a future without him, her regret over breaking it off with Michael. She thought of the tweets her husband had been sending her, of the reminders of the love they'd once felt for each other. She thought of the wishing tree tags she'd collected in the past weeks—all those wishes for a happy future for Owen and Shea, all those people who were rooting for them. And somewhere in all of those things there was enough hope for her to tell her sister what she wanted to hear. "You're not crazy at all," she said. "You and Owen have something special."

"I thought you and Michael had something special too, though."

Ivy just nodded, unsure of what to say. "I think we did. I just didn't know it. I didn't have enough life experience—nothing to compare it to. I convinced myself there was something . . . better out there."

"And was there?"

The question hung in the air between them. Ivy could almost see it there, like a cartoon bubble with the words inside. She wanted to tell Shea the truth about Elliott, about what he'd done and what had happened since, about how she'd run away from him the same way she'd run away from them years ago. But something kept her from blurting out the details: pride or shame or privacy or, very faint, the possibility that she and Elliott could resolve things, and she didn't want her sister to hate him. She stared down at her hands.

"I'll just say this. There was something different out there. But different and better are not synonymous. Just because something's known doesn't mean it's wrong. New does not equal improved." She looked up to find Shea staring at her, reading between the lines as only a sister can do. She backpedaled, doing damage control. "I mean, I just don't want you to think that there's someone better out there for you than Owen."

But it didn't work. Shea pounced on the scrap of revelation. "Ivy, why are you here? And why don't you ever mention Elliott? Would you just tell me what's going on?"

Tears filled her eyes. "I can't really talk about it yet." She shifted away from Shea, her knees pointing toward the door she wanted to run through. "Okay?"

"I'm sorry for whatever it is," Shea said. She reached out and squeezed Ivy's hand. "And I'm sorry I sent you away that day when we went shopping. I was mad at you, about Grandmama's dress. Mom's dress." Shea ducked her head. "I've been mad at you about a lot of things."

Ivy nodded. "Because of what happened with Michael." This was the conversation she'd been waiting to have for five years. They would finally say what they'd both needed to say, finally lay it all out on the table. And once it was out, maybe then they could put it all away.

"I was sad about Michael—mostly sad for him because he was so upset. Because I care about him, of course. He's like the brother I never had, and I'm not real keen on how you've been messing with his mind lately." Ivy nodded, bracing herself for what was next. "But mostly I was mad at you for having the courage to do what I never could." Shea looked over at her. "You went off and made this whole other life. You broke free from the . . . sadness that hung around here after Mom and Dad split. And I was mad because I felt like I had to stay here and pick up the pieces. Like because you left I had to stay—and all my fantasies about doing exactly what you did went up in smoke."

Ivy tried to take in what Shea was saying. She wasn't mad for the reasons she'd always thought. "You weren't mad at me for breaking things off with Michael? For marrying Elliott?"

Shea gave her a "duh" look. "If you didn't want to be with Michael, I wouldn't have wanted you to marry him. I knew you did the right thing for you."

"Wow" was all she said. "I never thought—"

"You never asked."

"I just assumed that you were mad. That you took Michael's side and you didn't want any more to do with me."

Shea chuckled. "And I assumed that you were so blissed out up there in the mountains, you'd forgotten all about us. That you didn't care about coming home."

"I thought I wasn't welcome here. I thought you all would never forgive me for what I did."

Shea reached out and wrapped her arm around Ivy's shoulder. "How could you think that? This is your home. We're your family. We might not agree with your decisions. We might have to talk things out. But we'll get through it." Ivy let that sink in. All this time, she'd had a family. She'd had a sister. It was like looking for her sunglasses when they were sitting on top of her head.

And then Shea said something that resounded in her heart. "Ivy, you took off before we could fix everything." And in her mind's eye, she could see herself packing to leave as Elliott watched, as he begged her to stay.

"I had no idea," she said. "All this time I thought you were angry at me."

"More hurt than angry, but I do get angry at you. I always will. But I want to be able to talk to you and work it out with you. Because you're my sister and I love you."

Ivy reached out and gave Shea a real hug, inhaling the scent of her perfume mixed with the ocean air. "Thank you," she whispered. She pulled back, making a joke just to defuse the intensity of the moment. "And to think I came out here to help you."

Shea rose from her seat. "You did help," she said. "Just by coming back here, you helped."

Ivy rose and followed Shea back into the house, both of them yawning and stretching. "I'm glad you're not calling off your wedding to Owen," she said to Shea's back.

Shea turned with a smile, her hand on the door. "Yeah, me too. He's a keeper."

"So what dress did you end up buying?" Ivy asked.

Shea waved her hand in the air. "That basic white dress. It's pretty enough."

She shrugged as Ivy smiled. "I know you'll look beautiful," Ivy said.

"We both will," Shea said and slipped into the house, blowing Ivy a kiss good night.

Ivy looked up. The sky was completely dark, the night that preceded the day.

Twenty-One

Everyone slept late the next morning, including Ivy, since the bakery was officially closed for a few days so that Leah could focus on the wedding. But Ivy decided to drop by anyway. She let herself in with the key Leah had given her, stopping in the doorway to watch as Leah moved efficiently around the kitchen area, the radio, as always, playing.

Leah glanced up and caught Ivy's eye, her face breaking into a wide smile.

"T minus two days and counting," Ivy quipped.

"I hope you came to help," Leah said. "I've got a mess here to fix." She gestured at Shea's ruined cake in the middle of the worktable. The middle was sunken and the edges were scorched.

Ivy walked closer, her eyes on the cake as if it might jump up and bite her. "Any idea what happened?" she asked.

Leah shrugged. "Sometimes it's pointless to spend too much time figuring out what happened or why. It's a mess and that's all we need to know. The main thing we gotta do is figure out how to fix it."

The look that passed between her and her aunt told her that Leah was talking about more than just the cake. Resorting to humor as a defense, she pretended to roll up sleeves she didn't have. "Guess we better get busy then."

"Heard you found Shea last night," Leah said as they got to work making a whole new cake.

"I didn't find her. She came home. But yeah, we had a good talk last night."

"Got things sorted out, maybe?"

She thought about how good it had been to clear the air with her sister. "Yeah, we talked about a lot of stuff."

Leah peered at her over her glasses. "So I guess you found out that your sister's not mad at you like you thought?"

"Yeah, I did." Ivy eyed her aunt. "Why didn't you tell me that if you already knew?"

Leah gave her a sassy look. "You never asked."

She laughed in spite of herself. "You think everything's going to be okay?" she asked, staying focused on the work so she didn't have to look Leah in the eye.

Leah, apparently sensing that she was asking about more than just Shea and Owen, gave her an answer that applied to them both. "I've always known you girls were going to be just fine."

"Even though Shea ran away? Even though the cake got ruined?" She looked over at Leah. "She thought that it was some sort of sign. It really freaked her out."

"Does she still think that?"

Ivy shook her head.

"Some mistakes mean something. And some mistakes are just mistakes. The trick in this life is to figure out which is which." Ivy thought about Leah's advice in light of all that had happened with her and Michael, and her and Elliott. Which one was a mistake that meant something and which one was just a mistake?

Her aunt thought about it for a minute. "I see couples in and out of here all the time. I've got a good nose for which ones will make it after all these years of baking their wedding cakes."

"So, will Shea and Owen make it?" Ivy asked.

Her aunt smiled. "I'll tell you something, I know Shea and Owen will make it the same way I knew you and Elliott would. I've got a sense about these things." She winked at Ivy and turned back to her work, singing along with the radio.

You're so wrong, Ivy thought, but she kept working.

"Have you thought of what you'll say for the toast at the rehearsal dinner?" Leah asked, making conversation. Her aunt knew that making public speeches was one of her least favorite things to do.

"Umm, can I just write something good on a tag for the wishing tree and leave it at that?" Ivy tried to keep her voice light but it was obviously shaking.

"I don't think your sister's going to be satisfied with that. Tradition dictates that the matron of honor make a toast. And you know this family and their traditions."

Ivy knew it was pointless to argue with Leah about it. She was only the messenger. She glanced up at the old-fashioned cake topper Leah kept in the shop, the one that had once stood on top of her wedding cake when she was a young bride, before her husband was killed in Vietnam. Leah had loved her husband but had only had a few short months with him before he was shipped off to war, never to return.

A sharp knock at the door made them both jump and Ivy looked up to find Lester there, holding flowers, his face as open and earnest as a young man. Gone was the frown he usually wore and in its place was an expression of hope as he held out the flowers to Leah when she let him in. "For you," he said and bowed as Leah blushed and glanced over at Ivy.

She watched with amusement as Leah, flustered, tried to find a container to put the flowers in. She finally settled on a flour bucket, filling it up with water and sticking the flowers in haphazardly. Ivy tried not to stare so Leah didn't feel even more uncomfortable. She was clearly embarrassed about Lester's romantic overture.

But Lester, on the other hand, seemed relieved to be out in the open with it. He put his arm around Leah and pretended to stick his finger in the batter as she slapped it away. The way they related to each other told Ivy that there was a history between them.

Lester attempted to whisper to Leah, but his deep voice had a way of defying a whisper. "Sorry," he said. "I didn't know your niece was here."

Leah looked over at Ivy and winked. "It's okay," Leah whispered back.

"I hoped you'd be done," he said. "I wanted to take you to lunch."

Without thinking, Ivy answered him. "Oh, you can take

her to lunch. I can finish here." Their faces answered her in two different ways: Lester looked relieved as Leah looked panicked. It was bad enough her secret was revealed. Worse yet that she was being asked to surrender one of the most important cakes she would make all year. A cake for her niece. A cake that would be on TV. And yet, as Leah looked at Lester, Ivy could see she saw more than that—she saw the potential for her own happiness, apart from the bakery, apart from even the family she loved. After flooding Ivy with advice on the cake, she let Lester escort her from the bakery. Leah, in that moment, was choosing something just for her.

It reminded Ivy of the time she'd done the same thing— when she'd decided to choose Elliott over Michael or her family. She'd been so happy when she married Elliott, danc- ing their first dance as husband and wife at the party that April threw for them while the guests gathered to watch. She hadn't even minded that the only guest who'd actually come for her was her aunt. Her attention had been fully on her new husband, this man who had captivated her atten- tion and imagination. In his arms she'd felt vulnerable and transparent yet safe and shielded.

They'd danced to "All the Way" by Frank Sinatra and felt—more than heard—the words. This was what intimacy was, she'd thought. Eventually other couples joined them on the makeshift dance floor but she'd barely noticed. There was a time, she remembered, when things had been good between them. And that time had happened when she didn't withhold any part of herself.

She turned her attention from the cake to the icing, her eyes falling on that cake topper again. The plastic bride and groom looked like they were dancing. She wondered if it made Leah sad to see it, a reminder of what was lost, or of what she once was blessed to have. She only felt sad when she thought of dancing with Elliott, and the words to the song they'd chosen to dance to. "When somebody loves you, it's no good unless she loves you all the way."

Her eyes filled with tears as the icing blurred in front of her. She hadn't kept her end of the agreement. She hadn't gone all the way, holding a part of herself back "just in case." Just in case she ended up like her mom—alone and sad, Carly Simon playing endlessly.

To love the way Elliott wanted was to take a risk that terrified her. She hadn't loved him all the way, and he'd known it—their genuine love had become a cheap counterfeit. And cheap counterfeits didn't last or have any value. He'd known it, and now she did too. The question was what she should do about it now that she did. It was impossible to love someone all the way without getting hurt. Michael would've been the safer, smarter choice—and this was her chance for a do-over.

She hurried through the remaining tasks of the day with her mind on the wedding ahead, turning up the music to drown her thoughts. She worked steadily and danced along.

~

That reporter, Vivienne, was in the front yard with Michael when Ivy got home. She was leaning too close to him, her smile an invitation that anyone with eyes could see. Ivy didn't know what made her angrier—that she was making a play for Michael or that she was there at all.

Ivy pulled around the news truck nearly blocking the street and into the driveway, shoving the car into park and sitting for a few minutes as she waited for one or both of them to notice that she was there. When neither of them did, she opened the car door and slammed it shut. Michael looked up at the noise, but Vivienne kept her eyes on him. Ivy and Michael traded looks. Hers said: Be careful. His said: It's none of your business. She walked right by them, keeping her head high as she climbed the stairs into the house.

She grabbed the day's mail, ripping into the final tags trickling in for the wishing tree. The rest would be hand-delivered by guests in attendance. She took a look at the tree. It was already pretty full. Everyone had something to wish the happy young couple. But Ivy hadn't thought of anything to write on a tag for her sister and Owen. The right words eluded her. She could hardly write, "Don't make the same mistakes I did." She thought of her earlier revelation about loving someone all the way. Maybe that would be her wish for her sister—that she and Owen could do what she and Elliott could not. Then she thought about making a toast and her stomach lurched.

There was a knock on the door. She turned to it, for-getting for a moment what she'd just seen in the front yard, expecting for the surprise she had arranged for Shea to be waiting on the other side. Instead she tugged the door open to find Vivienne blinking back at her, her makeup artfully applied, her eyes the color of clover. Her beauty only made Ivy dislike her more.

"I was hoping you'd reconsidered talking to me. I had a good conversation with your husband this morning." She leaned against the doorframe, looking at home in a way that was disconcerting to Ivy. "He says he's not sure he can pursue the story any longer, but I'm going to keep working on him . . ." She shrugged like Elliott's change of heart was just a trivial detail, but Ivy knew different. "I'm just giving you a chance to weigh in with your side. I mean, if you want people to hear it."

Ivy shook her head. "I don't have any intention of talking to you. And I'd appreciate it if you'd leave my family and friends alone." She emphasized "friends," hoping that the reporter would know that meant Michael specifically.

The clover-green eyes narrowed. "Your family and friends are the story I'm covering right now. Imagine my surprise when I realized that two of the stories I'm covering involve you and your family. I call that serendipity."

Ivy willed her face to be expressionless as she responded. "We'll just see about that," she said.

Michael pulled up outside in his yellow Jeep and honked the horn as the reporter gave her a little wave, turned, and sashayed down the steps. Ivy watched them go, hating Vivienne's ridiculous stiletto heels, her fancy skirt that didn't qualify as beach attire, and her overly red lips that transformed into a smile as she got into the passenger side of the Jeep, the wind whipping her perfectly fixed hair into a mess as they drove away together. Mostly what Ivy hated was that the reporter was in her spot beside Michael—and there was nothing she could do about that.

Ivy paced by the front window, eyeing the street. April had promised to arrive this afternoon, and she couldn't wait to see her. Upstairs she could hear Shea getting ready for her and Owen's last dance lesson before the big day. Ivy wondered what song they would dance to.

Minutes later Shea clomped down the stairs wearing her wedding shoes with a pair of shorts. She looked silly, and Ivy giggled. Shea pointed at her. "No comments from the peanut gallery. The instructor said I better get some practice wearing the shoes I'm going to be dancing in." She held up a bag. "I've got shoes to change into when we're done. We're going out to dinner after."

Ivy looked outside once more. "Are you leaving now?"

"Yeah, Owen will be here any minute. Why? You've been camped out by this window since before I got in the shower. What's up with you?"

"I've got a . . . surprise coming. For you. I was hoping it would get here before you left."

Shea clapped her hands together, smiling like the little girl Ivy used to pretend to be mermaids with. "I love surprises!"

"Yeah, I know. That's why I arranged this one, but it's late."

Shea glanced down at her bare arm and looked up. "Of course I'm not wearing a watch, but I don't think I have much time to wait."

"Oh, it's okay. I know you've gotta go. Hopefully it'll be here when you get back." She couldn't keep the disappointment out of her voice.

"Hey." Shea put her hand on Ivy's arm, the kindness and genuine feelings from the night before passing between them. "Whatever it is, I appreciate you thinking of me. It's nice of you to try and make my wedding special."

A knock at the door surprised them both. She hadn't heard the car pull into the drive. She grinned at Shea and raced to open the door first, calling, "I'll get it!" She blinked back at Owen's face on the other side of the door.

"Gee, Ivy, didn't know you were so excited to see me," he quipped. Apparently all was forgiven now that Shea was back.

She rolled her eyes and waved at Shea. "Your ride's here." She watched them go, enjoying Owen's amused gaze as he took in Shea's outfit.

"Hey, Shea," she called after them.

Shea stopped, shielding her eyes from the sun as she looked back at Ivy. "Yeah?" she asked. Ivy could hear the impatience in her voice, anxious as she was to try out her dancing shoes.

"What song are you dancing to?" she asked.

Owen nudged Shea and Shea smiled. "It's a surprise." She giggled.

Ivy saw the familiar car making its way down the street, headed toward their house in the nick of time. "Hey, speaking of surprises," she yelled, pointing at the car. "Here comes yours!"

Shea looked at the unfamiliar car and back at Ivy, confused. "What? You were expecting FedEx?" Ivy asked. April parked on the street and jumped out, waving a box at Shea as Ivy ran into the yard to meet her. Owen just looked confused as the women encircled him and Shea tore into the box, Ivy calling out erratic introductions as the tape was ripped from the box. Before she was even into it, Shea was already calling out, "Is this what I think it is?"

Ivy just smiled back at her and waited for her to see the folds of white silk hidden underneath aged tissue paper. Shea pulled the dress from the box and tossed the cardboard aside as she held her prize aloft, the dress waving in the wind like some oversize silk flag complete with lace and pearls. "Mom's dress!" Shea kept saying over and over, the smile on her face exactly what Ivy had in mind when she'd first conceived of getting April to bring it.

Shea turned to Owen. "Now I don't have to wear that ugly one I hate!" She reached out and hugged first Ivy, then April. "Thank you both so much!" She looked at April for a moment. "You must be April!" Tears flowed from all of them even as they laughed.

"I hate to break up this little party, but we better be going if we want to make dance class," Owen said, clearly looking for an escape from the flowing estrogen. Reluctantly, Shea handed over the dress to Ivy, with the promise that Ivy would take it in and hang it up. Tomorrow would mean a speedy alteration process if the dress would be ready for the nuptials. Ivy had already secured an expert seamstress —one of Leah's cronies—for the job. She held the dress up and inspected it. It looked like it would fit Shea perfectly. It helped that Margot and Shea were roughly the same size.

As she watched Shea and Owen drive away, she realized she wished her sister nothing but happiness. The thought comforted her. She'd already come a long way. Maybe that meant she'd make it the rest of the way too. She put her arm around April and squeezed. And now her best friend and trusted confidante would be beside her as she did. Everything felt perfect as they headed up the stairs into the house, the dress dancing on the breeze as they walked, just like it would dance when Shea wore it in two days. And Ivy had made that possible. But her feelings of goodwill lasted as long as it took for April to start talking, to confess that the dress wasn't the only thing she'd brought to Sunset with her.

Twenty-Two

The feeling between April and Ivy went from elation to devastation in the few seconds it took for April to reveal that she had brought Elliott with her. Dread swamped her. "What do you mean, April?" she asked, her voice a warning.

"Elliot's here," She repeated, her eyes begging her to understand.

"What?" She should have expected this. She had never told him outright that she did not want him at the wedding, just assumed that her message was loud and clear: no contact. She hadn't worked out what excuse she'd tell her family yet for Elliott's no-show, but she'd certainly determined she didn't want him here.

"Ivy." April switched tactics from beseeching to exasperation. "From what I can gather, you haven't even told your family yet what's going on. What was going to be your excuse when Elliott didn't show up? Having him here actually helps you, when you think about it."

"Thanks a lot. I appreciate your thinking of me." Ivy couldn't have been more sarcastic.

"If it helps you to know, it was kind of a last-minute decision," April admitted. "Elliott thought it was risky, but I talked him into it. At least I had the good sense to leave him at the hotel first," she said, as if that made a difference.

Ivy looked at her friend—the one person she thought would never betray her. "I just can't deal with this right now, April," she said.

"Then when will you, Ivy? How long are you going to keep running away?"

Ivy stood up, signaling the conversation was over. She went to the front door and opened it. "I'll let you know."

April left without further argument, but not without a "you're crazy and you'd better face up to life" look.

Ivy wanted to feel angry at April, but instead she just felt fearful over the thought of talking to Elliott now. Now when that reporter was there sniffing around for a story. Now when she was trying to retake lost ground with Michael. Now when the wedding was getting ready to happen in front of a nation's worth of viewers. *Now* Elliott was here.

Things couldn't be worse.

Ivy paced around in the living area, in front of the bank of windows, barely noticing the expanse of marsh in front of her. She stopped pacing when her phone rang and leaned down to pick it up. She looked at the display on her phone, grimacing at the number she saw: April, calling so soon after her hasty exit.

She was tempted to ignore it, giving her the cell phone equivalent of the silent treatment. But that would be childish, and maybe April was calling to say she was sorry and she was taking Elliott back where he came from. She answered with a hopeful note in her voice, drawing from a reservoir she was surprised she still had.

"There was something I didn't tell you," April said, going right to her point. "Something I think you should know."

More unexpected news was not what Ivy was looking for. She sighed into the phone. "What?"

"Your family knows. About Elliott. About the Twitter account."

So things could be worse. Her heart quickened and she sank into the nearest chair, gripping the phone tighter as she tried to process what April was saying. "What do you mean, they know? They haven't said anything. They've acted completely oblivious."

"Well, they know somehow. They've all been following him at least a week. Elliott said your mom apparently created an account just to follow him. Did you even know your sister was on Twitter? He told me as we were driving down here. He thought you knew—that they were following him for you, giving you reports or whatever." April paused. "He was hoping that you were reading what he'd been writing to you, or at least hearing about it from them."

Hanging on to the last shred of her pride, Ivy didn't confess that she'd read every tweet he'd written. "No" was all she said. "They weren't telling me about it."

Her mind raced through the possibilities of how they could know. Michael. She'd told him about the Twitter account on the night they went out to dinner. So why had her family said nothing in spite of the chances they'd had, all doing a good job of acting oblivious?

She realized that wasn't quite true. Just yesterday both her mom and her sister had danced around the subject, cracking the door open for her to walk through. But she wasn't ready yet. Not with the wedding coming up. Not when she was so mixed up about Michael.

Anger rose within her, running through her veins and warming her skin. Betrayal was everywhere she looked. First Elliott, then Michael, then April, now the rest of her family—people who were supposed to care, to want the best for her. She leaned against the back of the chair and closed her eyes, Michael's face coming to her mind as she did. Why did he do this to her?

"I gotta go, April," she said, already rising from her seat and looking for her car keys. She had to find Michael and ask him why he'd betrayed her.

"We'll just wait here," April said. "I mean, Elliott wants to see you before we go back."

"What if I don't want to see him?" Ivy retorted.

"You've been following his Twitter account. You know every word he's written even though you deny it. Ask yourself why that is and don't lie to yourself that it's just because you want to monitor what he's saying about you. You're checking it because you want to hear his apology, you want to accept it. Because you still have feelings for him and deep, deep down you hope that your marriage can somehow be saved." April sounded smug and very, very right. "And you'll never convince me otherwise." She paused for dramatic effect. "So be mad at me if you must, but you will eventually get over it. I did the right thing bringing him here and I stand by my decision."

"Must be nice to be you. So sure of yourself," Ivy spat, sounding snippy and childish. Maybe someday she would understand April's bold move. Maybe someday they would laugh about all this. But first she had to confront Michael and find out why he of all people had betrayed her too.

∾

As she drove around trying to spot the yellow Jeep in Michael's usual haunts, she thought about all that had happened between them in the last several weeks—how his hesitation with her had been palpable at first but had progressed to a tolerance that was a relief. From there they'd made slow progress to an understanding of what had doomed their relationship in the past. So what if he had turned away from her overtures last time they talked. With a few more weeks, they might've made it back to good friends. And from there, who knew?

She longed to turn back the clock, to go back to the night the photo was taken that she still had up in her room, the one of her and Michael, Shea and Owen. Michael had asked her to marry him at the gazebo near the pier that very night, kneeling down as children rode by on bicycles and elderly couples shuffled past. Some people stopped when they realized what was going on. She'd tried to listen to the words he said, but they were words she already knew—things they'd said to each other for as long as they could remember. The moment other girls dreamed of was, for her, one that had happened already, the details a mere formality. And even as she said yes and he kissed her and the people clapped and wandered back to their own lives, she'd felt a little pang for what she didn't have—and for how unfair it was to Michael that she couldn't muster up the same excitement he had.

After his proposal they'd met Shea and Owen for dinner on the water in nearby Southport, the mood festive as they all talked about the wedding. A nearby diner had snapped that photo, the sun setting in the background as the camera captured their radiant faces. But the ring Michael had put on her finger hadn't fit and she'd spent most of the evening feeling it slip, worried that it would fall off.

She thought about all that Michael had to be angry with her for. She hadn't just broken their engagement. She'd taken the coward's way out, shipping his ring back in a box with a note, staying in Asheville with Elliott instead of returning to Sunset Beach. Everyone had been so angry with her, she'd been afraid to come back and face them all. So she'd started a new life, dodging them for years because she was embarrassed, ashamed of her behavior. And she'd blamed them for it because they didn't show up on her doorstep and beg.

She pulled into the pier parking lot and walked over to the gazebo where Michael had proposed, taking a seat in the same spot she'd been sitting in then, wishing she could change what had happened after that moment in time. But as she closed her eyes and tried to picture Michael's face, it was Elliott's she saw. Elliott proposing to her not long after they met, holding his grandmother's ring as they sat beside the stream beside one of April's cabins, the earnest look in his eyes as he begged her not to marry Michael.

He'd slipped Michael's ring from her finger, replacing it with the one he held. Michael's had been bigger, prettier, shinier. But Elliott's had fit perfectly without having to be resized. Elliott's ring had meaning attached to it, a heritage that didn't involve her scheming, dreaming family, a chance to make her own way. She'd said yes to Elliott, feeling giddy and hopeful and . . . happy. So happy.

She looked down at her hand, at the ring she'd chosen to wear. She hadn't taken it off at Sunset because she wanted to fool her family. But also because somehow it hadn't felt right to take off her wedding ring. Not yet. She spun it around on her finger, noting that it needed cleaning. She'd neglected it like she'd neglected so many things.

She stood up and, for lack of anywhere else to go, headed for home. She aimed her car down the now-familiar street. As she passed the McCoy house, she gave it a cursory glance, not expecting to see the yellow Jeep in the drive. But it was. She turned abruptly into the drive and parked.

Not rehearsing what she would say to him, she knocked on the door, a staccato succession of sharp sounds.

He opened the door and blinked at her before moving out of the way and gesturing for her to enter. "Not sure I'm in the mood for whatever this is about," he mumbled as he shut the door.

Ignoring his comment, she looked around. "Is she here?"

He wrinkled his brow. "By *she* I would guess you mean Vivienne?"

Ivy gave him her best "duh" look from their teen years. "Is she?"

He crossed his arms in front of him, looking amused. "No. She had some work to do. Some story she's covering. She had to do an interview with some guy who's in town."

Ivy felt her blood pressure spike as she put two and two together. No doubt who Vivienne was interviewing. Her hands clenched by her sides, but she chose to ignore them. There was nothing to protect anymore. Everyone knew about Elliott's Twitter account and their separation. In a way, she realized as she stood facing off against Michael, knowing that her secret was out freed her. She didn't have to hide anymore. "Will you go for a walk with me?" she asked.

He shrugged, looking like he couldn't care less, which she tried to ignore. He followed her out of the house, sliding on his flip-flops in the doorway before they headed down the stairs. They walked stiffly along 40th Street, away from the house, him keeping a careful distance.

After a stint of silence, she finally spoke up. "I guess I should thank you."

"Thank me? For what?" he answered.

"For telling my family about me and Elliott. About his Twitter account."

He stopped walking and turned to look at her. "I didn't tell your family anything."

She responded quickly. "Well, did you tell Owen? That's the same as telling my family, you know."

"No, I didn't tell anyone. It wasn't anyone else's business. And it was your decision when you wanted people to know." He cocked his head at her for a moment before he continued walking. "I kept my promise to you." The last comment was quieter, so faint she wasn't sure she heard him right.

She knew he wasn't just talking about this time, this promise. He was talking about all of them. The ones he'd kept versus the ones she hadn't. Without thinking about it, she reached out, took his hand, and squeezed it. She was surprised when he squeezed back, and didn't feel bad when he let go. They continued on in silence, making their way to the center of the island, back to the gazebo she had just visited. Though they never discussed it, it seemed they knew where to go without speaking. It was as if her wish to start over was being granted. She snuck a look at Michael, thinking of how she'd felt when he drove away with Vivienne.

They took a seat on one of the benches in the gazebo. She was careful to avoid the one she sat on when they got engaged. "Feels weird being back here," he said. He wiped his palms on his shorts and looked away.

"Yeah," she said. "It sure does." She looked out at the ocean, noticing that the traffic had sure picked up since she arrived. People wandered around, some carrying fishing poles, some carrying cameras, some carrying beach chairs. She took a deep breath of the briny air. "But it feels good too."

"Maybe for you."

She looked over at him, the pain on his face unmistakable. She thought of what Owen had said when he was angry the other night, about Michael's conflicting emotions over her return.

"I'm sorry," she breathed. "I—"

"You know what you told me, that one time I got you to talk about it?"

She remembered he'd called from the beach house and she'd answered thinking—hoping—it was her mother calling to tell her she was coming to her and Elliott's wedding after all. It had been a sneaky thing to do on his part, and she'd been angry. More because it hadn't been her mom on the other end of the phone than because of what he'd done. She was always taking things out on him. She'd felt comfortable doing that, entitled even. "I hardly remember anything from that time in my life. It was a . . . confusing time."

"You said that he was the one person you were meant to be with. That you never knew love could feel like it did with him." He pressed his mouth into a thin line. "And I knew right then I had to let you go."

"But I think I was wrong."

He shook his head. "You weren't. When you said it, I felt it go through me, the truth of it. I knew I'd lost you and I knew that, as hard as it was going to be, I had to let you go."

"And you did," she said.

He gave a wry little laugh in response. "You make it sound so easy."

"Well, you've made it look easy since I got here."

"That's just because you missed the past few years." He leaned over and nudged her with his shoulder. "It was a process."

"Is that why you've been so distant with me?"

He nodded. "Yeah, I just figured I better keep my distance. Don't want to lose the ground I've gained."

They were silent for a few moments. It was time to let Michael go just the way he had let her go. Not because it was the easy choice but because it was the right one. She'd known in the bakery today what the right thing to do was. And in this moment it was clearest to her. It was time to find whatever Leah had seen that made her believe in Ivy and Elliott. She rose from her seat. "I'm sorry for all of it. For taking the coward's way out and sending you that letter instead of facing you. I had a lot of growing up to do."

He didn't disagree with her, just barely nodded, his mind, she knew, revisiting the pain of that time—recalling what it felt like to open that letter, see his ring carelessly shoved in an envelope by the coward he'd once wanted to marry. Elliott wasn't the only one seeking forgiveness so that he could move on.

She leaned down and picked up a stray shell on the floor of the gazebo, studying it instead of his face. "Think we've taken the curse off this place by coming here together?" She gestured at the gazebo.

He gave her a small smile as he rose to his feet. "I have to be honest, this is the first time I've come back here since then. I just couldn't revisit the scene of the crime."

She nodded. "Understandable, considering. Thanks for coming here with me."

They fell into step, walking back to 40th Street together. He reached over and gave her shoulder a familiar squeeze, much like something he would've done back when they were kids, before they became a couple and friendship, pure and simple, had defined their relationship. She missed that feeling and leaned into it, and him, her head resting on his shoulder as they walked together. She felt more comfortable with him at that moment than in any other since she got to Sunset.

At that moment she heard her name being called. She popped her head up to see Elliott standing across the street, wearing his running clothes and dripping with sweat, his eyes wild with jealousy and something that resembled accusation. He jogged across the street until he was standing directly in front of them, his eyes moving from her to Michael and back again. "I guess I deserve this," he said, breathing heavily. His face was red, his eyes bloodshot. He looked terrible, like he hadn't slept in days. He'd lost weight too, his normally muscular frame looking gaunt. It was all she could do in that moment of seeing him again after all this time not to reach out and hug him. But she didn't get the chance because Elliott turned and ran away, leaving her to stand on the street with Michael, the two of them watching him go.

Twenty-Three

When Michael left her on her doorstep, he looked at her for a long moment, his kind eyes making her wish that things with him could've been simple. "Sorry about that back there," she managed.

He smiled. "He loves you," he said.

She shrugged, feeling more than a little uncomfortable talking about that with Michael. It was one thing to discuss their problems with him, it was another thing entirely to discuss the love she felt for the man who caused their breakup. "I guess," she mumbled, her eyes on the door, her escape from the awkwardness.

"I needed to see that. To know that he loves you. And that you're going to be just fine, Fore."

She laughed in spite of herself, blinking back the tears at the mention of the nickname that recalled their history in a single word. "I'm glad you think so."

He reached out and touched her nose with the tip of his finger. "And don't worry about me. I'm going to be fine too. It's all good." He turned to walk away and then turned back. "Save me a dance at the wedding?"

She smiled and nodded, then slipped inside the house to call Elliott, wondering if he would take her call and surprised to find herself hoping he would. As she closed the door, her eyes fell on the wishing tree, focusing on a new tag that read simply, "I wish you a life filled with passion and adventure." The wish could've been applied to her and Elliott in the beginning of their marriage, they had so believed that those two words would define them as a couple.

When they got married, Ivy saw Elliott as her fresh start, her chance to make things different from the way they'd been back home, her way to take control of her own life instead of handing it over to her mother and Michael. Their life in Asheville was completely other than her life at Sunset. She and Elliott had hiked to secret waterfalls and visited out-of-the-way apple stands, laughing as the sweet juice dripped down their arms. They'd found Appalachian craftsmen and bought unique pieces for the house they bought together, the one with the fantastic view of the mountains that she just had to have. They'd made friends who felt like family and spent holidays with those friends, ensconced in the cocoon that was their world together. She'd learned to love the smell of pines and crisp mountain air as much as the coastal scent of the air at Sunset. And though she missed dipping her toes in the Atlantic, she found that a brisk mountain stream could feel a lot like waves.

For a time she'd told herself it was enough, that Elliott

made up for her missing family. But sometimes she longed for her mom and sister, wanted to laugh with Shea with the ease she once enjoyed, united in their deliberate and relentless jokes at Margot's expense. She wanted to answer her mother's phone calls without her whole body tensing. She wanted to be forgiven and accepted. And in her longing and loss, she'd gradually pulled away from her husband, not keeping the promises she'd made to him on that day they danced to "All the Way" as husband and wife.

As she listened to the phone ring on Elliott's end, she realized that all that time she only wanted what he had asked her for. She hung up the phone without leaving a message, hoping that she would get a chance to tell him what she had discovered about forgiveness since she'd been at Sunset—how forgiving meant freedom, both for the person giving it and the one receiving it. How she had withheld forgiveness because she could, because it was all she could think of to do to punish Elliott. And how wrong it was to do that when at the same time she was seeking forgiveness of her own. Maybe she could explain that that was what she was doing as she walked along with Michael, drawing from the forgiveness he had offered like a well so that she could then turn and offer it to Elliott. Maybe she could make Elliott understand what a gift Michael's forgiveness had been. And maybe she could muster the humility it would take to own her part in their marriage coming apart.

She opened her computer and sat down in the den, not bothering to hide what she was looking for if someone walked in. Her mom and sister apparently knew all about Elliott's tweets anyway. She wanted to ask them how they knew—if it wasn't Michael who told—and why they hadn't said anything. She watched as the site loaded, thinking how strange it was that she wasn't angry that they'd kept it a secret.

She sat back and smiled as she typed in Elliott's handle. She read over his profile: "Hi, my name is Elliott and I'm an idiot. I plan to use this forum to explain why, in hopes that my wife will read it and forgive me." She read through his posts, the ones that begged for her attention, the ones that recalled the days before they lost sight of each other, the ones that told her he remembered who they once were, just like she did.

Soon she would have to face what he'd done. She might even ask him some questions whose answers would be hard to hear. They would need to go to counseling, probably for a long time. But she had a man who wanted to be with her, who wanted to do the work it took for that to happen. Her husband was not acting like her dad had, and that was worth noting. He hadn't continued the affair. Yes, he'd made a dreadful, hurtful mistake. But he was truly sorry. And, as so many of Elliott's followers had commented, true repentance wasn't all that common. She and Elliott, it seemed, had something. She'd felt it in the street as he'd stared at her, that broken look on his face. She found herself wanting to find out what that something was.

She hovered the mouse over the button that said "Follow," knowing that as soon as she pressed it, he would get a notice that she had followed him. A hopeful smile spread across her face as she clicked on the button, sending a message into cyberspace that she hoped would change things between them. She had no idea where this change would lead them, but for the first time since that day in April's cabin, she wanted to find out.

∽

She fell asleep right there in the den, waiting for someone to come home so she could ask them about the secret they'd kept from her—the secret about her secret. Curled up on the couch with her laptop resting on the floor beside her, she dreamed of being in the ski lift, gliding over the snowy wonderland beneath. In the dream she could see the deep blackness of a sky dotted with stars, feel the cold air entering her lungs. But when she reached for Elliott's hand, it wasn't there. She woke up, feeling more alone than she'd felt since she made that solitary drive to Sunset, uncertain of how her family would receive her, yet certain she couldn't stay in Asheville with Elliott.

She heard voices nearby—a man's and a woman's. Still lying down, she turned to look in the direction the voices were coming from. Her mother and father were standing by the wishing tree, their heads bent toward one another. Since they hadn't noticed she was awake, Ivy was able to observe their body language, the way they seemed . . . inclined toward one another. And they were smiling. She hadn't seen her mother smile around her father in years. She thought back to the mystery of who her mother had been talking to, how Leah had seemed to know but wasn't willing to divulge who it was. She'd been protecting her sister's new happiness, forgiving her brother-in-law for what he'd done so many years ago.

She watched in horror as her father leaned in and began kissing her mom—and it wasn't just a peck. She sat up and hollered out, "Mom!" Her mother jumped backward, straight into the wishing tree, knocking it to the floor. The pot smashed, the wishing tags scattered across the floor, and the marbles rolled in all directions.

Ivy sprang from the couch and raced over to the wishing tree, gathering the broken bits of pottery into her lap. The pent-up tears from the day—no, her whole life—finally spilled as she looked down at the broken tree. One of the branches had snapped off, another was bent, and some of the tags were wrinkled too. She bent her head down, closed her eyes, and sobbed.

She felt her mother's arms go around her and her father's hand on her shoulder. "I'm sorry, darlin'," she heard him whisper. She wondered which part he was sorry for—leaving her mother all those years ago, kissing her mother, keeping their newfound relationship a secret, or breaking the tree.

But he didn't elaborate because Margot sent him away. "Let me," Ivy heard her mother say. She looked up in time to see his back walking away, his shoulders slumped, not ramrod straight as she was used to.

"I was going to tell you when you woke up. We came here to tell you and Shea, but she wasn't here and you were asleep," Margot said.

"So you just decided to make out instead," Ivy sniffled. She didn't miss the little smile that comment triggered in her mom. *Ick*, she thought.

"It's . . . complicated," Margot said. She busied herself with gathering up the tags from the tree. Ivy felt her begin to remove the pieces of broken pottery from her lap and looked up to find her mother's eyes seeking her own.

"Are you okay with it? I mean, your dad and I . . ."

"I guess so." She was relieved to realize that her mom thought her tears were about them, not about . . . everything else.

Her mom held out a hand. "Let me help you up." Ivy took her hand, then stood awkwardly. She stumbled into the kitchen and retrieved plastic grocery sacks to gather the marbles and collect the broken pieces to throw away. She walked back over to her mother, who was staring down at one of the tags, a thoughtful expression on her face.

She reached over and took it from Margot's hand, squinting down at the familiar handwriting. It was Margot's own handwriting, and Ivy guessed that she'd added it recently. "Even as you stand together, learn also to stand on your own," it said.

She looked up at her mother, who smiled sheepishly. "A hard-earned lesson?" Ivy guessed.

Margot nodded, taking the tag from her hand and placing it with the other tags. "One you're learning, being here."

Her mother's gaze held understanding and compassion, which gave Ivy the courage she needed to ask the next question. "Why didn't you tell me you knew about me and Elliott?"

"Because you didn't want me to know. And I understand that. You felt you had to protect yourself, because you were afraid of my reaction."

"Then how did you know?"

"Leah found your Twitter account one day after you were at the bakery. She said there was a look on your face as she talked about Twitter that made her think there was something you weren't saying. She said she just started looking around, and eventually she found Elliott's Twitter account. After that we all just started following him so we could try to . . . understand what you were facing. To explain a bit about why you were here and why you never mentioned him."

"Why didn't you just ask me? Why'd you sneak around behind my back?"

"Because I understood your hesitance to talk to us about what was happening. I understand the shame that comes with betrayal. And of course there were all of the things that we've never talked about from . . . before. I know you always thought that I was angry at you for marrying Elliott." Margot resumed gathering the marbles, the sound of them hitting the plastic as she dropped them in like a heavy rain falling. "But I wasn't—not for the reason you think, at least."

Ivy held her breath, waiting to hear the rest of what her mother had to say.

"I had a plan for your wedding. I was going to use your dad and I being forced to be together as an opportunity to get him back. I had it all planned—the music I was going to ask the band to play, the memories I'd bring up, the fact that he'd be here again, where we had so much history together. I just knew that it would be what he needed to realize the mistake he'd made and come running back." Margot sighed. "Back then it was all I could think about—how I could get him back. I focused on that so I didn't have to focus on the deep sense of shame I carried."

"And when my wedding was off, so was your chance." Ivy understood the lost chance she'd unknowingly created for her mom. Rational or not, it had been all she'd had to keep going.

Margot nodded. "And then I had to face the shame I'd been avoiding—that sense that I was all alone. Shea was still at college, you'd moved to Asheville to be with Elliott, and your dad was gone. It was like everything I'd lived for had shattered just like that pot." Margot pointed at the bag holding the pieces of broken pottery.

"So how did you get past it?" she asked. Ivy could remember when Margot finally started calling her again. Things were still strained between them, but her mother had made the effort to reconnect. By then, though, it was Ivy who was angry and hurt, Ivy who resisted the efforts her mother made, calling them "too little, too late."

"Your aunt helped. She dragged me to that crazy church of hers, told me to pray and read my Bible. It sounded so simple—too simple. But I started doing it because I couldn't think of anything else to do. And the crazy part was, it started working. No miracle in one day, but a gradual . . . hope started working its way through my heart. And I started realizing I wasn't alone like I thought. I never had been. God was right there, waiting for me to notice. And over time I let go of the fear and the shame."

Ivy thought back to her walk right after she came back, how she'd asked God to show her she wasn't alone. Weeks later, her mother was reminding her that she never had been. "I had to face being alone," Margot continued, "to learn that I wasn't alone." Finished bagging the broken pieces of pottery, she tied a knot in the top of the bag and placed it on the table where the wishing tree had sat before.

"I can't believe it's ruined," Ivy said. "All those wishes."

Margot smiled. "The wishes are fine." She patted Ivy's shoulder. "I'll show you." She winked at her and turned back to finish bagging the marbles. "Now the lost marbles, well, I can't make any promises about those."

Ivy started to laugh and Margot joined in, their laughter mingling with the broken pottery, mangled wishes, and lost marbles, making a kind of crazy sense.

℃

Ivy decided to walk to the Sunset Inn to find April and Elliott instead of calling first. She walked alone in the rosy glow of the setting sun, the wind blowing through the marsh grasses, making a silver rustling sound. She inhaled the fresh beach air and wondered how she could give all this up a second time. To be certain, a part of her soul lived at Sunset. But equally undeniable was the fact that a part of her soul also now lived in Asheville.

She walked down Beach Road, feeling spread out, strung out, and yet, happy. Peaceful. Her mother's advice had been good for her to hear. She could face whatever happened and not fear being alone. She could hang her wishes for the future on God and let him fulfill them however he saw fit. It was time to stop pinning those wishes on people who could not carry them any better than that tree. Every time she'd expected them to, she'd hurt them— and herself. Elliott and Michael, her mother and Shea, Leah and April had all suffered under the weight of her expectations, her needs. Needs and expectations only

God could fill. When she saw Elliott, she planned to tell him that.

Funny how she'd left Asheville fuming over the apology he owed her—and while he was totally wrong in what he'd done, she had come to understand that it was the weight of her expectations that had started unraveling their marriage long before he acted on his impulses. Elliott could not complete her. Elliott could not meet her needs. Elliott could not make her happy. And neither could Michael. She saw that now, all too clearly. She'd run to Michael, thinking a relationship with him would erase the hurt from Elliott, just like she'd run to Elliott, thinking a romance with him could erase the hurt from her father. But no one on earth could fix her, make her whole.

She needed a stronger foundation than wishes, nice as they may be. She needed more than just a rush of romantic feelings and a whirlwind courtship under starry skies. She needed to find what her mother had found, a strength outside herself to help her go the distance, to love someone other than herself. As wrong as Elliott had been, he wasn't the only wrong one. Ivy sensed that her first step was to tell him that, to own her part in what had happened between them. Beyond that, she didn't know what would become of them.

She smiled as the Sunset Inn came into view. The best part was, she didn't have to know. She would hang her wishes somewhere else from now on—on a sturdy branch that could support all her prayers, hopes, and dreams.

Twenty-Four

Ivy woke the next morning with a mingled sense of dread and anticipation. It was a day to be filled with the bridesmaids' luncheon and the rehearsal dinner, expected traditions with the added element of cameras and crew recording it all. She grimaced at the toast she had yet to write, yet another tradition she'd be held to. The thought of it all made Ivy want to crawl back into bed, but Margot and Shea appeared at her bedroom door looking like eager horses loaded in the gate, ready to charge ahead.

The doorbell rang as they were pouring coffee, and Margot got up to find a wrapped package sitting on the front porch. She brought the package into the house, and they launched into speculating over what could be inside, guessing everything from the practical (a wedding present delivered by a neighbor) to the truly romantic (diamond earrings from Owen that would perfectly match the dress April had delivered). It was Margot who found the tag marked "To Ivy" stuck to the bottom of the package. Shea's eyes gave away her surprise as she handed over the gift to Ivy, who was just as surprised as she was.

She fumbled with the wrapping paper, a fussy floral print that smelled faintly of mothballs. She was all thumbs underneath the weight of Margot's and Shea's curious stares. The only thing she could think of was Elliott and their heart-to-heart the night before. It would be like him to leave her some symbol of what he hoped was a new future for them, a future she'd promised to consider. He'd said that was all he could ask for and thanked her for the chance, his eyes earnest and intense as he cautiously reached for her hand.

The paper tore away to reveal a white box. When she shook it she heard the unmistakable clink of china rattling inside. She raised an eyebrow at Margot and Shea, who looked as perplexed as she was. She and Elliott had never registered for china, never found much use for the trappings of formality. She opened the box, anxious to see what waited inside.

It was a piece of china, but it wasn't from Elliott. She pulled the teapot from the box and set it on the kitchen table, thinking of her conversation with Michael that day in Mrs. McCoy's kitchen, when the memories had floated in the air along with the dust. Then she had hoped for a different ending for the two of them. He had been resistant, guarded, smart. He had known she wasn't done with Elliott, no matter how much she told herself otherwise. By keeping her in the friend zone, he had been a good friend.

"Hey, I recognize that teapot!" Shea said. Ivy looked up

and met her sister's gaze, so many things passing between them, the strength of their shared past forging this new, unexpected present. Shea was marrying Owen but Ivy would not be marrying Michael. And for the first time, that was okay. She'd found someone else, the person who, for better or worse, she was forging a life with. There was work ahead for each of the sisters, but now they wouldn't be doing it alone.

"It's from Michael. I . . . told him I wanted it." She glanced down at the card he'd included—no bigger than a business card with just enough room for a few short lines: "Take this home to remind you where you came from and that you have people who care about where you're going." She slipped the card into the teapot and placed the lid back on it. She would find a place for it in her own kitchen.

"Well, if he's cleaning out that house, I'm going to put in my order for what I want! Owen and I have a whole house to furnish!" Shea said, scampering off to call Michael, Ivy guessed, and lay claim to some free antiques.

Margot called after her, "Don't forget we've got the luncheon at eleven, young lady! And the fitting after that!"

There was no response from Shea. Margot turned back to Ivy and shook her head. "If we're on time for that luncheon, it'll be a miracle straight from God."

Ivy grinned, knowing the rest of this day would pass by in a blur. She wondered if all of the formalities and festivities leading up to a wedding weren't designed to distract the loved ones from focusing on the changes they were facing—parents losing the children they'd loved and raised, siblings losing the person they'd shared a home with, two people losing their individual lives as they promised to live for another, forever. Had she even grasped what she was saying as she recited her vows to Elliott? Could anyone really?

"How'd things go with Elliott?" her mom asked, tapping into her thoughts as only a mother could.

"We had a nice long discussion. We're . . . going to work on it."

Margot gestured to the teapot. "And Michael?"

"We'll always be friends," she said, thinking of the words he'd scrawled for her on the little card tucked in the teapot. She believed that things would work out for all of them. They had so far.

Her mother moved over to the wishing tree, sitting whole and perfect after the unfortunate accident and repair efforts. Her mother had even managed to find another pot somewhere, and the tree sat once again filled with tags bearing wishes for Owen and Shea. She still needed to add her own.

Ivy watched as her mom rehung some of the tags, filling bare spots. A few weeks ago that action would've driven her crazy, been taken as a criticism of Ivy's work. Now she saw it for what it was: Margot trying to make everything perfect for her girls, doing what she could with what she had just like anyone else.

"I remember putting this tree into storage after you called off your wedding," Margot said, still fussing with the tags so Ivy didn't see her face. "I shoved it a little too hard into a corner of that storage room, never dreaming I'd ever pull it out again. I didn't care if the pot got cracked and the branches broke because I didn't ever consider that something that was over could have a new life."

Ivy knew they weren't just talking about the tree. They

were talking about their marriages and the new life they were each embarking on—a life that required faith and forgiveness. She looked over at the teapot. Michael had extended her forgiveness, something she'd craved more than love or happiness or kindness. She had clamored after him, not knowing it was his forgiveness she sought. When she looked in Elliott's eyes last night, she'd seen that same hunger and known it was her turn to extend forgiveness.

"I'm supposed to give a toast at the rehearsal dinner tonight," Ivy said. She picked up the teapot to take it upstairs. "I still haven't figured out what to say." She sighed. "I don't do awkward situations very well, but I don't suppose I can run away this time." It was her backhanded way of apologizing to her mother for fleeing so many things.

Satisfied with the tree, Margot turned back to face her. She rested her hand at the base of the tree and gave Ivy a knowing smile. "Just tell everyone about the wishing tree and what it taught you."

She searched her mother's face. "You think that would be good? I just don't want to say something dumb."

"If you speak from your heart, you'll never sound dumb." Margot reached for her, and as Ivy stepped into her mother's arms, she felt safe and loved and more than a little hopeful that she could rise to the task. She would let her heart speak for her and trust it to have something valuable to say.

$$\sim$$

Ivy was surprised to see her father at the bridesmaids' luncheon, sitting off to the side sipping punch and making small talk with cousin Dory, who was really only there because of the cameras. Shea narrowed her eyes at her. "Opportunist," she muttered. "She thinks she's going to get discovered." Shea had never gotten over her making up an off-color nickname for her when they were twelve.

"No home training," Margot tsked from behind them, her eyes focused on cousin Dory, who looked up and caught them staring. They all gave a little wave, forcing smiles. Her father saw them too and his eyes lit up. When Dory looked away, the forced smiles gave way to real laughter.

Simon joined them, the relief on his face visible. Ivy wasn't the only one who'd learned a few lessons recently. Her mother's reappearance in Simon's life, combined with the failing business, must've softened her father, humbled him. He was, Ivy realized, genuinely glad to be part of this family event instead of merely tolerating it like the father she remembered. Her eyes filled with tears. That summer she'd aimlessly ridden her bike up and down beach roads and avoided her sad mother, she'd never dreamed this could be possible.

One of the bridesmaids called Shea over, and she tugged Margot along with her, leaving Ivy and Simon alone. "I can't believe you're here," she said. "In the midst of all this estrogen. I thought you were allergic."

Simon set down his empty punch glass on a nearby table and gave her shoulders a little squeeze once his hands were free. "I outgrew my allergies, I guess you'd say." They both laughed. "That Dory . . ." He gestured at the cousin. "She's a piece of work."

Ivy nodded her agreement. "I've got a reporter I should introduce her to. They'd be fast friends." She realized as she said it that her toast would be filmed. That Vivienne would be staring her down as she spoke. As she shared her heart, she would be exposed. "Excuse me, Dad. I'm going to go try some of that punch." She picked her way through the tables to reach the punch bowl, poured herself a glass, and sucked it down in one big gulp.

"That stuff's so sweet, it'll make you sick if you drink it so fast." She heard a familiar voice behind her just as she went to refill her glass.

She turned to find Leah, the expert on sweetness, standing there in a canary-yellow dress with matching hat. She looked out of place there, much less at home than in the bakery. Ivy didn't know if it was the yellow dress or the lack of flour on it.

Leah helped herself to a cup of the punch, clinking it with Ivy's as soon as she'd finished ladling it. "You did a good thing, coming here," she said. "Good for you. Good for us."

"Thanks." Ivy nodded, looking into her punch cup.

"Don't expect I'm going to talk you into staying here, though. Now that the big day's here and your job is done."

"I'm going to go back to Asheville, Aunt Leah. It's . . . time."

She looked up to find Leah smiling at her. "I told myself I'd support you no matter what you decided, but I have to say I'm glad to hear it. 'Course I'll miss you at the bakery. But Elliott needs you a whole lot more than I do."

Ivy couldn't resist. "And you have Lester."

Leah winked. "Indeed I do." She waved at Shea and Margot. "I see Simon's making an appearance. Wonders never cease."

Ivy smirked. "Guess he's got some work to do, huh?"

"Oh, honey, we've all got some work to do." Leah nudged her. "I'm proud of you for being willing to do the work. Loving someone, and living with them, is some of the hardest work you'll ever do. But it's worth it. I wouldn't take a thing for the time I had with my husband, short as it was. He was a good man. But he wasn't perfect either." She raised her eyebrows and bent closer to Ivy as if she were going to tell her a deeply held secret. "None of 'em are."

Ivy laughed so hard, she nearly choked on her punch. "I'm going to miss you, Aunt Leah," she said after she'd recovered enough to speak.

"Well, the good news is, now I expect you'll be back. It won't be like before, and that's a good thing."

"Yeah, it is." Ivy scanned the room as everyone began taking their seats. Servers began carrying in plates of grilled fruit, crab quiche, field greens with champagne vinaigrette, and a pasta salad with sun-dried tomatoes. Ivy's stomach rumbled in response. They'd never had time to eat that morning in the rush to get ready.

But Leah didn't seem to notice everyone taking their seats or the plates of delicious food being carried past. "Your mother told me you're going to talk about the wishing tree tonight when you do your toast."

Ivy rolled her eyes at her mother's ability to relay news at the speed of light, especially news about her. "If I get the courage."

Leah shook her head. "You will. You didn't come this far to stop now." She scratched her head, shifting the hat as she did. "You know that wishing tree tradition is special in our family."

"Yeah, Aunt Leah, I know."

"It was—" Ivy turned to stare at her aunt as her voice broke. "It was special to me too." Leah began fishing around in her purse, searching for something as Ivy waited. After a few seconds she produced a yellowed piece of paper with a frayed ribbon looped through it. "This was from my wedding. I thought you might like to see it."

Ivy forgot about the people eating, the delicious smells. She took the treasured memento from Leah's hands and read it, her eyes taking in the faded ink, the obviously masculine handwriting. She looked up at Leah, blinking away tears as she tried to hand it back to her, but Leah shook her head and gently pushed it away as her eyes also brimmed with tears.

"He wished he'd come back to me from Vietnam. But he didn't. And for a long time I was alone, and lonely. But I had you and your mom and your sister. And later I had a business, a future that—while it wasn't what I'd wished for—was good. And now, I have this wonderful life." A tear escaped the corner of her eye, making a track down the length of her cheek through the carefully applied foundation and powder Leah usually eschewed. "Wishes don't always come true, but joy? Joy is always possible. That's what you should tell everyone tonight."

She took a deep breath, composing herself as Ivy did the same. "I think your mama's fixing to blow a gasket if we don't sit down." She tucked her hand into the crook of Ivy's elbow and steered her toward the table where Shea and Margot and Simon sat waiting for them. Ivy tucked the tag into her own purse, thinking that it would fit perfectly in her teapot, nestled beside Michael's note, another little reminder of where she was from, and where she wanted to go.

~

She was going to be brave, but she wasn't going to go first. She listened patiently as friends and family stood at the rehearsal dinner that evening to pay homage to Shea and Owen, sharing funny stories and happy memories, giving wise advice and making dumb jokes. She reached into her purse and rubbed her thumb along the tag Leah had given her, bolstering her courage. When it was silent again, she stood up before she could chicken out, her eyes scanning the gathering of familiar faces and coming to rest on her sister's. Shea gave her a smile and a wink. She did her best to ignore her wildly pounding heart.

"Hi, everyone, I'm Shea's sister, Ivy, and the matron of honor. I was also in charge of preparing the wishing tree, which is a tradition in our family that goes back for generations. You'll see it tomorrow at the reception, but tonight I just wanted to share what I've learned from it." She took a deep breath and plunged ahead.

"Over the past few weeks as I've read many of the wishes for Shea and Owen, I've come to appreciate just how special it is to have people who care enough not only to send you wishes but to be there for you when those wishes don't come true." Without meaning to, her eyes flickered over to Michael and quickly away. She wondered if anyone noticed. "Someone told me today that wishes don't always come true, but joy is always possible." Her eyes found Leah's.

"These past few weeks, I've watched my sister and Owen pull together when things got hard, and I've seen them find joy. I have no doubt that with our wishes, but more especially our prayers, behind them, they'll be able to keep doing so and have a wonderful life together." She raised her glass. "To wishes," she finished, grateful to be done.

Everyone around her raised their glasses too, repeating the phrase, "To wishes!"

She sat down with a big smile and found the one face she most wanted to see at that moment. "Good job," Elliott mouthed from his seat beside April. He gave her the thumbs-up sign, and she ducked her head, embarrassed. But also pleased and proud. She thought of what Leah had said about finding joy and knew what wish she would hang on Shea's wishing tree: a wish for joy to win out even when wishes didn't. She was living proof that was possible.

Twenty-Five

The music was loud, the guests happy, the food plentiful, the bride glowing. And Ivy had heard more than once that she looked especially pretty herself. She looked down at the beautiful blue dress she was wearing, silently thanking her sister for not making her bridesmaids look hideous just so she could look better, as some brides were apt to do. She looked up to see a cameraman zeroing in on her. She gave him a little smile and wave, looking, she was sure, completely goofy as she did. Oh, well, it didn't matter. They were happy, the wedding was done, and all that was left to do was have a good time.

She spotted April just then, talking to a handsome groomsman, a rapt smile on her face. She caught Ivy's eye and motioned that she was coming over. "I didn't mean to interrupt what looked like a promising conversation," Ivy said, giving April a hug when she reached her.

Ivy glanced back over at the groomsman, who was staring after her. With a coy grin she said, "He'll wait."

The two of them laughed, the tension that had existed between them slowly dissipating. "Guess I owe you another apology," Ivy said. This dance of forgiving and being forgiven was one with many complicated steps, but she was learning.

"It's okay. I knew I was taking a risk bringing Elliott here, but I had to try it." April gave Ivy a deliberate grin and stuck her tongue out playfully. "Besides, I knew you'd forgive me."

"Oh, you did, did you?" Ivy grinned back.

"What do you think?" April gestured toward the groomsman, a friend of Owen's from college, who reminded Ivy of a pest from her elementary school days—but she didn't dare say that.

"Cute," she said. And then with a smile, she added, "But he's nothing like my Rick." The reference to *Sleepless in Seattle* made them both burst into laughter.

Elliott approached, looking shy and uncertain. "What's so funny?" he asked, looking from Ivy to April.

"Inside joke," April said. She looked at them both with raised eyebrows. "I'll just get back to my prospect over there and leave you two alone." She glided back over to the groomsman before another single girl could get her hooks into him. Ivy watched her go, giving her the thumbs-up sign when she glanced back at them.

"Do you wish we had had this?" Elliott asked, gesturing at the commotion all around them, the flickering candles on the tables, the guests, beautifully dressed, dancing and laughing. His tone was wistful, as if he understood for the first time what she'd given up for him.

She reached for his hand and squeezed it. "In a way, yes. I made a mistake not having a wedding, not letting my family get to know you. But you have to admit, what we did was wildly romantic."

They shared a smile, and she allowed herself to savor it. They too had a history now. And if they worked hard enough, maybe a future as well.

Seemingly emboldened by her warmth, he said, "Have I told you how beautiful you look?"

A pang crossed her heart as she remembered who else he may have said that to. But she resolutely pushed it aside. "You haven't, but you may certainly say so."

"Then by all means let me say it: you look stunning. It's really not fair to the bride." He grinned at her, his grin flickering a bit when he looked over and saw Michael. "He keeps looking over here. I think he feels uncomfortable coming over."

"He might," she observed. Her eyes found Michael across the room, on the edge of the dance floor, talking to Vivienne, who caught her looking and turned away. Vivienne was still mad that Elliott had cancelled his Twitter account and retracted his interview, refusing to give her the story she so badly wanted. "I only started it to get to you, not to anyone else," Elliott had told Ivy two nights ago on the screened-in balcony of his room at the Sunset Inn. "Now that I've got your attention, I don't need it. I'd rather have one woman in particular than a bunch of women following me." They'd watched the boats passing by on the Intracoastal Waterway as they'd talked into the wee hours. "I don't deserve a second chance," he'd said.

It wasn't just true of him. No one deserved grace. It was a free gift. And it was her turn to give it in the same way it had been given to her. She couldn't get caught up in the what-ifs. That was where faith came in: trusting that no matter what became of her and Elliott, she would be okay. She could stand alone.

She looked over at her mom and dad, dancing and laughing right next to Lester and Leah.

As the song ended, her father looked over to see her watching them and whispered something in Margot's ear. The two of them left the dance floor hand in hand as they made their way over to her and Elliott. "Don't look now, but here come my parents," she said to Elliott.

"Good, I like your parents," he said, finishing off the drink he was holding. "Can I get you one?" he gestured.

She smirked at him. "Coward."

"Not at all, I'll be right back." He winked. "Promise."

"So, that cake is quite a creation," her dad said, nodding his head in the direction of the cake on display. Margot had never made it all the way to them because she had stopped to talk to one of her many friends in attendance. "I hear you were the one who saved it."

She looked over at it again, pride swelling in her heart. "I guess." The cake did look beautiful.

"You know, now that I've closed up your branch, I might be talked into venturing into something else. A second location of the bakery, maybe? In the mountains of North Carolina? Call that one Mountainside Bakery?"

She could see her father's wheels turning, ever the businessman. She had to admit she'd had the same thought. But she wouldn't let herself take her dad's help to do it. If she did open a bakery in Asheville, it would be on her own.

She put her arm around her dad and squeezed. "I love you, Daddy" was all she said as she planted a kiss on his cheek, her lipstick leaving a dark-pink imprint on his skin. She was wiping it away when the DJ announced it was time for Shea to have her dance with her father. Ivy nudged him toward Shea, who was beckoning him back to the dance floor, the first strains of "The Way You Look Tonight" beginning to play. Their dad always did love Frank Sinatra.

Owen sidled up to her with a cat-that-ate-the-canary grin on his face. It was his big day, so Ivy refrained from making a smart comment like she usually would've. They stood and watched the bride dance with her father, Ivy regretting that she never got that moment. She saw Owen glancing at her out of the corner of his eye and turned to look at him.

"Sorry I called you a bored housewife," he said.

"I knew you didn't mean it," she teased.

Never one to get too mushy, he replied like a sullen adolescent. "I mean, I kinda did, at the time."

She looped her arm through his and pulled him close enough to kiss his cheek. "Congratulations, you got a good one."

Owen's mom was waving him over to the dance floor and he started to join her, but not before turning back to grin at Ivy. "I did, didn't I?" He reached over to give her a high five, then dashed away.

Elliott returned with two drinks in his hand, presenting

hers with a flourish. He looked handsome in his suit and tie. She'd managed to forget how handsome he was. It was coming back to her now. They traded smiles and fumbled with conversation almost as if they had just met. The fumbling awkwardness was kind of nice, a far cry from the mundane state their relationship was in before.

"So, the wishing tree is quite the hit," he said. "I heard some women talking about it. They were discussing their wishes." He nudged her. "Good job."

"Thanks." She took a sip of her drink, staring down into it.

"Did you write something yet? A wish for them?"

"No, not yet. I . . . haven't had time to get over there."

"Do you know what you're going to wish for them?" His tone had gone from playful to serious, and she looked up to meet his gaze.

"What I said last night—that even though wishes don't come true, there's always joy to be found. I've learned that in the past few weeks." She looked at the celebration going on around them, so much joy to be had.

"I know what I'd wish," he said. "I'd wish for Owen to always feel about Shea the way I feel about you at this very moment."

She gave him a coy look, trying to keep things light, not move too fast into this new marriage they were trying for. "And what is that?"

"That he has something precious, something that should always be treasured and never overlooked."

She was fumbling for how to respond to his perfect answer when Margot appeared out of nowhere and grabbed Elliott's arm. "Come on, Elliott, I need a dance partner!"

She giggled, giving Ivy a little wave as she pulled him toward the dance floor. This dance, Ivy knew, was her mother's version of a peace offering, her way of bridging the gap between the family and Elliott. She was grateful for the way everyone was making an effort.

With nothing better to do, she followed her mom and Elliott until she came to the edge of the dance floor. She stood and watched as Michael danced with Vivienne, her dad danced with Shea, Owen danced with his mom, April danced with the groomsman, and Leah continued to cling to Lester like a lovesick teenager. Any other time she would've felt left out to not be paired off, but this time it didn't bother her. She stepped out onto the dance floor, watching the other couples glide around her. Later she would give Michael that dance she promised him and take a spin around the floor with Elliott too. But for now, she was fine to sway back and forth without a partner. She wrapped her arms around herself and smiled, completely content to dance alone.

Reading Group Guide

1. Ivy doesn't want to be alone. Do you think her interest in Michael is fueled by that fear or real feelings?
2. Can you draw a parallel between the wishing tree and Ivy's marriage to Elliott?
3. Have you ever had to face someone you hurt in the past? Did you address the situation head-on or avoid it like Ivy?
4. Was Ivy right to give Elliott another chance? Why or why not?
5. Was Michael right to keep his distance from Ivy? What do you think would've happened if he hadn't?
6. The reader never sees the conversation that took place between Elliott and Ivy when they finally talked. Why do you think the author chose not to include that particular scene in the book?

7. *The Wishing Tree* is a story about forgiveness. Name the people Ivy had to offer forgiveness to through the course of the story and, if you're comfortable, share a forgiveness story from your own life.

8. How does the last sentence of the book parallel to Ivy's prayer on the beach when she first arrives at Sunset? What does that last sentence mean to you?

Acknowledgments

A big thank you goes out to:

My mom, who remains my biggest supporter.

My family: six kids and one husband who pull together when I need to write and tell me often they are proud of me.

Ariel, who amazingly still claims me as her best friend.

Ariel and Kim, who make She Reads possible.

John Pierce, who helped me understand my characters better.

Michael Hauge, who challenged me to determine what Ivy wanted.

Becky Philpott and the team at HarperCollins Christian Publishing who brought this book to you, dear reader.

Carolyn Wright, who opened the real Seaside Bakery in Sunset Beach, NC, to me and my family and let us taste her delicious, beautiful wedding cakes.

ACKNOWLEDGMENTS

The gracious staff of Daphne's Bakery in Mint Hill, NC, who let me ask a lot of questions—and even gave me samples—the best kind of research!

April Adams Mangum, who inspired the character of April with her good heart and irrepressible spirit.

Erika Marks and Kim Wright Wiley, who are my faithful writing friends.

Lisa Whittle, Shari Braendel, Rachel Olsen, Lisa Shea, and Paige McKinney, who are still my friends even when I'm MIA because I'm on deadline.

My readers, who inspire me to keep telling my stories. Especially those who write to tell me "the rest of the story."

The One I hang my wishes on. Thank You for fulfilling this one.

An excerpt from *The Guest Book*

one

The first thing Macy Dillon noticed when she entered her mother's house on her dead father's birthday was the missing pictures. The front room—a place she and her brother Max had dubbed "the shrine"—was usually filled with photos and mementos from her father's short life. It was a place Macy had a habit of breezing through, if for no other reason than to avoid the memories the room evoked. But this time she paused, noticing space where there had once been pictures, gaping holes like missing teeth. Macy looked down and saw some boxes on the floor, the framed photos resting in them. Perhaps her mother was just cleaning. That had to be it. Macy couldn't imagine her mother ever taking down the shrine. She glanced up, her eyes falling on one of the photos still standing. In it, her father, Darren Dillon, stood beside Macy on the pier at Sunset Beach the summer she was five years old, the sun setting behind them, matching smiles filling their faces.

"Mommy? Is that you? We're back here making Grandpa's birthday cake!"

Macy followed the sound of her daughter's voice coming from the kitchen, feeling the pang she always felt when she heard her daughter refer to Darren as Grandpa. He died years before Emma was born, so she had never known him as a grandpa who doled out candy and did magic tricks. Instead, Emma Lewis knew her grandpa only through an abundance of pictures and stories. Her grandma had made sure of that since the day she was born.

Macy made her way to the back of the house where the sunny kitchen faced the backyard. The large bay window gave a perfect view of the tree house and tire swing she had loved as a child. Earlier this spring, Macy's brother had refurbished both so Emma could enjoy them. Macy smiled at the thought of Max's kindness toward the little girl who had come along unexpectedly and who had, just as unexpectedly, stolen all their hearts, as though they had been waiting to breathe again until the day she was born and injected fresh life into what had become a lifeless family.

Macy leaned down and kissed the top of her daughter's head, then touched her mother's back lightly, noticing the slight stoop to her shoulders that had come with the weight of both grief and age. "You guys sure look busy in here," she said.

Emma stared intently into a bowl where a creamy off-white substance was being turned blue by the food coloring her mother slowly dripped into the bowl. "Grandma's letting me stir," she told her mother without looking up. "We're making blue icing for Grandpa's cake 'cause it was his favorite color. Right, Mommy?"

Macy's eyes filled with tears, surprising her, as she nodded. She could still see her dad pointing to the sky. "I think blue is God's favorite color too," he'd once told her. "It's the color of the sky, the ocean, and your eyes." He had tweaked her nose and tickled her until she giggled.

Looking away, Macy willed herself the emotional control she would need to get through the meal. She wished her mom, Brenda Dillon, wouldn't carry on this ridiculous tradition of marking the day with a cake and Dad's favorite meal, wouldn't continue insisting that Macy and Max join her in the morbidness. Macy had heard that other families moved forward after loss. But her family seemed determined to stay in the same place, trapped in grief. She hated involving her impressionable daughter in the grim annual tradition and wondered if she would have the courage to tell Brenda that she and Emma and her husband, if she had one, would no longer participate.

Emma smiled at her and looked up at her grandmother. "Mommy, did you tell Grandma what we're doing tonight?"

Macy tried to paste on a smile instead of grimacing at her daughter's mention of their plans for after the depressing dinner. She had hoped that Emma would forget and that Chase, Emma's long-time missing father, would back out, as Macy knew he was likely to do. When she agreed to the plans, she hadn't thought about them falling on this very night. She hadn't thought about anything besides making her daughter happy, keeping the radiant smile on her face by giving her whatever her heart desired. It was, Macy reasoned, the least she could do for bringing such a beautiful little person into her wreck of a life. If that meant sleeping in a tent in the cold of their tiny backyard at home, then that's what they would do. If it meant she had to invite the man who seemed to know best how to slip into the cracks of her heart, then she would go along with it.

Macy's mom looked at her. "What are you doing tonight?" Her eyebrows were already raised as though she sensed the answer would not be one of which she would approve. Brenda, a willing and hapless participant, had accompanied Macy through the drama that was her relationship with Chase. She had whispered cautionary advice to her daughter when Chase first pursued Macy. She had found a way to rejoice over Emma despite the lack of a wedding ring on Macy's finger. She had let Emma and Macy move in when Chase had suddenly left, just like everyone expected. She had encouraged Macy to find work and a place of her own. She had championed her daughter's single-mother status, telling people how proud she was of her daughter as Macy scraped her life together, renounced Chase completely, and moved forward.

When Macy didn't say anything, Emma rolled her eyes, a habit she had picked up, far too young, from the evil Hannah Montana. Emma knew every word to "Best of Both Worlds" and often forced Macy to put the song on repeat play.

"Since Mommy won't tell you, I will," she announced. "We are sleeping under the stars tonight . . ." she paused dramatically, "in a tent!"

Macy thought she had dodged the bullet of giving any more information than that. Her mother relaxed visibly.

"That sounds like fun!" her mother said, taking the spatula out of Emma's hands to give the thick icing a forceful stir, the lines of blue spreading and melding as she did. Macy watched, wondering if she had ever really stood and paid attention as her mother made the traditional blue icing for Dad's birthday cake. Had she always looked away in an effort to protect herself from the reality of what they were marking?

"It's going to be fun!" Emma said, sticking a small finger into the icing and scooping out a dollop she popped into her mouth with a giggle. "We're going to be like cowgirls. And we don't have to be scared, because Daddy's going to be there to protect us because he's a real cowboy."

Macy raised her eyes skyward, her hopes of dodging the taboo subject vanished. She could imagine Chase telling Emma he was a real cowboy, explaining his absence over the last five years in a made-up story. He was good at making up stories.

She looked at her mother, who was staring at her over the top of Emma's head, her frown knitting her brows together.

"Your daddy's going to come?" her mother asked Emma, still staring at Macy. "Really now."

Macy stared right back at her mother. "Emma invited us both," she said, feigning a stalwartness she didn't possess. "It was what she wanted."

"Oh, well then," her mother said, "if Emma invited you both then all's well." She shook her head slowly at Macy over the top of Emma's head. "Hey, Emma, why don't you go get our special Grandpa candles out of the buffet in the dining room? You know where I'm talking about?"

Emma nodded vigorously and scampered out of the room, eager to help. Sometimes Macy wondered if Emma ever shared the bizarre aspects of her life with her teacher or friends at school or day care. Disappearing fathers and dinners for dead grandfathers were sure to make people wonder about the environment the child was being raised in.

Macy just looked at her mother. "Don't," she said.

"Don't what?" her mother asked, hefting the bowl of icing onto the counter beside the freshly baked cake. She slapped a scoop of icing onto the center of the cake and began to spread it around a little too forcefully. Looking down at the cake, she added, "Don't tell you what a horrible idea it is for you to spend the night under the stars with Chase Lewis?"

A memory flashed across the canvas of Macy's mind. Chase leaning close to her, his breath on her face, igniting her insides as he always did whenever he stood so close. She could feel the heat of his body, the beat of his heart. She could hear his Texas drawl as, lips centimeters from her ear, he said, "We make a good couple, I think. Mace and Chase. We rhyme."

She pushed the thought of him from her mind and focused on trying to catch her mother's eye. "Emma will be there," she pointed out.

"A five-year-old is going to serve as your chaperone? You're really going to stand there and offer that up?" Her mother spun around, waving the blue-tinted spatula at Macy to emphasize her point. "You're smarter than that, Macy. Do I need to remind you where you were when he left?"

"At least I'm not in the *same* place I was then," Macy said, turning things back on her mother. "You're doing the *exact* same thing now that you were doing ten years ago. Nothing about your life's changed, Mom. At least things change in my life."

It was a weak argument, but it worked to deflect the heat she was feeling under Brenda's disappointed gaze.

Her mother sighed, lowering the spatula in defeat. She turned back to the cake and stood for a few seconds, not moving. Macy was about to launch into how awful it was that her mother kept special candles for a man who'd been dead for ten years when she heard a door slam and then, from the dining room, Emma's voice calling, "Uncle Max is here!"

Macy couldn't decide whether to thank her brother for his impeccable timing or curse him for interrupting. Something told her she wanted to hear what Brenda would've said if she'd been able to confront her.

Yet there was part of Macy that wanted to be saved from having to hear the truth. For just one night, she wanted to enjoy sleeping under the stars with her precious gift of a daughter and the man who had given Emma to her. Like a real family. There was nothing wrong with that.

‿

Max pushed back from the table and laid his hands across his stomach with a groan. "Mom, you outdid yourself, as always," he said.

Brenda smiled at her son and avoided looking at Macy, a holdover from their angry words in the kitchen. Dinner would've been a quiet affair if not for Emma and Max bantering back and forth.

Max was the quintessential uncle—silly, fun, a big kid himself—and Emma loved him.

Without saying a word, Brenda stood and began to clear the dishes from the table. Normally Macy would jump up to assist, but this time she let Brenda leave the room without offering to help.

Max turned to her. "Okay. What's up between you two?"

Macy shook her head. "Nothing I care to discuss with you, Uncle Max," she responded as she nodded her head toward Emma, who was making Goldfish crackers swim through the remaining gravy on her plate.

Max grinned and raised his eyebrows. "Hey, Emma. Why don't you go help Grandma in the kitchen?"

Emma left the Goldfish to drown in the gravy and ran to the kitchen, calling, "Let me help, Grandma!"

Macy stuck her tongue out at Max and rolled her eyes as he grinned in victory. "Okay, spill it, Sis," he said.

"She's mad at me. That's all." She gestured toward the clattering of dishes and running water coming from the kitchen. She guessed Brenda was taking her frustration toward Macy out on the dishes. "Why don't you go help her and be the good child in this family?"

He waved her suggestion away. "I'll go help in a minute. First I want to know why she's mad at you."

"Well, she doesn't approve of a decision I made. And, in my defense, I might have criticized her decision to have this dinner year after year." She pointed toward the shrine that was housed in the room adjoining the dining room. She almost commented on the missing photos but decided not to bring that up. "It doesn't bring him back."

Max shook his head, not bothering to look in the direction she was pointing. She lowered her finger, feeling somewhat ashamed. "It makes her happy to remember him in this way. It makes him seem close. What's wrong with that?" Max asked.

"I guess I'm just tired of living with Dad's ghost, of living in the same place. I want her to move on." She faced her brother, unblinking. "I want to move on."

He shrugged. "So move on, Mace. No one's stopping you." He paused, looking past her, out the window behind her. "Except maybe you?" He smiled at her. "You don't get to stick Mom with that. I have a feeling that whatever Mom's mad about has something to do with Chase. Am I right?"

It wasn't difficult to guess. Their usually unflappable mother got her feathers ruffled in a hurry whenever the subject of Chase came up.

Macy couldn't help but smile. "Yeah." She held her hands up. "You got me."

"And?" Max asked, showing his dimples even as he pushed her for the truth she didn't want to divulge. She loved her brother and often wondered why he wasn't married, rarely dated, and always seemed to mess up anything good that came into his life. Not unlike her.

She shook her head, knowing the absurdity of what she was about to reveal and bracing herself for Max's reaction. She told herself it was really no big deal—that Max and her mother were making more of it than it really was. She had spent the last few years getting stronger, creating a healthy distance between her and Chase. One night wasn't going to undo all of that.

"Well," she began, looking away from Max, down at the empty space where her plate had sat, at the round indentation still visible on the tablecloth, "Chase is back."

Max chuckled. "So I guess this is your version of 'cutting to the chase.'"

She looked up at him. "Ha-ha. Very funny."

She looked back down at the circle on the tablecloth, tracing it with her finger. "He's been coming to see Emma. That's all. He wants to be in her life. And he should. I mean, it makes her happy."

Max laughed loudly, and she looked up at him with a glare.

"Seriously, Mace, do you buy this? You obviously expect me to."

"Buy what?" She looked at him, willing herself to look like an innocent bystander instead of the initiator her family was painting her out to be.

"'Buy what?'" he mimicked her, chuckling to himself. "Look, I am not one to offer advice on love."

Macy snorted. "I'll say!"

He rolled his eyes. "You don't have to agree so readily," he grumbled, taking a sip of his sweet tea.

"If the shoe fits," she challenged, kicking him under the table.

"Ah-ha!" he said. "I'm not wearing shoes!" He stuck his tongue out at her and kicked her back with his bare foot.

She shook her head and laughed in spite of herself. She was thankful to have her brother, even if he was a pain. "I can take care of myself. Emma and I are doing fine."

"But?" he countered. "Something set Mom off."

"Emma told her that Chase is coming over to spend the night tonight. They're sleeping outside in a tent."

He raised his eyebrows and wiggled them. "And you will be . . . where, exactly?"

She closed her eyes and inhaled. "I promised Emma I would be out there with them." She paused as he slapped his hand down on the table like he had just won a bet. "But!" she continued. "But! I have thought better of it. And now I am going to tell Chase he can sleep outside in the tent with Emma, and I will be inside the house making good decisions."

"And when did you make this good decision?" Max asked, nudging her under the table with his bare foot.

She raised her eyes to meet his. "Just now," she said quietly.

The corners of his mouth turned into a half smile. "Good girl." He rose from the table. "Now I've got to go tell Mom that I talked you into doing the right thing." He pretended to rub an imaginary halo on top of his head, a long-standing joke between them. "It feels good to be the good one. For a change." He picked up his glass and Emma's glass, pausing before he left the room. "Good call, Sis. Keep being the smart, strong one. I know you can."

She flattened both of her hands on the tablecloth and breathed deeply, imagining the conversation she would have to have with Chase, dreading Emma's tears when she realized her plan of family togetherness was ruined.

She was glad Max believed she could be smart and strong. She wasn't sure he was right.

∾

"Emma! Let's go!" Macy hollered into the backyard, where Max was pushing Emma on the tire swing. She adjusted her purse on her shoulder and picked up the bag of leftovers Brenda was always faithful to send home with her. The bag contained enough food for two meals for her and Emma.

She smiled and turned to her mom. "You still cook enough food for an army, you know that?" It was safer to stick to a subject they could agree on, like food.

Brenda held up her hands. "It's a habit, what can I say? It's easier to cook for a crowd than for one person." Macy pretended not to notice when her mom's eyes got misty.

Brenda looked out at the backyard, at her granddaughter aiming her toes for the sky as Max pushed with force. "She's not coming in anytime soon," she observed.

Macy set the bag down on the table. "And Max isn't helping." She let her purse slip off her shoulder and placed it on the table beside the leftovers, keeping her eyes on Max and Emma the whole time. Max hadn't even tried to slow the tire swing. She could hear Emma's giggles through the closed door. Spring was in full swing, and summer would be here shortly. Macy relished the thought of longer days, evening trips to the ice cream parlor, and weekends spent by the pool. Maybe Chase would even be part of her summer. And maybe, with time, she could get excited about that prospect.

"It's staying light out longer," she observed. Weather and food: two safe subjects.

"Mmm-hmm," her mother said. "We're heading into summer."

Macy paused for a moment. "I promised Max I would tell Chase to sleep with Emma outside tonight while I stay in the house." She looked over at her mother to gauge her reaction.

Brenda put down the sponge she had been using to wipe the counters. "That's good, Macy. That's smart." She smiled at her daughter. "Max already told me."

Macy laughed and shook her head. "I knew he would. He still loves to tell on me even after all these years."

Brenda joined her at the table and they stood side by side, watching as Max finally helped Emma off the tire swing and the two of them started making their way back to the house, stopping every few steps to look at bugs or flowers. "He worries. Like me. Chase has this . . . hold on you that's not healthy. And as much as I love Emma and am glad for her place in our family, I have to say, she gives him access to you I'm not sure you'd allow without her."

Macy shrugged, grateful they stood shoulder to shoulder and not eye to eye. "You're probably right," was all she said.

Brenda opened the door to let Max and Emma in. A slight chill laced the air that blew in with them, and her mother shivered.

"I hope you're not too cold out there tonight," Brenda said. She looked at Macy and smiled in her knowing way. Her mother, Macy realized, didn't believe a word she'd said.

She started to argue with her, but bit the inside of her lip instead and smiled at the three members of her family, who were all staring at her expectantly.

Emma broke the awkward silence. "Mommy! Let's go!" She put her hands on her tiny hips and tapped her foot. Max and her mother suppressed their laughter as Macy shot them a look.

"That's enough, Miss Sassafras," she said, using a nickname the child had garnered as soon as she could talk in complete sentences, which had been early in her life. Macy blamed Emma's talkativeness on being raised around all adults. It had never occurred to Emma that she wasn't one too.

Macy started gathering her purse and the bag of leftovers again, but her mom stopped her. "If you could just wait a second." She put her hand over Macy's. Macy lowered her brows and looked at her mother, then at Max. Brenda smiled back at them, suddenly looking like a child who had a secret she was bursting to tell.

"Mom?" Max asked. "Is everything okay?"

Her mother laughed, the sound erasing the tension. "Oh, sure. Everything's fine. I just . . . I had an idea, and I've been a bit nervous about mentioning it to you kids. And now . . . well . . . now I've gone ahead and made the plans, and I'm just hoping you two will warm to it." Her smile flickered for a moment. "Because I have to have your involvement for it to work."

Max pulled out a chair at the kitchen table and slumped into the seat. He dropped his head into his hands. "I'm afraid to hear the rest of this," he said, his voice muffled.

Macy slipped into the chair beside him and pulled Emma into her lap, whose eyes were darting from Max to Macy to her grandmother as if they were involved in a tennis match. Emma yawned and leaned her head back onto Macy's shoulder. Macy knew it wouldn't take long for her to fall asleep in the tent with her daddy.

Brenda's voice brought Macy back to reality. "It's not going to require much from the two of you. Just some time off work."

Macy looked up at her mother, alarmed. She needed every penny from every hour of work she could get in order to be able to meet her monthly bills. And her mom knew that. Brenda held up her hands. "And I will help out with any lost income."

Macy relaxed and smiled back at her mom.

"The last time we all went on vacation together was ten years ago." Brenda looked at Emma with a wry smile. "Your grandpa had just died, and we were all very, very sad, sweetie. The beach was your grandpa's favorite place in the whole world, and it was just . . . awful . . . to be there without him. Every corner of that house"—she looked at Macy and Max—"remember the house we used to visit every June?"

They nodded in unison. Unbidden, an image sprang to Macy's mind: the name of the house—Time in a Bottle—on a plaque hanging beside the front door. Her dad had whistled a few bars of the Jim Croce song every time he walked in. To this day, she never caught Jim Croce on the oldies station without tears forming in her eyes.

"Every corner of that house was filled with memories of

him. We decided not to go back, because it was too painful for any of us to be there." Brenda smiled at Emma.
"Now I think that was a mistake. I think we should've kept
going, should have pushed through the hard memories and
made new ones. I've . . . regretted . . . that decision. So
this year"—she took a deep breath—"this year, as we mark
ten years without your grandpa, I started wondering how I
could make that . . . significant."

Max looked up, catching on. "So we're going to the
beach?"

Macy pictured him at fourteen years old, laying out
shells on the kitchen table, a smug smile on his face. She
shot him a look as the unpleasant memory surfaced.

"What?" he asked. "What'd I say?"

Her mother waved her hands to silence him, and Macy
wrapped her arms around Emma.

"Is Uncle Max right?" Emma asked. "Are we going to
the beach for real, Grandma?"

Brenda smiled and nodded. She looked much the same
to Macy as she had ten years ago, only softer, like a drawing
whose lines had blurred slightly over time and with wear.
Her mother, Macy realized, was still an attractive and not-
so-old woman. It was too bad she had devoted ten years
to living with a ghost. Macy smiled back at her and wondered if maybe—just maybe—this trip was some sort of sign
that Brenda was ready to stop living in this haunted house.
A haunted house that was now missing a few pictures. If
so, Macy would do whatever Brenda needed to make the
trip happen. She would pack up her daughter, take time off
work, and head back to the place they had all once loved, a

place tainted by loss yet still—she imagined—beautiful and breathtaking. She could do beautiful and breathtaking. In fact, it sounded like just what the doctor ordered.

"I've reserved the house for two weeks," Brenda said.

Macy could scarcely believe she'd be returning to Sunset Beach for two whole weeks. Two weeks of sun and sand and swimming, of bikes and beaches and blue skies. Two weeks in a place that—until moments ago—she had tried hard to forget about. Her mind flashed to a guest book lying open on her lap, a drawing of a sand dollar filling the page. The corners of her mouth turned up reflexively.

Two weeks away from real life sounded just short of heaven. Macy kissed the top of Emma's head and looked over at Max before asking Brenda the only question she had left to ask: "When do we go?"

two

Macy was almost home when her cell phone rang in her purse. She scrambled to fish it out while keeping her eyes on the road. Max's face lit up the screen. Emma had taken the photo, and it was horribly off center, with the top of his head cut off mid-forehead. But the picture made her smile every time she saw it. "You took longer to call than I thought you would," she said.

"You sure agreed to that beach trip fast," he said. She heard the sound of a beer can being opened and grimaced. She didn't bother to reply as she heard the sounds of him drinking deeply. "Ahhhh," he added. "That's better."

"Where are you?"

He paused. "At a friend's."

Macy wondered—but didn't ask—what his *friend* looked like. "Just be careful. Don't—"

He sighed in frustration. "I didn't call you to get a lecture, Sis. I could call Mom for that."

"Okay. Excuse me for caring." She turned her car into the driveway of her tiny rental house but didn't cut the engine.

"You sure got out of Mom's in a hurry," she said as she looked at Emma, who had fallen asleep in the backseat, her head lolling uncomfortably to one side. Macy laid her head back on the headrest. She should be racing around; Chase was due any minute, and she was nowhere near ready.

"I had to be somewhere," he responded a bit too quickly.

"Are you sure it's not because you didn't like Mom's plans for the beach?" She had stayed for a bit after Max left, planning the trip with her mom. Both of them had had giddiness in their voices as they spoke of the trip. It had been an unexpected but welcome end to a morbid birthday tradition.

He exhaled loudly into the phone. "I just don't think it's wise, going back there after all these years. Dredging all that up."

"Dredging all what up?"

She heard a feminine giggle in the background of wherever her brother was. He didn't respond for a moment as she heard him take another long pull from his beer. "Dredging up the memories of Dad and the beach. Those were . . ." His voice trailed off as if he'd run out of words.

She waited a moment. "Were what?" she asked, looking at the clock on her dashboard. The minutes were ticking away, and she needed to get inside. She had left the house a complete mess and didn't relish Chase walking into that. She had hoped to shower before he showed up, but remembering

Brenda's and Max's admonishments earlier, maybe it was better if she didn't.

"They were good times," Max said, "but they ended when Dad died."

Macy could recall the good times at a moment's notice. She thought of her dad and Buzz, the man Macy had always thought of as their family's "beach friend," returning from a day of fishing, their faces red and their eyes dancing as they pretended to chase her with the fish from the cooler.

"I'm not sure our good times should've ended just because Dad died. I think that's what's wrong with all of us." She smiled at Emma, who had roused from her nap, her eyes looking far too tired for a backyard campout. "Someone told me earlier today that I need to move forward. Well, I think we all do. I agree that I definitely do, but it would be really nice to move forward together, doncha think?"

Only silence came over the cell phone line. "Max? You there?"

"Yeah."

"I'm going to support Mom on this. I think it sounds fun. A real vacation would be nice. I hope you'll come."

"Doesn't sound as if I'll have much choice," he grumbled.

"There! That's the spirit!" She laughed. "Glad to hear you're jumping on the bandwagon! I love your enthusiasm!"

"You're crazy." She could hear the smile in his voice.

"Yeah? Well, I hear that craziness is a family trait. So I get it honestly, big brother. Have a great night with your *friend*."

The female giggle was getting louder, and Macy heard the sound of another beer being popped open.

"I plan to," he said, and hung up. Macy hoped she wouldn't be getting one of Max's infamous midnight calls later.

As her hand reached for the door handle, headlights swung into her driveway behind her. She had no choice but to plaster a smile on her face as she opened the door. She couldn't help but whistle a few bars from "Time in a Bottle," imagining ocean waves and sandy beaches as she helped her daughter out of the car and turned to face the rest of her evening.

∽

Macy heard the sounds of the door downstairs being opened and heavy footsteps crossing the linoleum.

"That didn't take long," she said aloud, rolling off her bed and tossing aside the magazine she'd been pretending to read as she waited for the inevitable.

While they'd been sitting around their campfire, Chase had thrown out enough hints about his plans for after Emma was asleep that Macy had expected this. She knew he wanted to get to know his daughter, but his motives for coming over weren't exactly pure. Part of her was flattered, as desperate as that made her sound. She had missed the companionship of having someone around. But she'd promised Brenda and Max—and herself—that she'd try to be wise about this relationship this time.

She met him on the stairs, intending to talk, but he covered her mouth with a kiss, halting her words. She used both hands to push him away, smiling as she broke free and brushed past him. She headed to the kitchen before he could grab her again.

He followed her, his body exuding heat even though it was cold outside.

"You can't leave her out there like that. What if she wakes up?" Macy asked, peering out the kitchen window into the tiny backyard where the small tent stood.

He wrapped his arms around her from behind and pressed his lips into her hair. "You're such a mom," he teased.

She turned to face him, their noses nearly touching. She could feel his breath against her face. He smelled smoky and sweet—like fire and singed marshmallows.

"I've been a mom for five years," she said, a reminder of the time he had missed, the length of time he'd stayed out of her life—and Emma's. She crossed her arms in front of her and pressed her back against the cold glass of the window, creating as much space between them as possible.

He wrapped his hands around her forearms and pulled her closer, erasing the space she'd just created. "You know, you could be a little happier that I'm back. That I chose to come back. For you."

She jerked her thumb in the direction of the tent where their daughter slept. "For her. You came back for her. Don't forget that. Because no matter what happens with us, Chase, I want you to be here for her." She thought of the sad dinner she and Emma had had earlier. She thought of the hole a father's absence can cause. "She's important."

He chuckled. "I'll be there for her. Don't worry so much." He hugged Macy close again, his chin resting on top of her head, feeling at once familiar and strange, cozy yet frightening. "Trust me," he added.

A laugh bubbled up from inside her, uncontained.

"What?" he asked.

"I struggle with trusting people," Macy mumbled into his T-shirt. "And you're one of the main reasons for that."

She pushed away from him, finding it easier now that she'd been without him so long. "Now get back outside and keep your eye on the real reason you're here."

He started to argue but she held up her hand. Chase needed to be here for Emma; but she was realizing she wasn't sold on the idea of him being here for her.

∽

After Chase stole back out the door he'd snuck in, re-joining their sleeping daughter in the tent under the stars, Macy congratulated herself for being strong. Once upon a time, she'd been helpless to his charms, but not anymore. She fell asleep making herself promises and slipped into a dream that took her back to Sunset as a child.

Her dad was holding her high above the waves as she looked down at their foamy tops from her perch on his shoulders. When her dad set her down on the sand, she ran along the beach, scooping up the tiny, fragile, pastel-colored shells she called butterfly shells.

"Look, Daddy," she said, holding them out for him to marvel over.

"They're beautiful," he said. "Just like you." He tweaked her nose and helped her put the shells in a plastic baggie to carry safely home.

"I think these are going to win the contest for sure," she said.

"I think you're right," he said, turning back to begin packing up for the day.

She studied the shells for a moment—trying to decide if she liked the pink one or the purple one better. When she looked up, her daddy was gone. She scanned the deserted beach, calling for him.

She woke up to a dark room, her heart racing, the space beside her in bed empty like always. She sat up, gathered the covers close around her, and wished she could close her eyes and return to the dreamworld where her father had been—if only for a few minutes. She had heard his voice, seen his smile, felt his warm hands holding her. In the dream, he had been alive. The talk of Sunset Beach had brought him back to her.

She smiled as she remembered the contest they'd had years ago, and how mad she'd been when she lost to Max with the shell he'd found. She'd thought of it almost immediately when Brenda had brought up Sunset Beach.

The year she was five, her dad had thought it would be fun to have a family contest to see who could find the best shell, with everyone voting on the winner. The prize was twenty dollars, and Macy had set her sights on a doll she could buy with the money. She'd scoured the beach daily, submitting several possible shells based on whatever the ocean offered up as she combed the shore for treasures. She'd felt certain that her best entry was the butterfly shells, tiny yet perfect, a trio of pastel colors. Max, being the ornery teenage boy he was, hadn't participated the whole week, and as the week drew to a close, Macy started counting her money in her mind, dreaming about her parents taking her to get that doll.

But on their last full day at the beach, Max had snuck out at dawn and found a large, perfect conch shell, its interior a glossy petal pink. Even Macy had had to concede that his shell was the best. But not without tears, and not without an especially emotional outburst at Max. He had waited to enter his shell until the last minute, just to be mean, knowing Macy would think she had won the contest. She'd told him he couldn't come to her wedding, the meanest thing she could think of at that moment. Max had merely turned away from her, leaving her fuming as tears tracked down her face.

Later that afternoon, their dad had announced that there was a second-place prize he'd forgotten to mention, and he and Macy had piled into the car to buy real pastel colored pencils so she could draw a picture in the guest book he'd found her flipping through. Since she was too young to be able to write about their trip in the guest book, he'd suggested she draw a picture that reflected what they'd done that week. Seeing a way to immortalize her precious butterfly shells, Macy had seized on the idea. Riding to the store with her dad, she'd caught his eye in the rearview mirror, seen the kindness and love that radiated from his gaze. And though she was still angry at Max, she'd been happy to have the new colored pencils, thrilled to be able to draw in the guest book, and certain she had the best daddy in the world. Years later, she thought about how winning second prize ultimately changed her life.

She burrowed back into her cozy nest of blankets, thinking about her mother's plans and finding herself wishing the trip wasn't so long away. A getaway to the place she'd once run from might just be the answer her heart was searching for.

She pulled the photo from the drawer she kept it in. Through all these years, it had occupied that honored spot—the top drawer of her nightstand, reachable at all hours of the day and night. The photo was creased from an unfortunate run-in with a notebook that had been carelessly thrown on top of it years ago, the crease running just to the left of the boy's ear, cutting the sand dollar he was holding neatly in half. As always, she smoothed the crease with her fingertips as she peered at his face, thinking, as always, about where he might be now, what he might look like. A smile filled her face as she pressed the photo to her heart and reflected on her mother's announcement. She was going to be near him, possibly even close enough to see him, maybe even to know him.

She pulled the photo away from her just far enough to be able to see again the image of the six-year-old boy holding his prized sand dollar, waves crashing in the background as he smiled for the camera. His smile came complete with dimples. He—you could already tell—would grow up to be incredibly handsome.

She squinted her eyes at the image until it blurred. The boy in the photo was no more. Somewhere out there was the man this boy had become, bearing the same dimples, the same smile, the same brown eyes that had seen every picture she'd ever drawn for him. Just like she'd seen his for her. Somehow she'd find a way to see him again, her past and future meeting on the pages of a guest book she'd never forgotten. She hoped he had not either.